the Birds, the Bees and Other Secrets

Frances Garrood has worked as a nurse and as a Relate counsellor. She lives with her husband in Wiltshire.

the Birds, the Bees and Other Secrets

FRANCES GARROOD

PAN BOOKS

First published 2008 by Macmillan New Writing

This edition published 2010 by Pan Books
an imprint of Pan Macmillan, a division of Macmillan Publishers Limited
Pan Macmillan, 20 New Wharf Road, London N1 9RR
Basingstoke and Oxford
Associated companies throughout the world
www.panmacmillan.com

ISBN 978-0-230-73626-9

3 5 7 9 8 6 4 2

A CIP catalogue record for this book is available from
the British Library.

Typeset by Intype Libra Ltd, London
Printed in the UK by CPI Mackays, Chatham ME5 8TD

Visit www.panmacmillan.com to read more about all our books
and to buy them. You will also find features, author interviews and
news of any author events, and you can sign up for e-newsletters
so that you're always first to hear about our new releases.

*In memory of my mother, who
took me out of school to pick primroses.*

One

October 2001

Outside the hospital window, a maple tree sheds golden leaves into the autumn sunshine.

'We ought to be able to die like that.' Her eyes follow the leaves as they drift downwards. 'Beautifully.' She pauses, her hands whispering over the sheets like small frightened animals. 'Not like this, all thin and ugly.'

'But Mum, you're not thin and ugly!'

'I'm not stupid either.' Bird-like eyes challenge me out of a face which has become gaunt almost beyond recognition. 'Not stupid, Cass. You can't fool me.' She sighs, and the sigh is so slight that it scarcely lifts the crisp white sheet covering her. 'The cancer may have eaten my body, but it hasn't got my brain.' A sudden smile; a glimpse of the old Mum. 'It wouldn't dare.'

I smile back, and take one of her hands in mine. It feels unbelievably tiny and fragile, and I hold it like a small precious thing which I must be careful not to break. All of her is precious now; now that I am about to lose her. Her smile, the blue of her eyes, her sense of humour, her total unselfconsciousness, her incorrigible optimism. I find myself studying her greedily, absorbing every detail, for although she is so changed, I don't want to forget a single thing about her.

'I wasn't a very good mother.' Her voice is pensive. 'I never really meant to be a mother. I'm not sure – not sure what I meant to be.'

It may have been true that, at the time, my mother wasn't sure how she had managed to produce children, but she certainly made up for any ignorance of her own by trying to ensure that the same fate never befell my brother or me. The fact that she furnished us with the information at an age when it was of no use to us whatsoever was neither here nor there; my mother had, in her own words, 'done her duty'.

This duty took the form of her (again to use her own words) 'gathering' us to her, and telling us the facts of life.

'I believe in being frank,' she informed us, years later, and with some pride. 'I think children should know these things as soon as they can understand them.'

But my brother and I didn't understand them at all. Bewildered by her inventive use of props (an egg from the larder and a jam jar full of tadpoles) and baffled by her garbled tale of eggs and passages, of body hair and bleeding, poor Lucas had nightmares for weeks, while the whole episode (apart from the tadpoles – how I longed to be allowed to keep those tadpoles!) passed me by completely. It seemed to bear no relevance whatsoever to my own narrow childish life, and so I filed it away at the back of my brain (retrieval later on was

2

to prove tricky) and forgot all about it. Long after my brother had stopped waking in the night, screaming with fear, I was still blissfully ignorant of where I'd come from, nor did I care. I had more important things to think about.

Two years later, I was to have my first real encounter with, as it were, the facts of life in action.

Awakened one night by what sounded like cries of pain coming from my mother's room, I ran into her bedroom to find her apparently writhing around under the bedclothes with her new friend, the (as I realized, years later) aptly named Mr Mountjoy.

'Mum! What's happening?' I stood panic-stricken in the bedroom doorway. 'Are you – are you hurt?'

My mother, who was rarely lost for words, emerged from under the covers, pink and dishevelled, and came up with an inventive if baffling explanation.

'We were looking for a button.'

Mr Mountjoy stifled a kind of choking noise, and my mother gave a rather odd little smile and sat up in bed. While she was careful to pull the counterpane up with her, I couldn't help noticing that she didn't appear to be wearing any clothes.

'It's all right, darling. There's nothing for you to worry about. Mr Mountjoy is . . . helping me.'

Mr Mountjoy, apparently intent on continuing the search, disappeared under the bedclothes again and my mother waved her hand in the direction of the door.

'Go back to bed now, angel. Everything's going to be fine, I promise you.'

But I didn't think that everything seemed fine at all. My

brother and I had never known our fathers (we had one each, our mother had told us, as though that were something to be pleased about), and I for one wasn't used to finding strangers in her bed. Certainly, she had had men-friends, but if she had slept with them (and I must now assume that she had), I had never had any knowledge of it.

'That Mr Mountjoy was in Mum's bed last night,' I told Lucas as we walked to school together the following morning. 'What do you suppose they were doing? She said they were looking for a button, but they weren't wearing any clothes.'

'Honestly, Cass! What do you *think* they were doing?' Lucas, with his full two years of seniority, was apparently better informed than I was.

'I don't know,' I said crossly. 'I wouldn't ask if—'

'OK, OK. I'll tell you then.' Lucas paused portentously. 'They were having sex, of course.'

'Having sex,' I repeated. 'I see.'

But of course, I didn't see. In fact I remained totally ignorant of all matters sexual until a biology lesson at school several years later, in the course of which the hapless Miss Wilson took us on a whistle-stop tour of reproduction, moving seamlessly from the buttercup, via the rabbit, to sex in human beings.

'You didn't tell us any of it! *Any of it!*' I accused my mother, when I got home from school. 'Everyone else knew, but me. And all that about buttercups and rabbits – you never mentioned buttercups or rabbits!'

'I don't know anything about buttercups and rabbits, but I did tell you about people. I told you everything.' My mother looked bewildered. She had been playing Beethoven's Emperor Concerto on the ironing board. It was one of her favourites, and the record player was turned up so loud that we could hardly hear each other speak. 'I told you when you were five,' she shouted, obviously referring to the gathering together of Lucas and me. 'I told you all you needed to know.'

'But I didn't need to know it then. I needed to know it for now,' I shouted back. 'So as not to look silly in front of everyone else!'

'You must have forgotten. How was I to know you'd forget something so important?' Mother's fingers began to move up and down across the back of one of my school shirts, and she had a dreamy expression on her face.

'And I wish you'd listen,' I yelled. 'I wish – I just wish I had a normal mother!'

This was certainly true. While I loved my mother dearly and was not on the whole a conventional child, I didn't always appreciate her many eccentricities. She was one of those people who conduct their lives with no apparent reference to the rules of normal behaviour. The piano-playing was only the tip of the iceberg, and in fact apart from when I was trying to talk to her, or when I had friends round, I didn't mind it too much. But she seemed incapable of editing the thoughts as they floated into her head, and this could lead to fearful misunderstandings. If someone was looking ill, or tired, or, worst of all, just plain ugly, my mother wouldn't hesitate to tell them so. In shops and cafes, on buses and in the school playground, she was an endless and rich source of embarrassment.

Conversely, she would pay outrageous compliments to total strangers, and this could be almost as embarrassing.

'Did you know, you have the most wonderful eyes?' she once informed a rather forbidding-looking young man on a train. 'Sort of treacle toffee, with a touch of—'

But before she could finish her sentence, the young man had got up and moved to another compartment.

'Well!' said Mum, much annoyed. 'How rude! Can you imagine why anyone would want to be so rude?'

Both Lucas and I could well imagine why the young man had found our mother's company less than congenial, but we wisely kept our counsel.

And then there was the somewhat eccentric domestic set-up in which we passed our childhood. True, the rambling and dilapidated Victorian house (a legacy from a long-dead aunt) was spacious, and the jungle of a garden offered plenty of scope for our imaginations, but the place was a social mine-field. There was the Lodger in the basement (always referred to as the Lodger, although the actual individual enjoying this title changed so frequently that we had trouble keeping up with who was supposed to be living there). Up in the attic, there was my mother's Uncle Rupert, who had been with us for as long as I could remember. He was a rather fey, ineffec-tual man of wispy appearance and indeterminate age, who lived off the dole and spent his time inventing things. Think-ing of things for Uncle Rupert to invent was a regular family pastime, and so he was never short of ideas, but he rarely came up with anything which could be considered even re-motely useful.

Mum, however, wouldn't hear a word against him.

'Rupert's so clever,' she would say, ironing his shirts (between piano concertos). 'He could have gone a long way, you know.'

Lucas and I often wished Uncle Rupert would do just that, for his lengthy occupations of the only bathroom, the pacing of his heavy boots across the floorboards above our bedrooms, the smell of his clothes (aniseed balls, stale sweat and tobacco) and, as I approached puberty, his covert appraisal of my developing body (never enough to complain to Mum about, but certainly enough to inspire a healthy revulsion) did nothing to endear him to us.

'Does Uncle Rupert have to live with us?' I asked once. After all, none of my friends had resident uncles. Theirs were the kind of uncles who were only seen on family occasions, and if they did visit, they came sweet-smelling and wholesome, bearing gifts of toffee, and if you were lucky, money.

'Of course Uncle Rupert has to live with us,' replied my mother, shocked. 'You must understand, darling. He has nowhere else to go.'

Other people who often had nowhere else to go were, variously, my mother's friend Greta, an exile from her native Switzerland who spoke little English and cried a lot; a tramp called Richard, who played the ukulele outside Woolworths and for whom my mother had a soft spot ('Not a tramp, Cass,' she chided me once, 'Richard's a Homeless Person.' 'But he calls *himself* a tramp,' I objected. 'That's different,' said Mum); an actor called Ben, who had fallen on hard times but had once had a walk-on part in *Coronation Street*; and the nice man from the chemist (Mum's words) who kept falling out with his landlady. These people didn't all come to stay at once, of course, but they turned up at regular intervals to spend a few nights on the put-u-up in the living room and join the queue for the bathroom. Whether, like the Lodger, they paid my mother anything towards their keep Lucas and I never did find out. Nor did we discover whether any of them were into hunting for buttons. But we did resent their regular intrusion into a household which was at best disordered and at worst chaotic, for what our mother seemed to forget was that we, too, had nowhere else to go, and that moreover, this was our home. Quite often it felt more as though we were all living in a hostel.

What I didn't realize until years later was that my mother was desperately lonely, and that her greatest dread was to wake up one morning and find that she was no longer surrounded by people. If there was no Lodger, she would visibly droop (I thought at the time that this was due to lack of revenue), and would send Lucas and me several times a day to our corner shop to ask if anyone had enquired about the advertisement she had placed in their window. If the phone was silent, she would fret that it might be out of order ('nip round to the phone box and give us a quick ring, Cass, there's a pet'). If no one called round, she immediately assumed she must have done something wrong. Flighty, insecure, by turns manically happy or beset with a sadness bordering on despair, she was not a restful person to live with.

But it was by no means all bad, and in fact my friends envied me my haphazard upbringing, for I was given the kind of freedom they could only dream of. We climbed trees and constructed tunnels underneath the hay bales in the local farmer's barn, and our mother turned a blind eye. We stayed up late with her, listening to unsuitable programmes on the wireless, and went trick-or-treating at Halloween long before the custom had caught on this side of the Atlantic. When Lucas remarked once that raw cake mixture tasted so much better than the finished article, and couldn't he have an uncooked birthday cake, Mum said what a lovely idea, and of course he could. The cake was consumed with spoons out of bowls, and while several of the party were ill that night, all agreed that it had been worth it. Their parents, however, evidently did not think the exercise had been worth it, and at least two of Lucas's friends were banned from our house for some time afterwards.

'We did have fun, didn't we?' It's as though she is reading my thoughts. 'Do you remember the time I sent a note to school and we went picking primroses?'

'Oh yes!'

A blue and white spring day, a dapple of bright new leaves, and the primroses like stars in the chalky soil, their faces turned to the sun. We picked the slender pink stems, sniffing the perfume of the flowers, and filled a basket with them, then sat on our coats on the ground ('Don't sit on the wet grass; you'll get piles.' 'Piles of what?' 'Never you mind.') to eat our picnic lunch of crisp rolls and ham and apples. It never occurred to me at the time to question what we were doing. My mother always reasoned that we were her children, and if she wanted us out of school for a day, then that was her right.

'What did you say in the note?'

'What note?'

'The note you wrote to the school on the primrose day.'

'I forget.' Her eyes start wandering again, then return with a snap. 'Oh yes! I said you had your period!'

'Mum!' I was ten years old at the time, my chest as flat as a board, my body smooth and hairless as a plum.

'Well, what did you expect me to say?' And of course, as usual, there is no answer to that.

'And Deirdre and the cowpat. Do you remember that?'

Blowing up cowpats with Lucas and his friends in the field behind our house, choosing a nice ripe one ('crisp on the top, with a squidgy middle,' advised Lucas, the expert); our excitement, watching the smouldering firework, waiting for the explosion; and the sheer joy when a particularly messy one erupted in a fountain of green sludge, splattering the blonde ringlets and nice clean frock of prissy Deirdre from next door. Oh, Deirdre! If you could see yourself! We rolled in the grass, kicking our heels, convulsed with mirth, while Deirdre, howling and outraged, ran home to tell her mummy what bad, bad children we all were.

'What'll your mum say?' one of Lucas's friends asked anxiously.

'Oh, Mum'll laugh.'

Mum laughed. She tried to tell us off, but was so proud of the inventiveness of Lucas, and so entertained at the fate of prissy Deirdre, that she failed utterly. But she promised Deirdre's mother that we would all be 'dealt with'.

'Whatever that means,' said Mum, dishing out chocolate biscuits and orange juice. 'Poor child. She doesn't stand a chance, with a mother like that. But I suppose she had it coming to her.'

'I wonder what happened to her?' she muses now.

'Who?'

'Prissy Deirdre.'

'Married, with a nice little semi with net curtains, a Peter-and-Jane family and a husband who washes the car on Sundays.'

But Mum is no longer listening. She is drifting away from me again, her eyes wandering, her fingers plucking at the sheets.

Mum rarely if ever told us off, and not only appeared to trust us implicitly but often sought our advice. We were always invited to be present when she interviewed prospective Lodgers, and although these meetings were rarely the formal, fact-finding missions she fondly imagined them to be, she always listened to what we had to say. As we grew older, she would even seek our views on her latest man-friend, although in this she tended to disregard our opinions and go her own way.

'Can't you see he's just after somewhere to stay?' Lucas exclaimed on one occasion (the gentleman in question had no job and no visible means of support).

'So that suits us both, doesn't it?' Mum cried gaily. 'He can live here with us!'

'But Mum! He's just using you!'

'And I, my sweet, am using him.' She patted Lucas on the head. 'One day, you'll understand.'

Money, or rather, the lack of it, was an ongoing problem, and to this day I'm not sure what we lived on. True, there was the Lodger, and Mum did have a variety of odd jobs, but she quickly became bored with them, and was out of work more often than she was in it. In this as in every other area of her life, there would be sudden bursts of industry, where she would appear to be holding down several jobs at once. Then her maternal conscience (a flighty thing at the best of times) would kick in, and she would be at home for weeks on end, baking amazing cakes from recipes of her own invention and making strange-looking garments on her ancient Singer sewing machine. The cakes were always different and always odd-looking – sometimes burnt round the edges, often flat as pancakes – but they were invariably delicious. The garments – usually made from, and looking exactly like, old curtains – we hid at the backs of drawers and cupboards until she had forgotten about them. Sometimes she worked from home, as on the occasion when she took a job packing bottles of cheap perfume in little boxes. The perfume-packing regularly fell behind schedule, and the whole family, plus the Lodger and sundry hangers-on, would end up helping her out. The smell of that perfume – 'Gardenia' – haunted me for years afterwards.

On one memorable occasion when finances were particularly bad, Mum decided that she would capitalize on Lucas and me, and to that end she decided to take us along to a modelling agency.

'You're both good-looking children,' she told us, as she scrubbed and brushed us into shape. 'I'm sure they can use you for a catalogue or something.'

I was enormously excited. It would never have occurred to me to think of myself as model material, but perhaps Mum knew something I didn't. With high hopes of fame and glamour, not to mention days off school, I allowed myself to be dressed in a hideous flowery frock passed on to me by a friend of Greta's, and off we set. But the woman at the agency shook her head.

'No, no. Not the girl,' she said, after I had paraded in front of her. 'I'm afraid she's not suitable. The boy, now . . . The boy we can certainly use.'

At the time, it seemed desperately unfair, but when I look back now, I can see that Lucas's high forehead, clear complexion and dazzling combination of blond hair and brown eyes must have made him an exceptional candidate. But to Mum's credit, she turned the offer down. If the woman wouldn't accept us both, then she shouldn't have either of us.

'They come together,' she said grandly, as though we were some sort of double act. 'I can't allow you to have Lucas without Cassandra. It just wouldn't be right.'

Lucas, it has to be said, appeared to be much relieved at these tidings. He had been worrying for days about what his friends would say if he were to turn up in their mothers' favourite magazines advertising cutesy children's clothes, but I was bitterly disappointed. I think it was the first time in my life that I realized my looks were unexceptional. Never a particularly vain child, I had nonetheless hitherto been quite pleased with what I saw when I looked in the mirror. Mum had always told me I was pretty; I had therefore had no reason to believe otherwise. Now, it seemed, I must accept that there was room for doubt, and I never quite regained the cheerful confidence in my appearance which I held in those early years.

Was my childhood a happy one? As with many childhoods,

the memories are so tinged with nostalgia that it is hard to be objective, but there were certainly some wonderful moments, and there is no doubt that I was much loved.

But when I was fourteen, everything was to change.

Two

May 1961

Up until that time, while I was of course aware of my essential femaleness, I had given little thought to myself as a sexual being. Puberty may have been well on the way, but I was not particularly impressed by its manifestations, and had I not had to put up with the regular leerings of Uncle Rupert, I probably would have ignored it altogether. My breasts at that stage were poor little things, barely disturbing the surface of my chest and certainly not requiring the services of a bra; and any other bodily changes were not sufficiently interesting to exercise my mind more than fleetingly. I knew that I was turning into a woman, and I was quite pleased about that, but unlike many of my friends I was in no hurry. I had the good sense to recognize that childhood doesn't last forever, and that I should enjoy its advantages while I could.

Even now, after all these years, I still find it astonishing that innocence can be destroyed so quickly and so thoroughly in just a few brief minutes. One day, I was an ordinary child when I got up in the morning (as ordinary as it was possible to be in our household), but when I went to bed that night, I was someone else altogether. And yet nothing had actually been done to me. I had suffered no physical harm. I suppose, when I could bring myself to think about it objectively, I had been lucky. I had had a lucky escape. But at the time, lucky and escape were two words which seemed to have little connection with what happened to me on that awful day.

Apart from Uncle Rupert, who had gone to bed early, I was on my own in the house. My mother was out pulling pints at the local pub (a new job, and one which she appeared to be enjoying enormously), Lucas had gone to the pictures with his friends, the put-u-up was temporarily out of commission, and even the Lodger was away for the weekend. The only sounds were the ticking of the grandfather clock in the hall (a funny lopsided tick, strangely comforting in the silent house) and the occasional swish of tyres as a car drove up the road past the house. I never minded being on my own – after all, I had never had any reason to – and I felt relaxed and happy. The weekend stretched invitingly before me, and if I could get my homework done now, I would be free until Monday morning.

I don't know how long Uncle Rupert had been watching me, but it could have been for some time. I rarely closed my bedroom door, as one of my mother's more sensible house rules was that no one was allowed into anyone else's room without permission, and I had been fully absorbed in what I was doing. So it was with some shock that when I looked up I found him standing behind me, looking over my shoulder. He had a habit of shuffling silently round the house in his slippers, appearing unexpectedly in odd places, so his arrival in itself was not particularly disconcerting. But his rather odd demeanour together with the fact that he had entered the room unannounced immediately rang alarm bells.

'Hello.' Uncle Rupert placed an unwelcome hand on my shoulder. 'How's it going, then?'

'Fine. It's going fine.' My hands were clammy and I wiped them on my grey school skirt. 'I – I'm doing my homework,' I added, more for something to say than anything else, as it must have been perfectly obvious what I was doing.

'You're growing into a very attractive young woman,' Uncle Rupert said, as though I hadn't spoken.

'Am I?'

'You know you are.'

There followed a pause, in which Uncle Rupert appraised my body unashamedly. I felt as though he were peeling the clothes off me garment by garment with his pale, fishy eyes, and I tried to stand up.

'No. Stay where you are.' Uncle Rupert squeezed my shoulder. 'I like looking at you sitting there.'

Why didn't I just get up and leave the room? Why didn't I at least move away, as my instincts told me to? But it was as though I were suddenly paralysed, unable to move or even speak. To this day, I can still see the books spread out on my desk, the maths problem, with the rectangle half-drawn and my pencil and ruler lying across the page, the tiny fragments of rubber where I had erased a false start. I can smell the woody scent of pencil sharpenings, and hear the wheezy, unsavoury breaths of Uncle Rupert as he stood, as motionless as I was, his hand still on my shoulder.

My eyes met Uncle Rupert's, and there was something in his gaze which I had never seen before; something sinister and predatory; something which sent prickles of fear up and down my spine.

'I need – I need to finish this.' My mouth was dry, my heartbeats pounding in my ears. 'Before – before Monday.'

'Plenty of time for that,' Uncle Rupert said. 'After all, it's the weekend, isn't it?' He reached behind him and closed the bedroom door. 'I thought you and I could play a little game, while we're on our own. Just the two of us.'

'What – game?' I had never in my life known Uncle Rupert play games, and couldn't think what he meant.

'Just a little game. A little secret game. You'll see.'

'No, please—'

'Now Cassandra, you know me.' He had never called me by my full name before. 'There's no need to be afraid of me. No need to be afraid of old Uncle Rupert.'

'Please. I – I need to get a drink.' I made as though to get up.

'Later. You can have a drink later. After our little game.' He pressed me back into my chair with surprising force. 'Be a good girl. Be a good girl and everything will be fine.'

By this stage, I was beginning to panic. Uncle Rupert was gripping my shoulder more firmly now, effectively anchoring me to my chair, and I knew I didn't have the strength to push him away. There was no one else in the house to respond if I were to call out. The bedroom window was open, but I doubt whether anyone outside would have heard me, and even if they did, what could they do? I had no choice but to stay where I was and hope beyond hope that he would soon tire of this game of his and leave me alone.

But Uncle Rupert had only just begun.

He moved closer. I could smell the stale tobacco on his breath as he stooped over me, and feel his leg pressing against my own. The rough material of his sleeve brushed my cheek as he took my hand in one of his.

'I have something for you,' he said. 'Something special. I think you're going to like it.'

I tried to pull my hand away, but he held on to it firmly. His own hand was unpleasantly damp, and I could feel his untrimmed fingernails digging into my palm.

'Look on it as a little present. A present from me to you. A very special present.'

Slowly, very slowly, he began to pull my hand towards him.

'There's a good girl.' His voice was soft, conspiratorial, and there was a faint smile on his face as he drew my hand inside the folds of his dressing gown.

For a moment, I didn't know what it was that I was feeling; a toy, perhaps, or some kind of practical joke. But only for a moment. Then, I knew. I was innocent and I was totally unsuspecting, but as he covered my hand with his own and began to move it gently back and forth, I realized with a horror beyond any horror I had ever felt before what it was that I was holding; what it was that Uncle Rupert was doing.

'There. Isn't that nice?'

Nice? *Nice?* I was speechless. Nothing could have prepared me for this. *Nothing.* Not my mother with her cosy chats, not Miss Wilson with her tales of rabbits and buttercups, not the innocent body of Lucas, remembered from the shared bathtimes of our early childhood – none of these things could have prepared me for anything so utterly, hideously, appalling.

For a moment I was so shocked I could barely breathe. Then, at last, I found my voice. And screamed.

Summoning up all my strength, I pushed Uncle Rupert away. Taken by surprise, he stumbled backwards, giving me the chance to get to my feet and throw the door open. I tore down the stairs, half-sobbing as I screamed, stumbling on the loose piece of stair carpet, tripping over Lucas's school shoes lying in the hallway. I pulled open the front door and fled down the garden path, out of the gate and along the road. I had no idea where I was going; I only knew that I had to get away. I had to put as much distance between myself and Uncle Rupert as was humanly possible, and I had to do it fast.

I don't know how far I would have gone had I not fallen, literally, into the arms of Greta, who was apparently about to surprise us with one of her unscheduled visits.

'Cassandra!' Greta dropped her suitcases and pressed me to her bosom. 'The matter is what?' (Greta's English had improved over the years, and while it was still somewhat eccentric, it was at least comprehensible, if only in parts.)

'Uncle Rupert!' I sobbed into the collar of her ancient overcoat.

'Iss ill?'

'No. Not ill. Horrible!' I raised my streaming face. 'Uncle Rupert is horrible, horrible, *horrible*!'

'Iss horrible?' The tears, which were never far away,

welled sympathetically in Greta's pink-rimmed eyes. 'Why iss horrible?'

'I can't tell you.'

'Uncle Rupert iss nice man, I think,' said Greta, stroking my hair.

'No! Uncle Rupert is not nice man! Uncle Rupert is disgusting old man! I hate him!'

'No hate Uncle Rupert,' Greta admonished (she had always, inexplicably, had a soft spot for him). 'You make mistake, I think?'

'No! No mistake!'

But of course I couldn't tell Greta what had happened. At that moment, I couldn't have told anybody, and besides, in a situation such as this, the language barrier would have proved too great. I didn't know the German for what Uncle Rupert had done, and Greta was unlikely to understand the English, even if I could have brought myself to say the words.

'We go home, yes? Nice-cup-of-tea?' Greta didn't herself like tea, but she had learnt that this was what the English resorted to in times of stress, and she was obviously anxious to remove me from the street before I made more of a spectacle of myself.

'No! We can't go home! Uncle Rupert's there!'

'Uncle Rupert no hurt,' said Greta firmly, taking my arm in a surprisingly strong grip and steering me back down the road in the direction of the house. 'I take care.'

What could I do? I had nowhere else to go, and no money, and it was getting dark. I wasn't sure where my mother worked, and even if I had known, I could hardly burst into a crowded pub with my unwelcome tidings. Besides, I would probably be safe with Greta there. Something told me that Uncle Rupert was unlikely to stage a repeat performance in her presence.

As it happened, by the time we got home, there was no sign of Uncle Rupert. The house was quiet, and his bedroom door was firmly shut. Greta set about putting the kettle on and hunting for the teapot while I sat at the table and shivered. I shivered with cold, I shivered with fear, but most of all, I shivered with shock. Up until now, home had been safe; it had been a haven. The people who came and went were a disparate lot, but they were basically OK, and I had certainly never felt remotely threatened by any of them. But now, all that was spoiled. My room – my own bedroom – had been the scene of Uncle Rupert's ghastly activities. Would I ever be able to go in there again?

Just then, we heard my mother's key in the front door, and she came into the kitchen.

'Why, Greta! How nice!' Mum embraced her. 'Well, this is a lovely surprise, isn't it Cass? Cass?' She looked at me closely. 'Whatever's the matter?'

'She no like Uncle Rupert,' said Greta, pouring boiling water into mugs. 'She run away.'

'You ran away? Cass? What's all this about?'

'Uncle Rupert – Uncle Rupert – he –' I burst into tears again.

My mother turned pale, and it was at that moment that I understood. My mother knew. She knew what had happened, and that meant that she knew something about Uncle Rupert that none of us had known; something she should have warned me about; something she should have protected me from. I had always been aware that there was some dark secret in Uncle Rupert's past, and had hitherto assumed that it was in the nature of a personal tragedy. Now I realized that it was something far more sinister, and something which my mother should have taken a great deal more seriously when she invited him into our home all those years ago.

I stood up from the kitchen table and faced her.

'You haven't – you haven't asked me what happened,' I said, and my voice suddenly seemed distant and separate, as though it were coming from a long way away.

'My poor darling.' Mum tried to put her arms round me. 'You tell me all about it, then.'

'You know all about it.' I pushed her away. 'You *know*!'

'I couldn't have – I didn't – oh, Cass! What did he do? Did he – did he touch you?'

Just for that moment, all my hatred and my anger was directed at my mother; my mother, whom I suddenly held completely in my power. Because while I didn't fully under-stand the significance of her question, I suspected that if I were to tell her that yes, Uncle Rupert had touched me, she would have been dreadfully punished for what she had failed to do.

'Tell me, Cass! Tell me at once! What did Uncle Rupert do to you?' Mum gripped me by my shoulders and half shook me. 'You have to tell me!'

'Nice-cup-of-tea?' suggested poor Greta. 'Make better feel, no?'

'Shut up, Greta!' shouted Mum, still holding on to me. 'Can't you see this is a crisis?'

'Let me go!' I cried, trying to push her away. 'You let me go!'

'But you must tell me,' Mother said, more gently now, relinquishing her grip. 'You must tell me what happened. What did Uncle Rupert do?'

'But you already know—'

'No. I don't know. I know Rupert has one or two . . . strange habits, but I don't know exactly what he did to you, Cass. You have to believe me. I would never have left you on your own with him if I'd thought – if I'd thought you were in any sort of danger.'

I hesitated. I knew my mother loved me; I knew that she would have protected me with her own life had she been required to do so. But it was also clear that she knew Uncle Rupert was capable of posing some kind of threat. I was still angry with her, but I also desperately wanted her to know what had happened. I ached for her sympathy, for her indignation on my behalf, and most of all, for the familiarity and safety of being held in her arms.

I looked round the kitchen. We were on our own now, Greta having made a tearful and reproachful exit some minutes ago. I sat down again at the table.

'What did he do, love? Please tell me.' Mum sat down beside me and took my hand. 'I can't do anything about it if I don't know, can I?'

'He came into my room,' I began slowly. 'He didn't knock or anything. He just came in.'

'And?' Mum prompted.

'And then – and then he – he made me – touch him.'

For a few moments, my mother didn't say anything. She

just sat there, stroking my hand, and when I glanced at her, I was surprised to see that she too had tears in her eyes.

'Did he – did he do anything else?' she asked. 'Anything at all? Did he touch you?'

I shook my head.

'He forced me. He made me do it.' My scalp crawled at the memory. 'But I ran away. Greta found me.' I hiccoughed. 'Oh, Mum! It was horrible!'

'I can imagine,' Mum said grimly. 'Horrible. Quite horrible. My poor, poor darling.'

And then, quite suddenly, she too seemed overwhelmed by rage.

'Where is he? Where did he go?' she shouted. '*Where is Rupert?*'

'I'm not sure. In his room I think.'

'Right. You stay here, Cass. You hear me? Stay right here till I get back.' And she stormed out of the room and up the stairs.

A moment later, I heard her banging on Uncle Rupert's door, and I crept guiltily out into the hallway. After all, I reasoned, this was my disaster, not my mother's. I had a right to hear the outcome.

Muffled shouts came from (presumably) Uncle Rupert's room and I listened breathlessly. I had rarely seen my mother angry, and never as angry as this. What would she do? Would she kill Uncle Rupert? Should I call an ambulance, or the police, or maybe a neighbour? Supposing Uncle Rupert attacked Mum? Should I try to rescue her?

As I stood dithering, I heard Uncle Rupert's door open again, and my mother's voice on the landing.

'You promised!' I heard her cry. '*You promised!* I trusted you. I took you into my home, I left you alone with my children. And look how you've repaid me! I want you out of here first thing in the morning. Do you hear? First thing in the morning!'

It was a very long time before I heard of Uncle Rupert again. I was packed off to a friend's house early the following morning, and by the time I returned home, every trace of him had gone. His room was clean and empty. Even the curtains had been removed from the windows. It was as though he had never lived in our house at all.

Three

The months following Uncle Rupert's departure were difficult for all of us. I was still traumatized by my experience, and yet old enough to reason that it didn't make sense to mind so deeply about what had happened. After all, I had suffered no harm, I hadn't been attacked, the source of my upset had been removed. Life could and should go on as normal. And yet everything had changed.

Worst of all was the feeling of being unclean; of being *soiled*. That was the only way to describe it. Something had been dirtied; something that no amount of washing and bathing (and I did plenty of both) could reach. Something clean and wholesome and good had been taken from me, and young as I was, I knew that I could never have it back.

Nowadays, no doubt, I might have received counselling, but my mother knew nothing about psychology, and it certainly wouldn't have occurred to her to seek that kind of help. She did, however, recognize the depth of my distress, and tiptoed round my feelings with great tenderness, offering me little treats, letting me off household chores (much to Lucas's disgust) and generally treating me with kid gloves. She cooked my favourite meals, bought me the expensive coat I longed for (I never did find out how she managed to pay for it) and, in a bizarre moment of inspiration, sent a note to the school to excuse me from PE.

I have no idea how this was supposed to help, or indeed what she told the school, but I was delighted. I was not an athletic child, and I did not – and still do not – have the slightest idea how the ability to climb up ropes or do handstands could possibly equip anyone for life.

I'm not sure what my mother told the rest of the household, but they too seemed to treat me with new consideration in the weeks that followed. Lucas, the only one who knew the whole story, made an effort to be nice to me, although I could see that he couldn't understand what all the fuss was about. Greta made soothing noises whenever she saw me, and gave me presents of the Swiss chocolate sent to her by her cousin. Having apparently finally run out of alternative refuges, she was now permanently installed in Uncle Rupert's bedroom, which she set about embellishing with flowery curtains and pink wallpaper and faded photographs of her family (usually against a chocolate-box backdrop of hygienic-looking cows and snow-topped mountains). She invited me up to see her handiwork, and I admired it from the doorway, but I wouldn't go in, and she seemed to understand.

'Poor you little girl.' She patted me kindly. 'Better soon I think?'

The nice man from the chemist brought me violet bath salts and a new hot water bottle, and even the Lodger, a bespectacled college research student with enormous feet and acne, offered me chewing gum and asked after me when our paths happened to cross.

Taken up as I was with my own problems, I still couldn't help noticing the effect Uncle Rupert's departure had had on my mother. I had never thought her especially fond of Uncle Rupert. Although, as I later discovered, he was more a distant cousin than a proper uncle, she had known him all her life, and he had lived with us for almost as long as I could remember. While they had led largely separate lives, and I had never seen any signs of affection between them, there was no doubt that Mum missed him sorely.

On several occasions I caught her going into his room and just standing there, gazing out of the window between Greta's fluttering pink curtains, an expression of great sadness on her face. The music she played on the ironing board was sad and pensive; a Brahms intermezzo, Chopin's funeral march, Beethoven's Moonlight Sonata. The music poured out plaintively from our ancient record player as mother's hands moved slowly up and down pyjama legs and blouses and the ridiculous frilly apron Greta wore in the kitchen. Not much actual ironing got done in the weeks following Uncle Rupert's departure, but no one complained. Mum too was suffering, and without actually saying anything, everyone seemed to understand.

'Where is Uncle Rupert?' I asked her one day.

She looked at me blankly. 'Uncle Rupert?'

'Yes. Where is he? Where's he living?'

'He's gone away. A long way away. You don't need to worry about him any more.'

'Are you – are you very cross with him?' I ventured.

'Yes. Well, I was. I was very cross indeed. But you know, Cass, some people do things they can't help. It's – it's a bit like an illness.'

But try as I might, I couldn't see that what Uncle Rupert had done could possibly have had anything to do with his health. Years later, I wondered what my mother could have been thinking of, harbouring an ageing paedophile in the same house as her children. But then Mum had always been trusting, and if, as I gathered, Uncle Rupert had given her his word that he wouldn't misbehave, it was typical of her to have believed him. Trust was second nature to my mother. I never knew her to turn away a stranger or lock a door, and it was little short of a miracle that in a house with four outside doors, all of them unlocked, we were never once burgled. The only occasion upon which someone entered the house illegally, they crawled in through the larder window, and Mum was so entertained by the thought of the effort they must have gone to (it was a very small window) that she refused to report the intruder.

'After all, he only took a bottle of wine. Not a very nice wine at that. He's welcome to it!' she said. And the doors remained unlocked.

In addition to my other problems, Uncle Rupert's bewildering performance had done nothing to foster in me a positive image of the opposite sex. In the street or on buses, in shops and even at school (it was an all-female establishment, but we did have two male teachers and a caretaker), I was constantly and fearfully aware that every man had the same equipment as Uncle Rupert, and that presumably they were all capable of the same dreadful antics. How could any woman want the body of a man near her, let alone have close physical contact with it? Mother's searches for buttons took on a whole new meaning, and I shuddered.

'I shall never have sex,' I told my mother. She was lying in the bath, and I was sitting on the edge. I always found that this was the best time for confidences, partly because her nakedness made her somehow more accessible, and also because being locked in the bathroom with her made me feel safer.

'Of course you will. Why ever shouldn't you?' Mum's milky limbs shimmered under the water as she turned on the hot tap with her toe.

'Because of – you know. I just couldn't. It's *horrible*!'

'Actually' – my mother picked up a flannel, and began slowly soaping her arms – 'it's rather nice. You'll enjoy it when your time comes, Cass. Believe me.'

'No, I shan't. I can't understand how anyone can enjoy *that*.'

'When you love somebody, it's the most wonderful thing in the world.' Mum's voice was dreamy. 'Lying together, feeling so close. You wait, Cass. You'll be surprised.'

'Did you love all the people you had sex with?' I asked curiously.

'Oh, Cass! What a question!' Mum laughed.

'Well, did you?' I persisted.

'Probably not,' she confessed, pausing with the flannel in mid-thigh. 'I should have, but no. I didn't always.'

'Then why did you do it?'

'That's a good question.' Mum stepped out of the bath and reached for a towel. 'I suppose I wanted to feel needed.'

31

'But we need you! Lots of people need you! You don't have to have sex to be needed.'

'There's a particular sort of needed that I want to be.' She laughed again. 'You'll understand one day, I promise you. Anyway, you don't want to bother yourself with any of this now. You're much too young.'

But whereas a few weeks ago I might have agreed with her, now I no longer felt too young to think about sex.

I look back on that time now as one of the loneliest of my life. Kind as she was, my mother soon appeared too preoccupied with her own worries to pay more than passing attention to mine. Lucas was increasingly out with his friends, and seemed to think it was time I put Uncle Rupert out of my mind. And my friends, through no fault of their own, were unaware of my problem. I spent a lot of time lying on my bed, listening to music, or playing with the mangy and recalcitrant dog Mum had recently acquired (*'Dog found tied to railway line,'* the headline in the local paper had screamed, followed by a phone number for anyone who might like to rehouse the unfortunate animal. My mother had found this invitation quite irresistible, and had responded without hesitation). The Dog (like the Lodger, he never acquired a name of his own) seemed as disturbed and preoccupied as I was, and we were probably good company for each other.

'That's good,' said Mum approvingly, watching me encouraging him to fetch an old slipper from behind the sofa. 'It'll bring him out of himself. You too, Cass.'

The Dog and I looked at each other in a moment of complete understanding. My mother might fantasize all she liked, but we both knew that it would take more than a slipper to sort out our problems.

But I had underestimated my mother, for unbeknown to me, she was taking my troubled state more seriously than I could ever have imagined. And had I known what she was planning, I would have put up with any amount of neglect rather than face the ordeal which was to come.

Four

'Boarding school! You want to send me to *boarding school*?' I could hardly believe my ears when my mother disclosed to me what she obviously considered to be a truly inspirational idea. 'Whatever for?'

'It will do you good to get away,' Mum said.

'I don't want to get away! Why should I want to get away?'

'After – what's happened. You need a change. You may not want to go now, but you will when you see the school. It's a lovely place, all green and wooded and—'

'You mean you've seen it?'

'Well, not exactly.' Mum looked sheepish. 'But I've seen the brochure and heard all about it and it sounds just perfect. You and I can go and see it together, Cass. It'll make a nice day out for us. And they want to meet you, of course. And they'll need you to do a little test.'

'What sort of little test?'

'Oh, a bit of maths and English. Nothing too difficult. You'll sail through, Cass. It's just a formality.'

'But I don't want to go! Mum, please don't make me! I'm happy here, and—'

'But Cass, you're not happy. Anyone can see that. And the doctor says—'

'The doctor? You mean to say you've been talking about me to the doctor?' My mother seemed to have been taking her parenting duties to unusual lengths. 'And you've told him – oh no! You haven't told him about – about Uncle Rupert!'

'Well, I did mention there'd been a spot of bother at home. I didn't tell him exactly what had happened, though.'

It seemed to me extremely unlikely that the doctor would recommend boarding school as a cure for a 'spot of bother', but I was too upset to challenge my mother on this particular point. All I could see was that I, an innocent victim, was being punished for the disgusting behaviour of Uncle Rupert, and that it all seemed terribly unfair.

'And Lucas? What about Lucas? Is he going to boarding school too?'

'Of course not. There's nothing wrong with Lucas.'

'But there's nothing wrong with me!' I wailed.

'Oh, there is,' Mum said, patting my knee fondly. 'And you're the one who needs a bit of special attention.'

In vain did I weep and wail. In vain did I alternately rail against my mother and sulk in my room behind a loudly slammed door. Her mind was made up.

The day out to visit the boarding school involved a long and sticky journey in the ancient Rover belonging to the nice man from the chemist, who was the current occupier of the put-u-up in the living room. Of all the people who came and went in our household, he was the only one to own a car, and he obligingly offered his services as chauffeur for the day. It was his day off, and he fancied a day out in the country, he told us. Wasn't that lucky?

Naturally I was relegated to the back seat, where I sat and sulked for much of the journey, annoyingly aware that since the two grown-ups had their backs to me, my sulk was largely wasted. I was hot and uncomfortable, and the too-small girly-pink frock which my mother had insisted I wear strained across my developing chest. The sulk forbade my partaking of the picnic lunch Mum had brought and which she and her companion ate sitting in a field while I remained in the car, feeling desperately thirsty.

I remember lying on my back along the seat (no seat belts in those days), my knees drawn up, watching the tops of trees and flashes of blue sky skimming past, and thinking that I would never forget this journey or this awful day. The interior of the car had an antiseptic smell – perhaps something to do with the professional calling of its owner – and it reminded me of hospitals and the terrifying occasion when I had been wrenched screaming from the arms of my mother to have my tonsils removed, and this did nothing to improve my humour.

Now of course I realize that I was behaving like a spoiled brat; that had I reasoned with Mum rather than screaming at her, she might well have listened to me and let me stay at home. But my furious outbursts had only served to fuel her conviction that there was something seriously wrong with me, and her eccentric reasoning had persuaded her that boarding school was the perfect answer.

At the time I never thought about the sacrifices she was

prepared to make. Lucas and I were all she had; she mightn't have been the most consistent of mothers, but she adored us, and looking after and providing for us was her life. Too bound up with my own misery and my dread of being away from home, I never spared a thought for her feelings and how much she would miss me. As for the money involved, that never entered my mind. School had always been free, and I assumed that the same applied to boarding school. It wasn't until years later that I discovered my mother had put by what she thought of as an emergency fund for me and Lucas, and that most of this had now been earmarked to pay the majority of my school fees. I also failed to notice that a small watercolour – the only really valuable item in the house, and one I later discovered to have been by a well-known Victorian artist – suddenly disappeared. I know now that Mum hoped for a bursary, but she wasn't banking on it. She had learnt the hard way never to bank on anything. It was to her considerable credit that she made no reference to bursaries when she spoke of the test I was to take. She had told me it was a mere formality, but to her it could mean the difference between relative comfort and real hardship.

Towards the end of our journey, there was much discussion and consulting of maps, in the course of which Mum and the nice man from the chemist nearly came to blows.

'You said you'd do the navigating. I'm just the driver,' he pointed out, as they pulled into a layby to take stock.

'It was fine while we were going north. North is easy,' Mum said.

'What do you mean, north is easy?'

'You don't have to turn the map round, with north. South is much more difficult. Everything's upside down.'

'Oh, don't be ridiculous! Nothing's upside down. It's perfectly straightforward. You're just being a typical woman.'

'How dare you patronize me!' Mum cried.

'And how dare you shout at me in my own car!'

'Perhaps you're forgetting that you are currently living in my house,' my mother rejoined.

'And perhaps you are forgetting the advantages that arrangement brings you.'

Advantages? What advantages? I longed to ask, but didn't want to disturb my sulk.

'And perhaps you are forgetting who's in the back of the car!'

'Oh don't mind me,' I said, relieved to be able to break my silence without sacrificing the sulk. 'You two just carry on fighting. I hope we do get lost, then I shan't ever have to go to that horrid school.'

The arguing dwindled to curt little exchanges, the navigational problems appeared to settle down, and much to my disappointment, we arrived at the school fifteen minutes early.

'Sit up, Cass,' Mum said, as smooth tarmac gave way to crunchy gravel. 'We're here. Look! Isn't it lovely?' She seemed quite carried away. 'Imagine being part of all this!'

In spite of myself, I sat up and looked. But what I saw was very far from lovely. The dark mock Gothic building, turreted and menacing, looked like something out of a horror film. Bleak ivy-clad walls and small sinister windows did nothing to soften the effect, and the surrounding conifers and laurel bushes all added to an impression of deepest grey-green gloom. I almost expected to hear the howling of wolves and see the dark shapes of bats flitting round the chimney pots. It didn't help that the sun had now gone in and rain clouds were gathering above the shiny slate roofs.

'It was built by the Earl of something in 1890, apparently,' Mum continued. 'He wanted something unusual; something *different*. I believe he committed suicide in the end,' she added cheerily.

The interior of the school was cool and dim, redolent of floor polish and disinfectant and cabbage. In the main hallway were four huge leather armchairs with a polished wooden table in the middle. There were portraits on the walls, a vase of wilting lilies in a kind of niche, and a glass cabinet containing a collection of fossils. The only movement came from the motes of dust dancing in the shaft of daylight from the window halfway up the curved staircase. Of human life there was not a sign.

'Should we sit down, do you think, Cass?' Mum asked, still apparently overawed (the nice man from the chemist had wisely gone off to park the car and do his crossword). 'Or – ring something?'

'There doesn't seem to be anything to ring,' I said, too wretched to continue my sulk.

'We'll sit down, then.' Gingerly, Mum lowered herself into one of the chairs. She looked very small and vulnerable in her best summer frock, surrounded by all that creaking leather, and suddenly I felt sorry for her. Poor Mum. She was probably trying to do her best for me, but even I hadn't imagined that a school could be anything like this. My only ideas of boarding schools had come from my long-ago acquaintances with such jolly romps as 'Fiona of the Fourth Form' and 'Penny against the Prefects', and while I personally had never hankered after midnight feasts and pillow fights in the dorm, I could see that for some it might be fun. But I couldn't imagine anyone having fun in this joyless place.

'Ah! Mrs Fitzpatrick, I presume, and this must be Cassandra.' A tall thin woman with a wispy bun of greying hair appeared as though from nowhere, and we both jumped. After a brief struggle, Mum managed to extricate herself from her armchair, and we all shook hands. 'I'm Mary Armitage. Headmistress. Do come this way.'

She led us into a small office (more portraits, but no fossils), and after the briefest of conversations, sat me down at a desk laid out with paper and pens.

'Just a few simple questions, Cassandra,' she said, handing me a question paper. 'I'm sure you won't have any trouble. Your mother and I can go next door and have a cup of tea. I'm sure you could do with one after your journey, Mrs Fitzpatrick?'

Left to my own devices, I realized for the first time that this was of course my opportunity – my only opportunity – to rescue myself from the fate which was closing round me. All I had to do was fail the test! Why hadn't I thought of it before? If I failed the entrance test, the school would presumably no longer want me, otherwise there would be no point in having a test at all. At last my future was in my own hands. Joy and relief flooded through me. I could stay with Mum and Lucas and everyone else. I could play with The Dog and see my friends and I would never have to leave home again. I would show them! Of course, Mum would be disappointed, but she'd get over it.

I smiled and picked up a pencil. For the first time in my life, I was going to fail an exam.

But I had reckoned without my pride.

I paused, pencil poised, agonizing over my decision. To fail or not to fail. Fail. Failure. Such miserable, condemning, dismissive words. I looked again at the first maths question. It was temptingly easy. How could I – how could *anyone* – get such a simple question wrong? I sighed, and picking up a ruler, I set to work and drew a neat triangle.

Five

When news of my scholarship arrived, my mother was beside herself with pride.

'The top scholarship, Cass. Just think! *The top scholarship* for St Andrew's, and you've won it. I just knew you had it in you!'

This last was almost certainly untrue, for no one could have anticipated that I would acquit myself with such distinction. It was true that I was reasonably bright, but that bright? My only (private) conclusion was that the other pupils at this illustrious establishment must be particularly dim if someone like myself was able to shine among them.

Mum set to work at once to make preparations for the celebration party. In our household, modest as it was, any event was an excuse for a party, since my mother's idea of heaven was a houseful of people, and what better way to fill a house with people than to throw a party? While others might worry about gatecrashers, my mother welcomed them with open arms ('such a wonderful way of meeting new people, Cass'), and while lesser mortals concerned themselves with the possibility of spilt drinks and stained upholstery, my mother cared not a jot.

Of course, I didn't want a party at all. All I wanted was to be left in peace to grieve over my fate, possibly gaining a little sympathy in the process, but it seemed that the preparations for what was after all *my* party could go ahead quite comfortably without any reference whatsoever to me.

Mum spent days planning and baking, and everyone connected with our household was recruited to help. Greta made wonderful Swiss confections; Richard, it transpired, had a special recipe for sausage rolls (how on earth did a homeless person, never mind a tramp, come by such a thing, I wondered? but I knew I would be considered to be indulging some sort of unspeakable prejudice if I voiced my doubts); the Lodger was commandeered to put fiddly little things on cocktail sticks; and the nice man from the chemist had promised to open bottles and hand things round.

The guest list included everyone from distant cousins (most far too distant to be expected to attend) to ex-Lodgers and some of my own school friends. These last I declined to invite. It was bad enough having to leave them for what they would almost certainly see as posher environs than any they could hope to aspire to; to be seen to be celebrating the fact would be crass in the extreme. My own special gang of lively miscreants would disapprove of what they would certainly see as snobbish aspirations, and little Sally Mayfield, who dreamed of academic opportunities which could never be hers, would be jealous.

'What about Myra?' Mum asked. 'Surely you'd like to have Myra.'

I thought of the girl who had been my best friend since primary school; fiery, red-headed, naughty Myra, who had taught me to smoke when I was nine years old and with whom I had played dubious games of doctors and nurses at the bottom of the garden; Myra, who was privy to all my secrets (except Uncle Rupert), who despite my efforts to dissuade her was already a seasoned shoplifter, and who lived in a run-down house on the most notorious council estate. Not for the first time, I wondered whether my mother ever had any sense of what was appropriate.

'Myra wouldn't understand,' I said.

'What's there to understand? A party's a party. It'll be fun. *Fun*, Cass. Sometimes I think you've forgotten what it's like to have fun.'

In this, she was probably right. But then, was it entirely appropriate for someone my mother's age to spend so much of her time in pursuit of fun? In those years of my early teens, there were times when I felt that I was the adult and she the child, and that because of this unnatural and premature reversal of our roles, I sometimes had to be doubly sensible to make up for my mother's immaturity.

The party was a success. All my mother's parties were successes, as she didn't hesitate to remind me. It seemed as though everyone I had ever known was packed into our house, eating and drinking and laughing, some of them smoking strange-smelling cigarettes, others making uninvited use of the bedrooms to further their new-found friendships.

Richard had brought his ukulele; Greta sang along to an old gramophone record, accompanied by Mum on the ironing board; someone I had never seen before had brought

44

bagpipes; The Dog sat in the cupboard under the stairs and howled. The noise was indescribable.

I found Lucas sitting on the stairs drinking a pale liquid out of a bottle.

'Vodka,' he explained briefly. 'Want some?'

I nodded and took the bottle from him.

'It doesn't taste of anything,' I objected.

'It doesn't have to,' Lucas grinned. 'Have some more.'

I had some more, and soon discovered that Lucas was right. It didn't matter in the least what vodka tasted like; it was the effect that mattered. Very soon I was singing along to the nearest instrument (the bagpipes, as it happened; not an easy instrument to sing along to, but as I discovered, I simply had to open my mouth and the vodka did the rest).

At half past eleven, the neighbours started to bang on the door and talk about disturbed sleep and work in the morning. Mum smiled and apologized and invited them all in, and some of them even went home to fetch more bottles to replenish our diminishing stocks.

'Just think,' I said to Lucas, as we walked unsteadily towards the kitchen in search of more food, 'any of these people could be our fathers.'

'So they could.'

We rarely discussed our fathers, partly because there was nothing much to discuss, but partly because I think we each minded more than we let on how much we missed having another parent, but didn't like to tell the other how we felt.

'I hope mine wasn't a Lodger.' This was something I dreaded, because Lodgers – even the nicest and best Lodgers – somehow seemed to belong to an inferior species. This may have been because they inhabited the basement, or simply because I would have preferred my father to be at the very least a homeowner, not reliant on anyone else to put a roof over his head.

'Or Uncle Rupert,' Lucas said.

'Oh, no.' I shuddered at such a dreadful thought. 'Mum never fancied him, I'm sure. Besides, he's an uncle. A relation. You can't – you're not allowed to, well, do it with a relation, are you?'

'What's there to stop you?' Lucas grinned unkindly. 'Besides, he's only a very distant kind of uncle; probably not really an uncle at all. And Mum was very fond of him, wasn't she?'

'Not that kind of fond,' I said. 'Besides, we don't look like him, do we? I'd rather it was a Lodger – any Lodger – than Uncle Rupert!'

We sat on the floor eating slices of Greta's apple strudel, contemplating the mysteries of our paternity. I was feeling dizzy from the vodka, and depressed by the (albeit unlikely) theory that I might have been a product of the scrawny loins of Uncle Rupert.

Much later, when most of the guests had departed (some were still lingering in odd corners, and at least two were in my bed) and I was being very sick in the bathroom, my mother came in. She appeared cheerful and only mildly tipsy, and smelled strongly of the odd cigarettes.

'Oh, Cass. You're drunk. Poor you.' She sat down on the edge of the bath and held my head while I deposited the rest of my party food down the lavatory. 'You need to drink lots of water and then go to bed.'

46

'I can't.' I wiped my face and rinsed out my mouth. 'There are people in my bed.'

'How tiresome.' Mum stroked my hair. 'Never mind. You can come and share mine.'

It was years since I had slept in my mother's bed. In my early childhood it had been a place of refuge when I was ill or unhappy. When I had chickenpox, when I had flu, when my pet hamster died, I had sought – and been given – consolation between those sheets, and I can still remember the musky scent of my mother's skin and the sweetish spicy smell of the perfume she used to wear.

'Well, did you enjoy the party after all?' Mum asked, when we had undressed – I was wearing one of her nighties as I didn't like to disturb the occupants of my bedroom – and I had settled myself in what I had come to think of as the visitors' side of the bed (my mother always slept on the left).

'Yes. I suppose so.'

'Good. I thought you would.'

'Mm. Mum' – I hesitated – 'was Uncle Rupert my . . . my father?'

'Uncle Rupert?' Mum let out a peal of laughter. 'Good heavens, no. Whatever gave you that idea?'

'Something Lucas said.'

'Then I shall have to have a word with Lucas, the bad boy,' said Mum fondly.

'Then who? Who was my father? I really need to know.'

I had never pressed my mother on this subject before; she had always been so odd and evasive that I hadn't liked to. But a combination of vodka and the intimacy of sharing her bed had given me new courage.

'Why do you need to know?'

I felt that Mum was playing for time. 'I need to know where half of me comes from. I don't feel whole only knowing about your side.'

But when I came to think about it, I didn't really know that much about Mum's family, either. Her father had been something in the Foreign Office, but had succumbed to a heart attack when she was small. Her mother had been neglectful, and had more recently developed some form of dementia and, after Mum's vain attempts to keep her with us, been committed to an institution some distance away. I knew Mum felt bad about this, and she did contrive to visit my grandmother regularly, but she returned from these visits guilt-ridden and depressed. Her mother no longer knew her. She must have been one of the few people who really did think she was Napoleon (presumably since she was sufficiently deranged to imagine herself to be a French emperor, then the addition of a sex change was a minor detail), and obviously someone like my mother was considered far too insignificant to be granted an audience of any length with anyone so important. Apart from my grandmother (whom we never saw now as Mum thought it might upset us), there was only a sprinkling of cousins, most of them distant, and an aunt in New Zealand doing interesting things with sheep. Ours was not what you would call a close family.

'I think feeling whole is more about being at home and comfortable with who you *yourself* are,' Mum said now. 'I'm not sure it has much to do with your parents.'

'I'd still like to know.'

'Well, I never really knew my father, either.' Mum stroked my hair, her voice pensive.

'That's not the point, Mum. You knew *who he was*. I want to know who *my* father was.'

'Well, there's a bit of a problem there.'

'Why?'

'The thing is, Cass, that I don't know who he was, either.'

'How?' I sat up in bed, shocked. 'How can you not know who he was?' It seemed to me inconceivable that anyone should perform that incredibly rude act and not know with whom they were doing it.

'There were several men—'

'Lodgers?' Oh, please not Lodgers.

'No. We didn't have Lodgers then. Just men. People I met. People I got close to.'

'Oh, Mum!'

'I know. I didn't behave very well, did I?'

'So – so you've no idea at all?'

'It was a long time ago, Cass. I did wonder – of course I did – but then life became a bit hectic, and it went out of my mind. I know this may sound odd to you, but I had you, my beautiful little girl, and I reckoned we could all get by without fathers. After all, I did.'

At this point, I'm sure anyone with an ounce of spirit, any real heroine, would have declared that that was the moment when she decided to track down her real father; that nothing would stand in the way of her discovering his identity; that if necessary she would devote her life to the search for this errant – and probably completely unaware – parent. But while I certainly did want to know who my father had been,

49

I was on the whole content with my family, albeit small. My experiences of men hadn't been particularly positive, and I tended to agree with my mother that we probably didn't need one in our lives. What did shock me, and probably drove any other thoughts from my mind, was my mother's undoubted promiscuity. For while I knew she must certainly have slept with a number of men, I had no idea that her behaviour extended so far back into the past and that her memory of her encounters could be so scanty.

We must have drifted off to sleep after this, because I don't recall that we discussed the matter any further. In fact, the subject of my father was not to be addressed again for many years, and by that time I was able to understand a bit better why my mother had behaved as she had.

We awoke the next morning to find several dishevelled partygoers in the kitchen looking for aspirins and breakfast. Mum was in her element, and spent a happy couple of hours frying bacon and ministering to hangovers. One or two people even stayed on to help with the clearing-up, and I was allowed the day off school.

Six

Mum was packing my school trunk, the uniform list at her side, piles of clothes scattered over the bed.

'Skirts, navy, two. White blouses, five. Five white blouses? Whatever do you need five blouses for? Three should be plenty.' She ticked them off her list. 'Long grey socks, six pairs. Six pairs of socks? You've never possessed six pairs of socks in your life. What can they be thinking of? I'll send four.'

We had already been through all this in the uniform shop, so I didn't take too much notice. After all, no one was ever teased for having only four pairs of socks.

The knickers were another matter.

Typically, my mother had refused to buy underwear at the uniform shop where, it has to be said, the prices had been craftily hiked up to match the prestigious standing of the school. Knickers and vests could be bought anywhere, she reasoned. There was no point in paying the earth for knickers and vests.

'I'll get them, Cass,' she'd said. 'No need for you to come with me this time.'

She had returned in triumph.

'Really cheap, Cass. A bargain, and good quality, too. One hundred per cent cotton.' She tipped out her purchases onto the kitchen table. 'How about that?'

To this day, I shall never know how my mother managed to find royal blue knickers. School knickers, as everyone knows, come in bottle green, grey or navy. No one wears royal blue knickers. No one (as far as I know) even *sells* royal blue knickers.

'But Mum – they're the wrong colour.'

'Blue. They're blue. Nice bright blue knickers.'

'But the list says navy! I can't wear those. I'll get into trouble.'

'Don't be ridiculous, Cass. Of course you won't. Who's going to see them, anyway?'

'Everyone!' I wailed. 'Everyone will see them. I'll have to do gym in them. It says so on the list.'

'Oh, gym!' said Mum dismissively. 'What does it matter what you wear for gym? It's not as though you're going out in them.'

'The knickers are nice, I think?' Greta, slicing carrots, was as usual trying to pour oil on troubled waters and, as usual, completely missing the point. Normally I could cope with her well-meaning interventions, but on this occasion I could cheerfully have strangled her.

'I don't want nice knickers. I want navy knickers!' I raged. 'Is it so much to ask? I've got the wrong colour or number of everything else. Can't I even have the right knickers?'

But Mum was adamant. She had paid good money for those knickers, there was nothing wrong with them, and she certainly wasn't taking them back.

And then there were the name tapes. I had wanted proper name tapes with my name embroidered on them in swirly blue writing. But no. Mine had to be hand-written with a laundry marker on pieces of tape. Mum, usually so generous, also loved a bargain, and home-made name tapes, she assured me, were a marvellous way of saving money. Some were in my writing, some in Mum's, and a few in Greta's strange foreign-looking script. Even Lucas did a couple ('to remind you of me, because I'm not much good at writing letters'). Everyone complained about the length of my name.

'Cassandra Fitzpatrick,' grumbled Mum, writing it out for the umpteenth time. 'Why couldn't you have had a shorter name?'

'You gave it to me,' I pointed out. Personally, I would much prefer to have been called Jane. Even Susan would have been preferable to Cassandra.

'I didn't think. At the time.' Mum reached for another piece of tape. 'Besides, the Fitzpatrick bit wasn't my idea.'

'My *father* might have had a shorter name. He might have been Smith.'

'I never slept with anyone called Smith,' Mum said (fortunately we were alone together when this exchange was taking place). 'There was a Jones once,' she added thoughtfully.

'Could it have been Jones?'

'Too long ago.' Mum sighed. 'Oh dear. Isn't life complicated, Cass?'

I forbore to remind her that some of her life's complications were of her own doing, since I knew she was only too aware of the fact. Besides, by this time I was beginning to realize that the idea of my going away was as disturbing for her as it was for me, and I didn't want to risk upsetting her further. I myself was now resigned to my fate. It mightn't be as bad as I imagined, and my mother could even be right. A change might do me good. After all, as she frequently pointed out, I wasn't particularly happy at home these days.

'Two terms, Cass. Give it a couple of terms,' she'd told me. 'If you really don't like it after that, then you can come home.'

'Promise?' I wanted to make absolutely sure where I stood.

'Promise.'

'OK. I'll give it a go. But I really need to know I can come home if I want to.'

'Of course you can.' Mum had kissed the top of my head. 'This is where you belong. I'm just – well, I'm just lending you to boarding school. This will always be your home.'

At last the preparations were over and I was ready for my new life, with my second-hand trunk, my four pairs of socks, the dreaded blue knickers and all the other impedimenta of a new boarding school pupil. Most of my uniform and other belongings were not quite regulation, since my mother seemed incapable of following what were, after all, fairly simple instructions. Thus, my shoes, though black (regulation) bore an interesting little motif on the sides; my hockey boots looked suspiciously like football boots; and my towels ('two large, two small, white') were three medium-sized and blue. But apart from the knickers (of which more later) I didn't mind too much. I'd been raised as a non-conformist in matters of dress and habit, and there seemed no reason why boarding school should make any difference.

When the time came, I was given quite a send-off. Lucas lent me Blind Bear, his treasured childhood companion (its eyes had been removed by a vicious little boy in his class at infant school, a crime which Lucas had never quite managed to forgive); Greta contributed two of her favourite bars of Swiss chocolate to my tuck box (Mum's contribution was a jar of peanut butter, two packets of rich tea biscuits and an enormous box of Turkish Delight); and the Lodger pressed a ten-shilling note into my willing hand. As for the nice man from the chemist (we had now been invited to 'call me Bill' – inevitably, the name had stuck, and he was Call Me Bill until our acquaintance ended many years later), he presented me with a pretty little box of toiletries. I suspected that these were left over from last Christmas, since the soap smelled musty and the talcum powder refused to sprinkle, but it was a kind thought. Even Richard turned up with a battered copy of an Agatha Christie novel ('to take your mind off things') and Ben (who was, in his words, 'on location' filming an advertisement for socks) sent a card to wish me luck.

My transport consisted of a battered white van loaned for the occasion by an ex-Lodger. My driver was Mum.

'Are you sure?' I asked anxiously, when this arrangement was explained to me. 'Are you sure you know how to drive a van?'

'Of course I do.' Mum laughed merrily. 'Car, van – what's the difference? Just gears and brakes and a steering wheel. They're all the same when it comes down to it.'

But I wasn't so sure. My mother was an occasional and erratic driver (she had never actually owned a car) with – as in other areas of her life – her own rules. I was an unwilling passenger at the best of times when she was in the driving seat, and to my unpractised eye the van didn't look at all the same as a car.

'You can't see out of the back,' I objected. 'There's no window.'

'Wing mirror,' said Mum. 'That's all you need, really. A wing mirror. We'll be fine, Cass. Trust me.'

I longed for Call Me Bill and his Rover, but the Rover was out of commission with engine trouble, and in any case, my mother was evidently eager to chauffeur me herself.

'It's the least I can do, Cass,' she said. 'We'll take a picnic, like last time, and The Dog can come too. It will make a change for him.'

In the event, it made an unwelcome and terrifying change for all of us. The van rattled and bounced all over the road, ricocheting off kerbs and verges; Mum, trying to drive and map-read at the same time, cursed and fumed; and The Dog whimpered miserably in the back as he scrabbled back and forth in his attempts to avoid the wildly slithering and very heavy trunk. As for me, I clung to the edges of my seat and closed my eyes, praying for this horrible journey to end as soon as possible.

We were too late to have our picnic, and in any case, I doubt whether either of us could have eaten anything; and when we eventually arrived at the school, the skies opened up as though on cue and welcomed us with a spectacular thunderstorm.

Seven

It is hard now to recount my initial experiences of boarding school. Everything was so new, and so entirely different from anything I had ever known, that my memories of those first few weeks are a jumble of mixed-up impressions and emotions, all of them tinged with the appalling homesickness.

I had never in my life been homesick simply because I had never been away from home. Very occasionally I had stayed overnight with a friend, but I much preferred my friends to come to me, and in this they were more than happy to concur. For my friends adored Mum. No one had a mother like mine, apparently; a mother who appeared unshockable and one to whom they could talk about anything (frequently, inevitably, sex – my friends had a voracious curiosity when it came to matters sexual, and my mother was always happy to answer their questions; no question ever fazed her, and if she didn't know the answer she would make one up). My mother would also allow us all to stay up half the night eating unsuitable food and giggling and listening to Radio Luxembourg ('turn out the lights, when you're done, Cass, and try not to make too much noise'). Even in her more depressed moments, Mum was unfailingly hospitable and kind, and would put herself out to make sure we all had a good time.

So homesickness was an entirely new experience. Of course I had expected to miss my home and family, but nothing had prepared me for the physical pain and the sheer wrenching grief which overwhelmed me, usually at bedtime, but often suddenly, unexpectedly, during the day. Some little thing – a word, an image, a small imagined unkindness – would set me off, and the pain would surge up through my chest, threatening to choke me. I tried not to cry, and usually succeeded, but I shall never forget how it felt. At night in bed, I would hug Blind Bear to me, chewing on his ears (one eventually came off altogether) to stifle the ache in my throat, thinking of Mum and Lucas and everyone else carrying on with their lives without me. I would imagine Mum bending over to kiss me goodnight, ruffling my hair as she pulled the blankets up under my chin; the pencil of light from the passage shining under my bedroom door; the cosy familiar sounds of someone running a bath, milk bottles being put out on the doorstep and The Dog being let out for a final run (three times round the lawn, a quick pee against the gate post, a triumphant yap and back in again).

From my initial impression of the school on that first visit, I had half expected it to incorporate the combined elements of a horror film and *Tom Brown's Schooldays* (a story I loved, but not one in which I would like to have taken part), but in fact it was not unpleasant. The teachers were kind on the whole, and my fellow-pupils reasonably friendly. My name blended in perfectly with the Fionas and the Camillas and the double-barrelled daughters of the higher echelons (I think it was the first time in my life that it hadn't been singled out for censure and accusations of snobbery), and I was enough of a chameleon to be able to disguise the hint of Norfolk lilt which was part of my heritage. Of course, by no means all my peers were either posh or wealthy – and some, like me, had earned their places through scholarships and bursaries – but they were in such contrast to the girls in my previous school that at times it felt as though I were living with the combined female offspring of the entire aristocracy.

Next to the homesickness, my biggest problem was having to conform to set rules. Of course my previous school had had its rules, but the classes were large, the pupils a disparate lot and discipline a problem, so most of us managed to get away with all kinds of deviations. Thus, our uniform varied considerably from girl to girl, badly executed (or hastily copied) homework was often overlooked, and our meals (most of us took packed lunches) were of our own choosing. Besides, we were only at school between the hours of 9 a.m. and 4 p.m. After that, our day was our own.

Not so boarding school. Every minute of every day was regulated. Apart from a few brief hours at the weekend, we had little time to ourselves. Ruled by the clock and the school bell, we were shunted from one activity to another; from bed to breakfast, from supper to prep, from piano practice to PE; we were like army recruits scurrying round a barracks, always under pressure and often (in my case) late.

Bedtime was particularly hard for me (in bed by 8.30, lights out at 9) as I had never in my life had a bedtime. Of course I had heard of bedtimes – most of my friends had bedtimes – but I had never had to abide by them myself. My mother reasoned that if we were tired, we would go to bed, and in this Lucas and I were fairly sensible. It may have been because we had never had a bedtime to conform to that we had no reason to rebel, and in fact we were usually in bed in good time. To be told to go to bed at a particular time was a different matter altogether, and seemed a terrible infringement of my freedom. Deprived of my customary hour of reading, I was often unable to sleep, and would lie in the dark listening to the regular breathing of my companions, clutching Blind Bear and longing for home.

Likewise, meal times. In our household, these were rare, not least because my mother was often at work. There was always food around, and we were encouraged to help ourselves when we were hungry. Sometimes Mum cooked for us, but often we (or whoever else happened to be around) prepared our food. Lucas and I were quite accomplished cooks, used to combining whatever ingredients we found in the larder, and we both enjoyed experimenting with new dishes. Some of these may have seemed odd to an outsider (Lucas's sardine omelette was a favourite), but to us it was just the way things were done. If you were hungry, you prepared yourself something to eat. It was as simple as that.

At school, the meals were regular, overcooked and bland. From the breakfast toast (limp and leathery) through lunch (usually some kind of meat, always liberally anointed with the same lumpy gravy and accompanied by sad-looking boiled-to-death vegetables) to supper (something on toast followed by cake or biscuits from our tuck boxes; mine was empty by the end of the second week) there was a sameness in our diet which took away all the pleasant anticipation I had hitherto associated with food.

Throughout all this, although thoughts of Uncle Rupert himself were mercifully beginning to fade, I was often haunted by fears and nightmares. Sleeping in an unlocked dormitory with seven other girls I felt exposed, but I tried to console myself with the thought that perhaps there was safety in numbers. I might not be able to secure the door, but should an intruder strike, there were more of us to choose from, and my bed was furthest from the door.

My favourite moment of the week was the hour on Sundays that was allocated for us to write our letters home. Most of my schoolfellows found this a terrible chore, and sat chewing their pencils and gazing out of the window, but for me this was the nearest I got to talking to Mum, and I made full use of it.

My own post (given out at breakfast) was meagre. Mum, it is true, endeavoured to write to me once a week, but often these letters were short and scrappy, written in odd moments at work or while waiting for potatoes to boil or a cake to be cooked, sometimes scrawled on the backs of envelopes or bills (on one occasion I received my news from home on the back of a bloodstained butcher's bill; not an epistle I felt tempted to cherish for long). What she wrote was often entertaining, but I felt cheated that she didn't devote more effort to her correspondence with her exiled daughter; that I obviously wasn't the priority I had expected to be. Lucas, true to his word, rarely wrote, and although Greta made an effort, her written English was so much worse than the English she spoke that her letters were often very difficult to understand.

Myra sent me the occasional note, but I think she was probably dyslexic (no one had heard of dyslexia in those days) and it would sometimes take me days to unscramble the hotchpotch of blots and characters her letters comprised. Altogether, my post bag tended to be a disappointment, and a disappointment at breakfast is not a good start to the day.

I kept all my letters in a box in my bedside locker, and together with my letters home, which Mum saved and which I still have in my possession, they make poignant, even nostalgic reading. Going through them now, I recall the pains I went to to avoid too much mention of the homesickness which dominated those early weeks, as I knew how much distress it would have caused. I was not an especially stoical child, but I recognized my mother's vulnerability, and tried my best to avoid adding to her problems. Yet when I read those letters now, and remember how I felt when I was writing them, I feel that pain almost as fiercely as I did then; and in spite of the many trials and tragedies that were to take place in the years which followed, I still think that the aching, solitary suffering of homesickness was one of the hardest things I have ever had to endure.

Eight

Dear Mum,

*This place is all right but not as nice as home. My bed
is a bit like a hospital bed, with a locker, but no flowers
of course. I sleep next to someone called Susannah who
actually snores (I thought only men snored) although
she says she doesn't. There are only nineteen girls in my
class, so the teacher always knows what's going on, and
no one is allowed to sit at the back (Myra and I always
sat at the back so that we could write each other notes
during class). We play a most peculiar game called
lacrosse, and I've got to have my own lacrosse stick (it
looks just like a fishing net) and I'm very bad at it.*

*I think I've got a best friend, although I'm not sure
how she feels about me. Anyway, we get on well and
make each other laugh. Her name is Helena (quite a
sensible name for this school) and she lives in a big*

house in Derbyshire. She is new too, which helps, but she is much better at lacrosse than I am.

The blue knickers are a disaster. I told you they would be. Our PE teacher is an enormous woman in a green tracksuit, and she has a very loud voice.

'What colour do you call those knickers, Cassandra?' she bellowed at me the first time we did PE, and I thought that was a pretty silly question, so I said 'red', and she put me in detention for being cheeky. But I really really do need navy ones, Mum. I'm not being fussy, and I don't mind looking a bit different, but those knickers make me look very different indeed. Helena calls them 'blue mers', which she thinks is very funny, but then she's got navy ones so it's OK for her to laugh.

The other girls are quite nice on the whole, although there's a gang who are a bit stand-offish and stay with each other in the holidays and make private jokes and tease poor little Monica, who is fat with sticky-out teeth and red hair. I try to be nice to her, but she's an awful wimp and very greedy. I offered her my biscuits and she took three.

Work is fine. I came second in a maths test, and my last essay was read out in class, but I got into trouble for setting fire to my lab coat when we were doing chemistry. I can't see the point in boiling things up in test tubes, although some of the colours are interesting.

Must go. Supper time.

Love from Cass xxx

PS   Please ask Lucas to write to me. I wrote to him every day when he was in hospital.

Darling Cass,

It was lovely to get your letter with all your news. I read it to everyone at breakfast, and they were all very interested. Call Me Bill said boarding school was obviously doing you good. Is it? Are you happy? You don't say, but I really want to know.

All is much as usual here. I think The Dog misses you as he keeps going up to your room and snuffling under the bed. Call Me Bill is sleeping in it at the moment, but of course I'll turn him out and give your room a good clean before you come home at half-term. I hope you don't mind, but it's turned very cold and Richard is sleeping in the living room. They say you can't have too much of a good thing, but if a ukulele is a good thing, then I assure you that you can. I almost prefer Lucas on the violin.

We've got a new Lodger. We found him in the local paper. He's a weaselly little man with tufty hair and eyes like tiny black beads, and he seems to be out at night a lot. Lucas thinks he's a cat burglar because he's the right size for climbing through windows and always seems to have plenty of money. I don't really care what he does as long as he pays the rent and cleans the bath after use. But I don't think I'll get fond of him. It's odd, isn't it, that there are the kinds of Lodgers one can be fond of, and those one can't. I don't think he's especially fond of us, either.

I'm sorry about the knickers, and can't understand why everyone's making such a fuss. I'll try to get some

more when I have time. I haven't much time at the
moment as I've got a new job as a waitress. Such fun,
Cass, and I get lots of tips. Greta thinks it's beneath
me, but what does she know? I don't think she's ever
done an honest day's work in her life, or any other sort,
come to that. But then she's got Private Means.

Lucas has a girlfriend! She is small and mousy, with
a stammer. I wonder what Lucas sees in her. Maybe she
makes him feel masterful. Masterful or not, Lucas's
hormones aren't helping his school work. He seems to
come bottom in everything.

Got to go. Making gingerbread men.

Love, Mum xx

PS   I hated chemistry too. I think it's a boy thing.

(This was the first and longest of Mum's letters. I think she
must have been missing me, or perhaps writing me letters was
a novelty. If that was the case, the novelty was very short-
lived.)

St Andrew's School
17th Sept. 1961

Dear Mum,

Who were the gingerbread men for? Isn't everyone too
old for gingerbread men now? Lucas certainly is, if he's
got a girlfriend. Talking of which, I don't suppose he'll
ever write now. I wonder what they do together. I can't
imagine Lucas kissing anyone. What's her name?

I'm OK, but I seem to get into an awful lot of
trouble. There are so many rules and regulations, and I
often can't remember what I'm supposed to be doing.

I'm either late, or in the wrong place, or I've forgotten some important piece of equipment. Talking of which, I REALLY need those navy knickers. Matron looked out a pair that had belonged to someone who left, but they are enormous and look even more ridiculous than mine. The elastic has gone all floppy, and I have to hold them up with my tie. Even then, I don't dare do too much leaping about in case they fall down. This may not seem very important to you, but at the moment I can't think of anything that would make me happier than some of my own which actually fit me. You asked me if I was happy, and the answer is not very, but the right knickers would be a start. PLEASE, Mum.

Does Call Me Bill have to sleep in my room? I don't like the idea of him poking around among my things, and I certainly don't like the thought of him in my bed. Why can't he get a place of his own? As for Richard, I always thought he rather took pride in being a Homeless Person. If he's living in our home all the time then he can't call himself one any more, can he? He certainly shouldn't put his HUNGRY AND HOMELESS notice round his neck. It's not fair on the people who give him money. The Agatha Christie he gave me has fifteen pages missing, so I shall never know what happened in the library.

The new Lodger sounds awful. Couldn't you find a better one? If you really think he's a burglar you could try going through his stuff when he's out. There might be a reward, and then you could stop being a waitress. It's time our family had some proper money. Helena is very rich and lives in a big house and has a horse of her own. She wants me to stay with her for half-term.

I came bottom in a chemistry test. I've never been

*bottom in anything before, but if I had to be, then I
think I'd choose chemistry to be bottom in. Tell that to
Call Me Bill. He might not like to sleep in the bed of
someone who comes bottom in chemistry.*

Love from Cass xxx

Hazelwood House
21st Sept.

Darling Cass,

*The gingerbread men were for Richard. He says they
remind him of his childhood. And of course he's
homeless because he hasn't got a home of his own. I'm
surprised at you, Cass. I always thought you were such
a kind child.*

*Call Me Bill saw your letter and took umbrage and
has gone back to his landlady with a bunch of flowers.
So you've managed to upset him too, and you're not
even here! I miss his car. It was useful for shopping and
the doctor.*

*Lucas's girlfriend is called Millie. Rather a silly
name, I thought. And I've no idea what they get up to
but I've told Lucas all about condoms, so they should
be fine.*

*I went to the market to try and buy your knickers,
but they only had pink or white frilly ones.*

Greta is having Spanish lessons.

*We've decided the Lodger isn't a burglar after all as
he's got quite a posh voice and washes a lot.*

*Please don't go somewhere else for half-term. We'll
really miss you.*

Love, Mum xxx

(I must have been very irritated by this letter of Mum's, for my reply had a waspish edge to it.)

St Andrew's School
24th Sept. 1961

Dear Mum,

I'm doing OK still, though I haven't cracked the chemistry yet. Miss Cole keeps me behind after everyone has gone to explain things all over again, but I still don't understand it. She says I don't concentrate. How can anyone concentrate on anything so boring? Yesterday we boiled up potassium permanganate in a test tube and then filtered it. What possible use is that to anyone? I spilt mine down my front and had to go and change.

Your last letter was very odd. For instance, what makes you think that someone with a posh voice who washes a lot isn't a burglar? I'm sure there must be clean burglars as well as dirty ones. Having said that, I never thought he was a burglar in the first place (although I've never met him).

Call Me Bill should never have read my letter. My letters home are PRIVATE. If he read it, then he deserves to go back to his landlady. I hope she gives him a hard time.

Don't bother about the knickers. Helena was so sorry for me that she wrote to her mother to say she had lost hers, and her mother sent some more, so I've got those (I'm not sure how you lose six pairs of knickers, but her mother didn't ask any awkward questions). Of course the market don't have navy ones.

They have cheap and nasty common ones. I would NEVER buy knickers from the market.

As for Richard, he's using you. It seems to me that everyone uses you, and you just don't realize it. And what does Greta want to learn Spanish for? She needs to have English lessons first. I hope she's still helping with the cooking.

Helena really wants me to stay for half-term. She says I can ride her horse. She's got an older brother, and acres of garden. I'm not usually jealous of people, but sometimes I'm a bit jealous of Helena.

I don't think I want to hear about Lucas and Millie.

Love from Cass xxx

Hazelwood House
5th October

Darling Cass,

I thought this picture postcard of the town hall would remind you of home. The Dog's been knocked down. Stitches in leg, but otherwise OK. Call Me Bill's landlady's allergic to flowers and threw him out again so he's back. Greta knitting you a cardigan. Please come home for half-term. Sorry this is so short – no room for more.

Love, Mum xxx

Nine

My mother moves restlessly on her pillow, her fingers pluck-ing at the sheet, her lips moving soundlessly.

'Are you in pain, Mum?'

'Pain,' she nods. 'Oh, such pain!'

I ring the bell and a nurse – one my mother particularly dislikes, all bosom and bustle and shiny badges – comes in with a syringe on a little tray.

'Roll over, dear.' My mother claws her way to the edge of the bed, exposing her painfully thin bottom. The nurse stabs with a practised flick of her wrist. 'There we are. All done. Time to sleep now.'

'"Roll over, dear,"' mimics my mother, as the nurse whisks out of the room. 'Like the bloody lottery. Silly cow.'

We exchange glances and smile. Oh Mum! I love you so much. Have I ever told you just how much I love you?

'Love you, Cass.' Mind-reader. Becoming drowsy. Begin-ning to drift off now, on a tide of drugs.

'Love you too, Mum.'

At this moment, I would give everything I have to spare

my mother her suffering, and yet over the years, she and I
have caused each other much pain, one way or another. That,
I suppose, is the price of love. But often I didn't realize how
much I was hurting her.

I must have hurt her badly that first half-term, and yet at
the time, I barely gave it a second thought.

For I did go to Helena's for half-term. I think that postcard
of Mum's clinched it. I had missed her so much, and imagined her missing me. I had pictured us rushing into each
other's arms when I returned home, my favourite meals being
cooked, perhaps even one of Mum's famous parties to welcome me home. I had already gathered that life at home was
progressing quite nicely without me, and I could just about
handle that. But I had hurried to fetch my post that morning,
and all I had received was that one lousy postcard. Up until
then, I had never even noticed the town hall, and I certainly
didn't need a cosy little reminder of its continued existence.

How I regretted sparing Mum all my tales of woe; the
homesickness, the nights spent weeping into my pillow,
the touching, cherished services of Blind Bear. Selflessly, I
had spared her feelings by not bothering her with emotive
accounts of my misery, and she had repaid me by letting Call
Me Bill into my bed and sending me a postcard instead of a
proper letter. However much information you put on a postcard (and there was very little on this one), there is something
careless and impersonal about a piece of correspondence
which is open for anyone to read.

One of our Lodgers, a snob and a name-dropper, who had
so many letters after his name that they took up more room

than his address (Mum thought he had made most of them up), used to send us what Lucas called boastcards. These would arrive from various distinguished venues where he disported himself in the company of those whose names he so frequently dropped, and were obviously intended to be read by – and to impress – as many people as possible. They were usually just addressed to Mum, but they fooled no one.

Thus, with that postcard, my mother had put paid to her chances of having me home for that first precious exeat. If she was going to treat me with such cavalier indifference, then two could play at that game. Besides, the idea of spending the half-term holiday in Helena's grand house appealed to me enormously, and although I still longed to go home, I would be back at Christmas and could see everyone then. I might even send Mum a postcard.

But Helena's house was not at all what I had imagined. There was no park, no tree-lined drive, no stone steps sweeping up to the front door. The house was big, it is true, but it was modern and ugly, with unpleasant orangey-pink brickwork and pretentious black and gold gates. There were certainly statues in the large, manicured garden, but these were poor imitations of armless Greek females swathed in drapery, stooping sentimentally over seats and flower beds, and there was a vulgar little Cupid peeing into a pond.

Inside, the house was a shrine to the gods of conspicuous consumption, from the gold-plated drinks trolley in the spacious living room to the lavatory paper holder in the downstairs cloakroom, which played a merry jingle from a Disney cartoon every time you took a sheet of paper.

'Do you like it?' Helena asked, when she had shown me round the house. 'My parents had it architect-designed.'

'It's amazing,' I said with absolute truth, and fortunately this seemed to satisfy her.

'I'll take you up to your room,' she continued, picking up my suitcase. 'Come on.'

I had envisaged us sharing a room, having cosy chats into the small hours, exchanging those confidences which are best shared in the dark. This was what I had been used to at home, where any visitors I had were accommodated on a mattress on my bedroom floor. This arrangement had suited my friends and me admirably, but obviously things were done differently in Helena's household.

'Here!' Helena flung open a door. 'This is yours.'

The room was vast, with an enormous double bed and even a small sofa. Everything was fussy and frilly, decorated in what my mother used to call 'bridesmaid colours' (peach, aqua, lilac), with matching fluffy towels laid out in the adjoining bathroom. In those days, it was almost unheard of to have one's own bathroom, but while I was impressed that I should have the use of one, there was something very insular and chilling about having one's needs catered for on such a solitary basis.

But despite my spacious accommodation, I was beginning to feel stifled; stifled by the opulence and the frills, stifled by the feeling that I was supposed to react in a way which I found almost impossible, and stifled by the heat. I had never in my life experienced central heating. Home was heated by a combination of open fires and electric heaters. If we were cold, we were told to put on more clothes, and in the winter we all used hot water bottles. Here, the heat was overpowering, and although it was a chilly week in October, the only occasions upon which I wore a sweater were when we went outdoors.

Helena's parents were kind and welcoming, but they were not what I would call homely people. Her mother was immaculate in her pale slacks, low-cut blouses and stilettos, with dyed blonde hair and lots of gold jewellery; her father was quiet and dark-suited, and seemed to spend most of his time at work.

'Where do you keep your books?' I asked Helena once, desperate for something to read (I had already finished the two I had brought with me).

'Books?' She smiled vaguely. 'We haven't really got many books, though Mum sometimes goes to the library.'

So I had to content myself with old copies of *Reader's Digest* and the heavy (and obviously unread) volume of *European Art Collections* from the coffee table.

The other disconcerting thing about a visit which was less than satisfactory was the change in Helena. I suppose we all alter according to our environment, but Helena was a different person when she was at home. Gone were the giggles and the pranks we enjoyed at school, and she spent much of her time phoning her friends or shopping with her mother (I was invited to accompany them but declined, since I had no money and didn't want to be in a position where I had to borrow any). The horse, Elvis, which was kept in an adjoining paddock, was my only consolation, and although I was a timid rider (I had never been on a horse before), I enjoyed grooming him and leading him down the nearby lane to graze (the grass in his field was sparse, and so far he had declined the hay that was on offer). I think Elvis was as lonely as I was, and so the arrangement probably suited him as well as it did me.

'Aren't you bored?' Helena asked me once. 'Just standing around watching Elvis can't be much fun.'

'I'm never bored,' I said, and it was true. While the discipline at home had always been pretty lax, the one thing Mum would never tolerate was boredom. If you had a brain to think and eyes with which to read, there was no excuse, she always told us, and in this she was successful, for I don't remember either Lucas or me ever being bored.

Strangely, I felt even more homesick at Helena's than I had at school. School wasn't meant to be homely, and I had never expected it to be so. But before my visit to Helena's I had anticipated at least a little of the comfortable domesticity of home. A cosy kitchen, cooking smells, Mum in her old apron, the busy sound of the wireless (BBC Home Service), people's various comings and goings; all these helped to comprise the atmosphere which I had always called home, together with saggy, old, comfortable furniture and dusty collections of books in every corner. In contrast, Helena's house was bandbox tidy, the cushions neatly angled on their corners on sofas and chairs, the pale carpet spotless, the air fragrant with lavender furniture polish. I tiptoed round the house, terrified lest I disturb or sully any of this perfection. I was grateful that I had tucked Blind Bear at the bottom of my suitcase, for without him I don't think I would have survived at all.

The day before we were due to return to school, Helena's elder brother, Alex, returned from boarding school for his half-term holiday. I had never given much thought to the sub-ject of Greek Gods, but seeing Alex for the first time, I knew immediately what one would look like. Tall and slim, with waving blond hair and sea-green eyes, he eyed me up and down when we were introduced and smiled a lazy teasing smile.

'So this is Cassandra.' His voice was unexpectedly deep, his handshake warm and firm. 'Well well. You never told me how pretty she was, little sister.' He turned mockingly to Helena. 'Perhaps you were jealous?'

'Oh, shut up, Alex!' Helena was obviously stung. 'Take no notice of him, Cass. He's like this with all my friends.'

'Only the attractive ones,' Alex said, unperturbed by Helena's indignation. 'And this one, Helena dear, is very attractive indeed.'

I shall never know how I got through the rest of that evening. Sitting opposite Alex at dinner, I was painfully aware of him watching me; of the teasing smile, the slightly raised eyebrow, and once, when I caught his eye, a knowing wink. I couldn't imagine that this sophisticated young man was actually still a schoolboy, having to wear a uniform and abide by rules and bedtimes just as we did. Helena had told me that he was seventeen, but to me he looked much older; certainly years older than Lucas. He seemed to treat his par-ents with the same levity as he did his sister, although they both obviously adored him; and if his manner towards them was more than a little high-handed, neither of them seemed aware of it. They questioned him closely, applauding his sporting achievements and exam results, laughing at his jokes, hanging on the most humdrum of his words. If they

77

had possessed a fatted calf this would certainly have been the occasion for it to be called into service.

I glanced at Helena, and felt for her. Poor Helena. With her indifferent academic achievements and average looks, how could she compete with such a brother? Hitherto I had never given much thought to sibling rivalry. Lucas and I had always been sufficiently fond of each other and sufficiently different in our abilities for comparisons to seem unnecessary, and Mum was not one to show favouritism. But there was no mistaking who was the favourite child in this family.

Later that evening, as I was making my way up to my room, Alex stopped me on the staircase.

'I meant what I said,' he told me.

'What? What did you mean?' I pressed myself against the wall, hoping he would go past me and let the matter drop.

'You're very pretty, Cassandra. Very pretty indeed.' He turned to face me, placing his hands against the wall on either side of me, effectively preventing me from moving on.

'Please – please let me pass.' I made as though to move away, but Alex merely laughed.

'Oh Cassandra, don't tell me you're shy!'

'No, of course not. I just want – I want to go to bed.'

'Bed? Did you say bed? What a very forward young lady you are!'

'I mean I want to go to my room.' My heart was thumping inside my chest like a trapped bird, and my palms were sweating. I longed for Helena to appear, but she had already gone up for a bath, and was unlikely to come down again. 'Please. Please let me go.'

'Why? Why should I let you go?' Alex seemed to consider for a moment. 'OK. I'll let you go. But you'll have to pay.'

'Pay?'

'Yes. A kiss. One little kiss, and then you can go. A small price to pay, wouldn't you say?'

'No. I mean, I'd rather not. Please let me go. I just want to go upstairs.'

'A kiss, Cassandra. I demand it.' Alex leant forward. I could feel his breath warm on my cheek and smell the wine he had had at dinner. 'One little kiss.'

I put out my hands to push him away, but he was surprisingly strong. His hands were on my shoulders now, his face close to mine.

'No! *No!*' I managed to get the words out before his mouth closed on mine, and then I screamed. All the terror and revulsion of my encounter with Uncle Rupert came back to me, and I screamed with a strength born of desperation. On some distant level I was aware that I was overreacting; that nothing serious could happen on a staircase in a house full of people, but the screaming wouldn't stop. It was almost as though it had nothing to do with me; as though some other part of me had taken over.

'Hey! Hey!' Alex looked as frightened as I was. He took me by the shoulders and shook me gently. 'Cassandra! I didn't mean anything. It was just a joke. Come on. Stop this noise, for goodness' sake!'

From different parts of the house, I could hear doors opening and hurrying footsteps. I had to get away. Stifling my sobs, I ducked under Alex's arm and rushed up the stairs, along the corridor and into my room, where I slammed the door shut and then leant against it, my chest heaving, the tears still streaming down my face.

'Cassandra? Let me in, dear. Whatever's the matter?' Helena's mother was outside the door, trying the door handle. 'Come on, Cassandra. You must tell me what's wrong!'

Reluctantly, I moved away from the door. I had no idea what I was going to say. I knew that if I told the truth no one would believe me, for I couldn't imagine Helena's parents ever thinking ill of their golden boy. I would be branded a liar, and Helena wouldn't want me for her friend any more.

Fortunately, Alex had come up with his own version of events.

'Alex said you thought you saw a mouse. Is that true, Cassandra?' Helena's mother came into the room and put her arm round me.

'No. Yes. Yes – I'm sure I saw a mouse.' I sat down on the bed. 'I'm sorry. It – it scared me.'

'That's all right, dear, although you did give us all a bit of a fright. After all, if it was a mouse – and I sincerely hope not; we've never had mice in this house – it's nothing to be afraid of, is it?'

I shook my head, unable to speak. I was furious with Alex. Furious with him for subjecting me to his unwanted attentions, furious that he should imply that I was the kind of girl who would be afraid of a mouse, and furious that he should lie to get himself out of his predicament, secure in the knowledge that I would probably back him up. I felt stupid and humiliated and ashamed, and all I wanted now was to be left alone.

But I had to endure all the fussing attention which

Helena's mother seemed to think appropriate for a deranged guest, and it wasn't until I'd had a hot bath ('leave the door unlocked, dear – just in case'), a mug of hot milk (which I hated) and a hot water bottle (which I didn't need) that I was finally left on my own.

Homesick and wretched, wishing myself anywhere but in this awful house, I eventually cried myself to sleep.

Ten

The injection is beginning to work and Mum becomes drowsy, her eyelids drooping, her twitching transparent hands loosening their grip on the sheet. I want her to sleep – of course I do – and yet we have so little time left together and I don't want to waste a minute of it. Apart from anything else, there's so much I want to ask her; so much that will die when she dies. How old was I when I took my first steps? Lost my first tooth? Stopped believing in Father Christmas? My whole childhood is sleeping with her on that pillow, and the bits I can't remember will go when she does. But how can I deny her the little respite she gets from her pain and her anxiety?

That term seemed endless. The weather turned bitingly cold, and we shivered as we scurried between classrooms, rubbing life back into our mottled thighs after games of hockey, where the only pain worse than the blow of a hockey stick against an unsuspecting ankle was a tumble onto the frozen pitch. We were always hungry, and there never seemed to be enough food. Meals were hurried (just twenty minutes for supper, before the start of evening prep), and we went to bed with rumbling stomachs.

Many relied on the contents of tuck boxes to stave off their hunger, and the arrival of food parcels – for that was what they amounted to – was greeted with great joy. Fortunate (and popular) was the girl who received a steady supply of provisions from home, but I was one of the unlucky ones, for in this respect, as in so many others, Mum proved unreliable. When I did receive a package from home it was as likely to contain something knitted by Greta (which I wasn't allowed to wear) or a book (which I didn't have the time to read) as the sweets and biscuits I craved. The navy knickers did finally arrive, tucked round two packets of peanuts, but the knickers were too late and the peanuts were musty-tasting. I suspected Mum had found them mouldering away at the back of a cupboard (no sell-by dates in those days).

My friendship with Helena resumed as though half-term had never happened. Perhaps there are some friendships which rely on a particular environment in order to thrive. No reference was made by either of us to what had been a pretty unsuccessful week, and nothing was said of Alex or mice. Had Helena questioned me on the subject of the episode on the stairs, I don't think I would have been able to dissemble as readily as I had to her mother. I suspect that, like most teenagers, Helena was not overly preoccupied with the ills of others, preferring to concentrate on her own problems (at the time, the likelihood that she would come bottom in the end-of-term exams).

My own school work was proceeding well. St Andrew's

was not an especially academic school, seeming content with its small but respectable annual clutch of university places, and most of the time I hovered comfortably near the top of my class. My chemistry results were consistently abysmal, but that didn't bother me. An inability to get by in French or an ignorance of English literature might be expected to carry a stigma, but no one was ever condemned for failing to shine at chemistry.

Piano lessons were another matter.

Perhaps to make up for the fact that she had never had piano lessons herself, Mum insisted that I should have them. Not for me the record player and the ironing board; I was to learn to play a real piano properly.

'It can't be that hard,' she had told me, before I started my new school, her hands moving lovingly up and down the back of one of Call Me Bill's shirts (she had taken to doing his laundry as well as everyone else's) to the accompaniment of a Mozart concerto. 'Lots of people can play the piano.'

What she had evidently failed to notice was that lots of people play the piano very badly, and we were both about to discover that I was one of them.

'I can't. I just can't,' I sobbed during my fourth piano lesson, when once again I had failed to understand how a scatter of dots and squiggles could be interpreted as musical notes.

'But you can read, can't you?' Mr Presley, a dapper little man who came to the school twice a week to teach piano, looked bewildered. 'It's the same principle. You translate letters into words. You do the same with music, only in this case it's notes. Now dry your eyes, Cassandra, and try again.'

I tried again. And again. But to no avail. How could anyone not only interpret all those lines and dots, but do it with *both hands at once*? By the end of the term, I had failed to master even the rudiments of 'The Jolly Farmer', a horrid bouncy little piece which was the launch pad of the musical career of all Mr Presley's pupils. And at my last lesson of the term, he gently suggested that I might consider giving it up. I could have kissed him.

I looked forward eagerly to Christmas: to the chaos and bustle of a house full of Mum's waifs and strays; to the bedraggled football socks which served as Christmas stockings and which Lucas and I hung up on Christmas Eve; and to Christmas carols from an old and very scratched record (we had to help it along in the middle of 'Silent Night', where it always got stuck).

I was much exercised as to how I was to travel home, dreading a repeat of Mum and the van, but in the event I was spared, for Call Me Bill took the afternoon off to bring her to collect me in his car.

'Here we are!' cried Mum gaily, getting out of the passenger seat and sweeping me into her arms. 'Oh, Cass! You've grown, and you're so thin!'

I forbore to take this opportunity to remind her that her contributions to my intake of food had been sadly lacking. There would be plenty of time for that later. As I succumbed to her embrace, I was aware of other girls watching us. Next to the Jaguars and the Mercedes, Call Me Bill's car looked shabby and tired, and Mum, swathed in several layers of faded cardigans and sporting a bright red knitted hat (Greta's handiwork, I had no doubt), appeared out of place among the tailored and coiffed mothers of my friends, but I didn't care. I was used to – even proud of – my family's eccentricities, and after my experience of Helena's household, I was also grateful.

The Dog, anxious not to be excluded from the reunion, leapt from the open car door and threw himself at me ('He so wanted to come,' Mum later explained. 'He couldn't wait to see you.' How on earth could she tell?), and completed our little display by making a neat deposit in the middle of the lawn. It was time to get going.

That Christmas was everything I could have hoped for. Mum, inspired by a posh magazine she'd seen at the dentist's, had festooned the bannisters and mantelpieces with swags of red ribbon and ivy, and there was a colourful wreath on the front door. All this looked rather incongruous when combined with our faded paper chains and the battered decorations on the Christmas tree, but it gave the house a more than usually festive feel, and in any case, none of us was too much bothered with matters of taste.

The house guests consisted of Call Me Bill, who didn't appear to have any family, the Lodger, who had fallen out with his parents, and a friend of Greta's who was over from Switzerland. Fortunately, Greta's friend was small and shy and fitted perfectly onto the sitting-room sofa (I refused to give up my bed, reasoning that I had been without it for quite long enough, and for once Mum understood).

If I had grown, so had Lucas, who seemed to have reached overnight that spotty gangly stage so common in adolescent boys; all bony wrists and Adam's apple and wispy suggestions of facial hair, which seemed designed to put off the opposite sex rather than the reverse (which I imagined to be what adolescence was all about). Certainly, the girlfriend had apparently ditched him in favour of an older model, but Lucas appeared unfazed. There were, he told me confidently, plenty more fish in the sea. I just hoped for his sake that the fish didn't go too much on appearances.

Otherwise, Lucas seemed much the same, and we quickly settled back into our easy bantering relationship punctuated with the odd comfortably familiar squabble. His school report was as bad as mine was good, but Mum seemed entertained rather than annoyed.

'Look, Cass,' she said, holding up a report in either hand. 'They're almost mirror images of each other. If I could add all your good points together, I'd have a perfect child!'

And there was something in what she said. For while I had contrived to come either top or second in almost every subject except chemistry, chemistry appeared to be the one subject in which Lucas had if not excelled, then at least passed unnoticed. Add to this the fact that he was good at sport and passable on the violin – while my sporting record had been as bad as my piano playing – and it would appear that between us Mum had indeed produced the ingredients for one perfectly rounded child (and presumably one dismal failure as well, but she obviously preferred not to look at it that way).

But throughout Christmas and the new year – through all the feasting and drinking, the partying and singing – there was something about Mum which wasn't quite right. She seemed to be throwing herself into the festivities with a kind of desperation, almost as though she were using Christmas as a diversion from some other far more serious matter. And as the three weeks of my holiday drew to a close, I became increasingly worried. Was Mum heading for one of her famous depressions? She hadn't had one for some time, and they didn't usually last long, but I dreaded a return of those black moods; of the overwhelming sadness and the weeping and the catalogue of regrets which haunted her on these occasions. As far as I knew, nothing had happened to precipitate such a decline; she had seemed happy, Lucas and I were reasonably settled, the house was as full as even Mum could have wished. And yet I knew that something was wrong.

'Is Mum OK?' I asked Lucas one day, while we were out walking The Dog. 'She doesn't seem – right.'

'I don't know.' Lucas picked up a stick and threw it for The Dog. 'I've asked her, and she says she's fine, but she's not herself.'

'It's not man trouble, is it?' Man trouble featured regularly in our mother's life, and although she tended to keep it to herself, and Lucas and I rarely even knew the identity of the man in question, the fallout of man trouble affected us all.

'I don't think so. I don't even think there's been a man recently, though you never can tell with Mum.' Lucas paused. 'She might tell you, Cass. After all, you're a woman.'

I wanted to say that no, I wasn't a woman, I was not yet fifteen, and still anxious to hang on to what little childhood I had left, but there was no point in trying to explain this to Lucas. Lucas, with his fake ID for getting into pubs and his eager anticipation of his provisional driving licence (one year to go) wouldn't understand at all.

I tackled Mum while she was drying her hair up in her bedroom.

'What's up, Mum?'

'Up? What do you mean, what's up?' Mum lifted and shook out a thick handful of hair. She had beautiful hair, a deep rich auburn; a colour she hadn't managed to hand on to either of her offspring.

'There's something wrong, isn't there?' I sat down on the bed beside her. 'Please tell me, Mum. I need to know. I can't go back to school, leaving you like this. I'll only worry.'

She turned to me, letting her hair fall back onto her shoulders, and placed the hairdryer on the bedside table.

'Oh, Cass. I'm in a bit of a mess. I don't know what to do.'

'Mess? What sort of mess? Is it money?'

'No. Not money.'

'What, then? You've got to tell me.'

'Something – something's happened, Cass. It – it's difficult.'

'So I see. But you'll have to tell me sooner or later, so you may as well get it over now.'

'You're too young. You shouldn't have to be bothered with this sort of thing yet.'

What sort of thing? What on earth could have happened to Mum which required me to be older in order to cope with it?

'Are you ill? Is that it?' I was becoming frightened. Perhaps Mum had some incurable illness. How would I manage? How would any of us manage without her?

'No. Not ill. Oh, Cass. Promise you won't say anything to anyone else if I tell you?'

'Promise.'

'And you'll forgive me?'

'Of course.' Why shouldn't I forgive her? What on earth had Mum been up to? I took her hand and gave it a squeeze. 'Tell me, Mum.'

'Well then.' She took a deep breath. 'There's no easy way of saying this, but – oh, Cass! – I'm pregnant. I'm going to have a baby.'

Eleven

January 1962

I eased myself off the bed and walked unsteadily over to the open window to get some air.

'Cass? Cass! Please talk to me. Please say something.' Mum's voice was small, almost childlike, and I was filled with unreasoning rage. How could she do this to me; to us? What could she have been thinking of? I could imagine – just – a scenario in which I might have to confess an unwanted pregnancy to my mother, but I had never in my wildest dreams imagined that it could be the other way round. It was all wrong. She was the adult. She was the one who was meant to be sensible and responsible, and although I knew only too well that I couldn't always rely on Mum to be either of these, she was still my mother.

'How?' My voice came out in a strangled croak, and I held on to the window sill, concentrating my gaze on the lawn outside, where Lucas was playing with The Dog.

'Well, the usual way, I assume.' Mum gave a little laugh.

I rounded on her. '*How can you?* How can you laugh at a time like this?'

'No. You're right. It's not funny. I'm sorry.' She looked down, her fingers plucking at the counterpane. 'But it's not the end of the world, Cass. It might even be – fun.'

'Fun? You call this fun? You announce that you're pregnant, and you think it's going to be *fun*? You've got no husband, in case you haven't noticed, and Lucas and I haven't even got fathers. Has this – this baby got a father?'

'Well, of course it had a father—'

'*Had*.'

'Well, yes. I mean—'

'I know what you mean. You mean this poor little sod won't know its father either!'

'Language, Cass!'

'*Language?* You talk to me about language? Mum, how can you expect me to show you any respect if you – if you go around behaving like this. At your age, too. It's – it's disgusting!'

'I didn't go around behaving like anything. And I'm not even forty yet, Cass. I'm not – old.' Her voice was a whisper now, and there were tears on her cheeks.

'Old enough to know better, though.' I had the upper hand now, and the feeling was not unpleasant.

'Yes. Yes, I suppose you're right.' She wiped her eyes with the back of her hand. 'But I hoped you'd understand.'

'I don't understand. I'm not meant to understand. I don't even want to understand. I just – I just want things to be the way they were!'

'So do I. Believe me, so do I.' Mum looked up at me. 'Cass, I'm so sorry. I really didn't mean this to happen.'

'And I don't suppose you meant Lucas to happen, or me to happen. We're all your – your little mistakes, aren't we?' I said bitterly. 'After all your little talks about birth control, too.'

'Well, you needed to know.'

'No. *We* didn't. *You're* the one who needs to know, and look at you!' I moved away from the window and came towards her. She looked small and vulnerable and beautiful, and at that moment, I hated her. 'This isn't just your life we're talking about. It's mine and Lucas's and – everyone else's. This is going to ruin everything.'

'We'll be OK, Cass. We've always been OK. We'll get by. And I've never looked upon you and Lucas as mistakes. You might not have been – well – planned exactly, but you're the best things that ever happened to me. I can't imagine life without either of you. And this baby will be special too. We'll make it special.'

'*We?*'

I was in no mood to extend a welcome to my unborn sibling or to have any involvement in this situation. Unmarried mothers still carried a stigma, and while Mum had managed to shrug hers off so effortlessly that we were barely aware of it, I knew that people talked about us. It seemed to me that just as everyone had got used to the fact that there was no father in our household, Mum was going out of her way to remind them.

'Cass, of course you're upset. I understand that. But

93

there's nothing more I can say or do.' She hesitated. 'Except, I suppose, get rid of it.'

'*What?*' Even I had heard unsavoury tales of gin and hot baths and women in dingy parlours armed with knitting needles. In those days before the 1967 Abortion Act, it was often the only resort for women who didn't have a very good medical reason to get rid of their unwanted babies.

'Well, I could. People do. I could – find someone to do it.'

The words hung in the air between us, serving only to fuel my anger. For with that clever little twist, Mum had some-how managed to shift her problem from herself onto me, and it felt as though she was asking me to make the decision for her; as though she was telling me that if I wanted her to get rid of her baby, she would.

'You can't ask me to do this!' I yelled at her.

'Do what? I haven't asked you to do anything!'

'Yes, you have. But I won't. I won't! This is your baby and your decision. Leave me out of it!'

'But Cass—'

'No. No more. There's nothing more to say. You got your-self into this mess, and now you've got to sort it out. I've got my own life to lead.' And I rushed from her room, slamming the door behind me.

'What on earth was that all about?' Lucas met me on the landing. 'Are you in trouble?'

'No. Not me. Mum.' I wiped my streaming eyes and leant against the bannisters. 'But I'm not supposed to tell you,' I added, remembering my earlier promise.

'Well, you'll have to now,' Lucas said reasonably. 'You

can't not tell me after all that racket you two have been making.'

'Well' – after all, what had Mum done to deserve my loyalty? – 'you and I are going to have a new little brother or sister. Isn't that nice?' I paused, enjoying in spite of myself that frisson of excitement which comes with being the bearer of bad news.

'You're joking!' Lucas's expression had changed from curiosity to horror.

'Ask her yourself if you don't believe me.'

'Are you sure about this, Cass?'

'Well, that's what she's told me.'

'I can't believe it. I thought she was past all that sort of thing. Well, the baby bit, anyway.'

'Oh, dear me, no. She seems to think she's still a spring chicken. I told her it was disgusting.'

'That was a bit harsh.'

'No, it wasn't. It is disgusting to go around flaunting yourself the way Mum does, and getting into trouble like this. Some example she is!'

'Oh, Cass, you know Mum. She'll never change. That's the way she is.' Lucas sounded suddenly very weary and very grown up and it infuriated me.

'You mean you're happy to let her go on making dear little babies until – until she can't any more? Is that what you mean?'

'No, of course not. I just mean that this is – must have been – a mistake, a one-off, and I suppose we'll just have to make the best of it.'

We. That word again. Well, Lucas could join in this new

cosy little game of happy families if he wanted to, but I certainly wasn't going to have anything to do with it. Hitherto, I had been dreading leaving home and going back to school, but now it offered a welcome escape. At least no one could ask me for help or advice if I wasn't here. At least at school I would have the security of being treated as the child that I still was, and not a cross between a best friend and an agony aunt to my feckless mother.

'Well, you do as you like, Lucas,' I said. 'You can see her through this – this crisis, happy event, however she likes to think of it. I'm off again in a week.'

'You mean you're still going back to school?' Lucas sounded shocked. 'Even after this?'

'You try stopping me.'

'Leaving me to – to deal with this?'

'No, Lucas. *No!* Leaving *Mum* to deal with this. This is her problem. We've got to let her sort it out herself. I'm sorry to be leaving you, I really am, but you don't have to be her nursemaid. You've just got to get on with your life, like me. She managed having you and me without any help. She's told us enough times. I'm sure Greta will make a wonderful nanny. After all, she doesn't seem to have anything else to do.'

'Does Greta know?'

'No one knows. Yet. But presumably they'll have to sooner or later.'

'Oh, Lord.' Lucas sat on the top stair and put his head in his hands.

'Quite.'

I knew I was being hard, but it was the only way I could

distance myself from the situation, for I knew that once I allowed myself to sit down and really think about it, I'd feel compelled to stay at home and help. To be fair, Mum hadn't suggested that I should, and it was unlikely that she would ask me to make any kind of sacrifice for her. Mum rarely actually asked for help; she simply made everyone aware of her problems, and sooner or later someone would offer whatever support was needed. There was a fragility about Mum which was hard to resist, but I was beginning to see through it. I know she never intended to trap or deceive any of us – in fact I'm sure that nothing was further from her thoughts – but her very neediness did it for her, and even if she wasn't aware of it, it was a powerful tool in getting her what she wanted.

'Lucky you.'

Lucas sounded bleak, and I felt genuinely sorry for him. Poor Lucas. He was just finding his way out of childhood into the heady world of girls and the right kind of jeans and consideration of his future career, and Mum, albeit unwittingly, had neatly plunged him into a situation which was bound to be a rich source of anxiety and embarrassment.

Once more, I was overwhelmed with anger, for whatever I might say, however brave and independent I might sound, I knew that fate had taken yet another cruel twist, and that life at home would never be the same again.

Twelve

'Octavia, I think. Octavia Fitzpatrick. How does that strike you, Cass?' Mum was driving me back to school in the borrowed van for the beginning of the new term. Once again, my trunk was making its unstable presence known in the back, but at least The Dog had been granted a reprieve, because I absolutely refused to take him with us. I myself had little choice if Mum chose to subject me to this ordeal, but there was no need to inflict it on a helpless animal. Besides, his yelpings didn't help Mum's concentration, and on this occasion I badly needed her to concentrate.

'What do you mean, "Octavia"? What are you talking about?' I held on to my seat and closed my eyes as we rounded a sharp bend in the road.

'The baby. If it's a girl. I think Octavia's rather nice.'

'Octavia's a ridiculous name.' I was in no mood to discuss names.

'It's a very old name. A classical name. I think it's rather nice.'

'It's inappropriate,' I countered. 'It means "eighth". You

have to have had seven children before you can have an Octavia.'

'Oh, don't be so silly, Cass. Of course you don't.'

'Yes, you do. Anyone can see you didn't do Latin at school.' Latin was one of my best subjects. 'In any case, isn't it time someone in our family had a normal name?'

'Lucas, Cassandra and Octavia,' Mum mused, ignoring me. 'I think they go together rather well.'

'Mum, we're not going to be travelling around together for the rest of our lives. We're not a circus troupe.'

'It would look good on Christmas cards,' Mum continued, undeterred. 'I'm not so good on boys' names, though. Have you any ideas, Cass?'

'I wish you'd just concentrate on looking where you're going.'

'Oh, Cass. What's happened to you? You used to be such fun.'

Mum may well have had a point. I still had the eerie feeling that as I grew older, she was becoming inexorably younger; while I was being asked to grow up and face my responsibilities, my mother was contriving to turn a blind eye to hers. If we continued like this, I thought, as we swerved round another corner, we might eventually pass each other; she tottering happily back towards childhood and I struggling to make my way in the world of grown-ups.

'Nappies,' Mum said, as we lurched into a lower gear. 'I got rid of all the nappies. Damn. I shall have to buy new ones.'

'Mum.' I took a deep breath. 'This is our last day together. Would you please, *please*, stop talking about babies!'

'Sorry, love. So. What would you like to talk about?'

Of course, I couldn't think of anything. Besides, I knew that whatever subject I might choose, I would be wasting my breath, for now that she had recovered from the initial shock, Mum was showing all the excitement and wonder which might have been expected of a first-time mother, and she seemed incapable of talking about anything else. Her thoughts were filled with cots and pushchairs, with the re-decorating of the tiny box room ('Pink or blue, Cass? Or would yellow be safer?') and with the prospect of labour ('I know it hurt, but I can't remember how much').

Her mood might have been more muted if the reaction of the rest of the household had been less enthusiastic, but by the time she told them her news – several days after her traumatic revelation to me – she appeared to have made a miraculous recovery from the subdued and emotional state in which I had initially found her, and her excitement was so infectious that she soon had everyone thinking what a brilliant idea it all was. I almost expected them to ask why she hadn't thought of it before.

'A little baby,' whispered Greta tearfully. 'Iss wonderful, no? I look after? I help, yes?'

'Oh, yes, Greta! That would be perfect!'

Call Me Bill, although initially shocked (Lucas and I privately suspected that Call Me Bill was sexually uninitiated, and likely to remain so), soon came round to the idea, even going so far as to say that a baby in the house would 'help to keep us all young'. Richard accepted the news with equanimity, and a visiting ex-Lodger – an ageing professor with a pronounced squint which had terrified me when I was younger – was fulsome with his congratulations. As for the neighbours, while they no doubt made the most of this nice little morsel of gossip, outwardly they appeared unfazed. One couple even made a coy appearance, bearing a little packet of bibs and a bunch of flowers, and I distinctly overheard snatches of conversation including such encouraging snippets as 'think you're amazing' and 'coping on your own . . . so brave'.

Lucas and I looked at each other. It was as we had anticipated. Once again, Mum had everyone on side, leaving us to struggle with any fallout.

I agreed with Lucas that, before I returned to school for the new term, we should at least attempt to establish the paternity of our new sibling. We had to accept that any trail leading us to discover the identities of our own fathers had long since gone cold, but we thought it unlikely that even Mum could have forgotten so recent an encounter as that which had resulted in her present condition.

After some difficulty finding her on her own (I suspected she had been avoiding us), we finally ran her to ground in her bedroom, sorting out socks.

'Mum. We need to talk to you.' I closed the door carefully behind us.

'Oh dear! You both look very serious.' Mum laughed, but she looked uneasy.

'Yes. We'll come straight to the point.'

'Please do.'

'Well, we – that is Lucas and I – we—'

'Who's this baby's father?' demanded Lucas, never one to

beat about the bush. 'We want to know, and the baby will certainly want to know. You owe it to us.'

'Do I?' Mum absently paired a blue sock with a grey one and rolled them in a neat ball.

'Yes. You do. After all this – this *disturbance*, you certainly owe us something.'

'Aren't I allowed a bit of privacy? I don't ask you personal questions, Lucas.' Another pair of mismatched socks. 'I don't know what gives you the right to ask me this.'

'What about the baby's rights? Doesn't it have a right to know its father?' I interrupted.

Mum sighed. 'All right. I'll tell you. But you're not to tell anyone else. Is that understood?'

We nodded.

'And you're not going to like this.'

No surprises there, then.

'Well' – Mum abandoned the socks and sat down on the bed – 'it was – it was someone I met at a party.'

'Someone you met at a party,' echoed Lucas.

'And,' Mum continued, 'before you ask, no, I don't know who he was. I don't know and I don't want to know. He was having a few problems and I – well, I cheered him up. I think he may have had a beard.' The last sentence she added as though this might somehow make it sound better.

'If you had time to find out about his problems and – cheer him up, you must know *something* about him.' Lucas sounded exasperated.

'It was very dark. We'd had a lot to drink.' Mum paused. 'I know. I'm sorry. It sounds awful, put like that, but that's the way it was.'

'But – but someone must know who he was. There can't have been that number of men drifting around in the dark with beards and problems!' I said.

'There were a lot of people, we'd all been drinking. He and I fell asleep on the sofa, and by the time I woke up, he'd gone. He might even have been a gatecrasher.'

'Oh, Mum. How *could* you?'

'I was lonely, Cass. *Lonely*. I don't suppose you've ever been really lonely, have you? I don't expect you to understand. One day,' she continued, 'one day, you may understand, and you may even forgive me. I didn't mean it to happen, and I certainly didn't mean to – to get like this, but I'm going to make the best of it. I didn't want it, I certainly didn't plan it, but now it's happened I really am looking forward to it. It'll – well, it'll give me a purpose. For when you two have left home. I'll have something – someone – to live for.'

I felt totally bewildered. Couldn't Mum see that Lucas and I would always love her and need her? That her life wouldn't come to an end simply because we'd left home (in fact, sometimes our house was so full, I used to wonder whether she would even notice our absence)? Evidently not. Mum's need to be needed was such that a third illegitimate child obviously offered an unexpected lifeline, for even if our house were suddenly to empty itself of all its waifs and strays, a baby, Mum's baby, would still be there. She had guaranteed herself another eighteen years' companionship (or so she seemed to think); a further eighteen years of being at the centre of another person's life. Little wonder, then, that she was so excited.

As for the baby's father, I think that consciously or unconsciously, Mum quite simply preferred her children not to have fathers. Although I'm sure that she never set out to be a single parent (in fact, she herself had said that she hadn't intended to be a parent at all, and I'm sure that was true), I believe she wanted us to herself; and I think she would have found it very hard had she had to share us with anyone else. Besides, she herself had never had a father – or not one she could remember – and I really think she considered fathers to be largely unnecessary.

It was a miserable grey January day with a leaden sky and a hint of snow to come, and I was feeling depressed. The long spring term stretched ahead of me, promising more frost-bitten days on the hockey pitch, more inadequate meals and more work. There seemed to be little to look forward to.

The daylight was failing fast, and the windscreen wipers squeaked as they battled with the first few flakes of snow. As we progressed, the headlights illuminated curtains of dancing snowflakes, and we skidded on the slippery surface. Once again, I closed my eyes and gritted my teeth. Experience had taught me that Mum drove better when uninterrupted (although that wasn't saying much) and although I wasn't looking forward to my return to school, it was preferable to ending up in a ditch miles from anywhere.

'I do love you, you know, Cass,' Mum said suddenly, leaning forward and squinting through the windscreen.

'I know. I love you too.'

'That's all right, then.' Mum patted my knee. 'We'll get by, all of us. We always do, don't we?'

'I suppose so.'

'That's my girl.' I could feel rather than see her smiling in the dark beside me. 'And I really will try to write more this term.'

'Not all about babies?'

'Certainly not all about babies.'

'And send tuck?'

'Of course.'

'Sensible tuck?'

'Very sensible tuck.'

'Thanks, Mum.'

'You're welcome.'

I found myself smiling too, for it was impossible to stay grumpy for long when Mum was in this kind of mood.

Thirteen

I fitted back into school and its routine as though I'd never been away, and although the cold and the hunger were sometimes hard to put up with, and the homesickness still tended to surface from time to time, I was surprised at how glad I was to be among my classmates again.

Possibly because of my reputation for noisy nightmares, I had been moved across the dormitory to a bed under a window, with the added bonus of a window ledge which could be used for displaying photographs and other personal possessions and which gave Blind Bear a nice view of the garden while I was having lessons. Whether the change of bed had any effect, or whether my head was so full of other things that it hadn't room for bad dreams I shall never know, but the nightmares appeared to have stopped, and unimpeded by lack of sleep I was able to apply myself to my studies with new enthusiasm.

'You are lucky,' sighed poor Helena, as she struggled with geometry and the idiosyncrasies of irregular French verbs. 'Mum and Dad were really upset with my results last term.

You seem to do it without even trying. I bet your mum was proud of you.'

'I think Mum's always proud of us,' I said. 'She seemed quite pleased, but she's not too bothered about exam results.'

'I thought everyone's parents were bothered about exam results,' Helena said. 'I'd love to meet your mum. She sounds amazing.'

'Oh, she is,' I assured her. 'She certainly is.'

But I wasn't too sure about a meeting between Helena and my mother, and I certainly wasn't sure about having my friend to stay (Helena was clearly angling for an invitation). How would Helena fit into our household, with its eccentric set-up and its modest mod cons? And – more to the point – how would she react to my mother's interesting condition? I hadn't yet told my friends about Mum's pregnancy because I wasn't at all sure how I was going to go about it, and I had a feeling that Helena at least might well be shocked. While I, with my unfortunate experiences, preferred to forget about sex altogether, my friends were at an age where the subject was endlessly fascinating; an age when much speculation went on (usually in whispers after lights-out) as to what it was like and whether one's parents 'still did it'. The received opinion was that most of them were probably too old; so irrefutable evidence that my own unmarried mother not only still did it but was currently proudly manifesting its conse- quences was bound both to fascinate and to shock.

In the end, Mum inadvertently managed to break the news for me by sending me another postcard, this time a reproduction of a portrait of a tiny Italian princess, which managed to fall into the wrong hands at breakfast.

'I like to think your new brother or sister will look some-thing like this,' she had written on the back. 'She looks like an Octavia, don't you think?'

By the time the postcard reached me, it had been all round the dining hall, and everyone knew about the baby. At the time, I even wondered whether Mum had done it on purpose, but then she wasn't to know that the card would be given to another girl by mistake, and besides, she would have taken it for granted that my friends already knew. Mum was never very good at secrets, and assumed that everyone else was the same.

'Gosh, Cass! Is your mum really having a baby?' Some-one asked, obviously impressed.

'I thought she wasn't married,' added Helena helpfully.

'She isn't,' I said, tight-lipped and fuming.

'Well, how did she—?'

'How do you think?' I retorted rudely. 'I thought you all knew so much about this sort of thing.'

'I only asked!' Helena looked hurt.

'Then don't,' I snapped. 'I'm off to finish some prep.'

My classmates gave me a wide berth until lunchtime, when a very plump, very plain (albeit double-barrelled) girl with the unlikely name of Fern could no longer contain her curiosity.

'Tell us, Cass. You must be excited! I've always wanted a baby brother or sister.' (Fern was an only child, and my uncharitable view was that her parents, having seen what their particular recipe produced, had long since decided not to repeat the experiment.)

'Perhaps,' I said, choosing my words carefully and trying

not to be unkind (people were often unkind to Fern). 'Perhaps it's different if your parents are married.'

'Ooh!' Fern's hand flew to her mouth, and her eyes widened. 'I forgot. I'm sorry!'

'Don't mention it,' I said coolly (I'd had time to calm down). 'But to answer your question, no. I'm not looking forward to it.'

'Why ever not? Don't you just love babies?'

'No, I don't.' If the truth be told I'd hardly ever met a baby, but current circumstances had not disposed me to feel kindly towards them.

'You'll be able to help with it.' Fern ploughed on, undeterred. 'Changing its nappies and feeding it and—'

'I shall do no such thing,' I interrupted. 'I want to have as little to do with it as possible.'

'You didn't really mean what you said, did you?' Helena asked later. 'I mean, about the baby. You must be – well – a bit interested in it. I'd love to have someone in my family who was younger than me,' she added with feeling.

'We're fine as we are,' I said. 'We don't need any more people in our house, and certainly not a baby. And I like being the youngest.'

'You might have a sister. Wouldn't you like a sister?'

'Certainly not!' For I had thought about this, and had decided that if the baby should be a boy (an eventuality which didn't seem to have occurred to Mum), then I would at least retain the distinction of being her only daughter.

'When's the baby going to arrive?' Helena persevered.

'I don't know.' And it was true. Amid all the excitement

and the trauma, I had completely forgotten to ask this rather crucial question. 'How long do babies take?'

'I don't know. About a year, I think.'

'That's all right, then. Anything can happen in a year.'

Thinking about it now, it seems strange that having been so thoroughly equipped with information regarding all the clinical details of the sexual act, no one had seen fit to tell us something as fundamental as the length of human gestation. But in my case at that stage ignorance was bliss, for having no idea of the imminence of the new arrival I was granted a brief reprieve from any immediate anxiety.

For the moment, despite frequent jolly reminders in Mum's letters, I tried to put the question of the baby to the back of my mind. For the first time since I started at St Andrew's, I was grateful that I had this separate world; a world of my own, which didn't include babies or Lodgers; a world where life was on the whole predictable and where other people – real grown-ups – made all the major decisions.

My fifteenth birthday took place towards the end of February, and was celebrated with a small but pleasing collection of presents from my friends and crowned by a surprise visit from Mum.

'Isn't this lovely?' she cried, when I was summoned to Miss Armitage's study to greet my unexpected guest. 'Miss Armitage was so kind to let me come' (birthday visits were not generally permitted). 'Call Me Bill brought me. He's waiting in the car. As it's Saturday, we're allowed a whole hour together.'

'How did you manage it?' I asked, when we were alone together.

'I told her what a difficult time you'd been having. She was so understanding.'

'What difficult time?'

'Oh, you know.' Mum said. 'This and that. Now, why don't you open your presents?'

As usual, Mum's enthusiasm was so infectious and our time together so short that I decided to leave the subject of the difficult time for the moment and enjoy her visit. I took her up to the dormitory ('Oh, isn't it quaint!' cried Mum) and she laid several parcels out on my bed. There was a new wristwatch from her, a strange little china figurine from Greta, and a box of fudge from Lucas. Call Me Bill's present, she explained, was chauffeuring her here. I couldn't expect a present as well (I didn't). Best of all, there were four packets of chocolate biscuits and a huge sponge cake dripping icing and jam.

'Oh, Mum! This is great!' I put on the watch and admired the cake. 'Thanks so much.'

'And now, perhaps I can meet some of your friends.'

'I think they're all doing things. They're – busy.'

'Not all of them, surely, Cass. I've been so looking forward to seeing them.'

'Well . . .'

'Are you ashamed of me?' She laughed. 'Is that it?'

'No. Of course not.'

'Well then.' She patted my hand. 'Introduce me to Helena, at least. I've heard so much about her.'

We found Helena sitting alone in our classroom, battling with the extra maths prep she had been given.

'Cass! Thank goodness! You can help me with this.'

'Helena, this is my mother.'

'Oh! I'm so sorry. I didn't see you.' Helena stood up and shook hands with Mum. 'You've come for Cass's birthday. How nice.'

'Yes, isn't it?' Mum gave Helena one of the radiant smiles she used to melt (and, I suspect, break) hearts. 'Oh, poor you,' she went on, seeing the screwed-up pieces of paper littering the floor and the pink and flustered face of Helena. 'I hated maths. Such a ridiculous subject, I always thought.'

'Me too,' Helena sighed. 'And Cass is so clever at it.'

'Isn't she? I don't know where she gets it from,' Mum said, inadvertently drawing attention yet again to my father-less state.

Helena, seeing the connection, blushed. My mother, who had no insight into her own lack of tact, did not.

'Oh, algebra.' Mum peered over Helena's shoulder. 'All that business of x and y. I never could make head nor tail of it. Why don't you leave that and come and have a piece of Cass's birthday cake?'

'That would be lovely—' Helena began.

'I thought we'd leave it until after supper,' I said quickly, for Mum had already outstayed her hour, and I feared repercussions.

'Midnight feasts in the dorm!' Mum clapped her hands girlishly. 'What fun!'

'No, Mum. Not midnight feasts in the dorm. Something to share with my friends after measly beans on toast. Come on. We'd better leave Helena in peace.'

'Then perhaps we'll meet again, Helena. You must come and stay with us some time. I know Cass would love to have you, wouldn't you Cass?'

'Of course,' I said, but without much conviction. I liked keeping my school and home lives separate, and suspected that any mingling of the two could lead to complications.

'Oh, I'd just love to,' Helena said. 'That's so kind of you.'

'We must fix something up, then.' Mum beamed at her, then looked at her watch. 'Goodness! I ought to be going. Come and see me off, Cass, and you can say hello to Call Me Bill. Goodbye, Helena. Hope to see you again soon.'

Later that evening in our dormitory, we divided up my birthday cake with a ruler (all we could find) and served it on sheets of paper torn from an exercise book. Like all Mum's cakes, it was messy but delicious.

'I think your mum's wonderful,' Helena sighed. 'I always get birthday cakes from the cake shop; all hard and dry and tasting of cardboard. Not a bit like this,' she added, wiping jam off her chin.

I had always rather fancied a posh shop-bought cake, with icing-sugar frills round the edges and my name in pink lettering, but maybe Helena was right. At least Mum went to trouble with her cake-making, even if the end results would never win her any prizes.

Altogether, it had been a most satisfactory day, and as I licked the last sticky crumbs from my fingers, I reflected that life was on the whole pretty good. I was doing well in my studies, I had just enough friends for the maintenance of self-respect without the risk of being crowded, and I had it on fairly good authority that there wouldn't be any baby for some time yet. Maybe Mum had been right about boarding school after all. It could be that it was just what I had needed.

Fourteen

'Cass.' Mum's awake now, her blue eyes lucid, her face still free from pain.

'Yes, Mum. I'm here.' I pull my chair closer.

'About my funeral.'

'Yes.' Oh, please don't talk about your funeral. Not now. Not yet. I'm not ready for your funeral.

'About flowers.'

'Yes?'

'I don't want no-flowers-by-request.'

'You mean, you'd like to have flowers?'

'Oh yes. Lots of flowers. I'd like everyone to send flowers.'

'I'll – I'll make sure they do, Mum.'

'That's all right, then.' A little sigh, eyes closed, resting. 'You can take the flowers home, you know.'

'What, all of them?'

'Yes. I want everyone to take some flowers home. Mustn't waste them.'

'That's a nice idea, Mum.'

'It is, isn't it?' She smiles. Looks almost happy. My mother loves planning things. 'And hymns.'

'Yes?'

'None of that lead kindly light stuff.'

'Not if you don't want it.'

'I don't.' She shifts restlessly. 'Nice jolly ones. Jerusalem. And that nice Welsh one.'

'Guide Me, Oh Thou Great Redeemer?'

'That's the one.'

'We'll have that one, then.'

'Cass?'

'Yes?'

'Where's Lucas?'

'He came last night. He'll be here later.'

'Perhaps he'll read something at the funeral.'

'I'm sure he will.'

'Do you think there'll be enough money for horses?'

'Horses?'

'To pull the coffin. I always fancied being pulled along by a team of shiny black horses.'

There isn't the money – there's never been any money – but what does it matter?

'Of course. If you want horses, you shall have horses.'

Another smile.

'They'll all notice me then, won't they?'

'They certainly will.'

Oh, Mum! Shiny black horses and lots of flowers. We can certainly manage the flowers, and perhaps we can run to one shiny black horse. I'll do my best. There must be someone who would lend us their shiny black horse.

*

My grandmother died suddenly that half-term. She too had wanted black horses to pull her funeral carriage. As she had explained to anyone who would listen, a team of black horses was only fitting. It wasn't every day that Napoleon was buried, and things had to be done properly. She had given her instructions in halting French, a feat which greatly impressed Mum.

'Her brain's shot to pieces, Cass, and yet she remembers that Napoleon would have spoken in French. I had to get one of the nurses to translate for me.'

Notwithstanding her damaged brain, my grandmother had managed to plan her funeral in minutest detail, although of course her grandiose ideas were out of the question. For there could be no cathedral service of thanksgiving, no grand procession, no reception for foreign dignitaries in her honour. The daughter of a Norfolk labourer, but with her position in life briefly elevated during her short marriage to my respectably middle-class grandfather, she would be buried alongside the other also-rans of the humble parish where she had spent most of her life.

When Mum received the news of her mother's death, she was distraught.

'Poor Mother. Poor poor Mother,' she wept. 'I should have done more. I should have kept her here. We'd have managed somehow.'

'We wouldn't, Mum. How could we have managed?' I reasoned. 'What with your work and – everything else.'

'But she should have come first. I ought to have put her first.' Mum reached for another handkerchief. 'What kind of daughter was I? You tell me that, Cass.'

I could have said that she was the sort of daughter who couldn't possibly have coped with an ageing incontinent Napoleon with tendencies to violence and sleepwalking, but my words would have been wasted. Mum had to grieve, and since it appeared that guilt was an integral part of the process, we had to allow this cocktail of emotions to run its course.

The funeral was fixed for the following week. Call Me Bill made most of the arrangements over the phone, since Mum was in no fit state to organize anything, and I was allowed to stay off school for a further two days in order to attend it. I myself was not especially affected by our loss, since I had scarcely known my grandmother and had had little recent contact with her. Even when I was small and she was in control of her faculties, I had been well aware that she looked upon children as an inconvenience at best, and so I had never had the chance to establish any sort of relationship with her. I did, however, wonder that a woman who appeared to be so cold and at times even ruthless could have produced a daughter as open and affectionate as my mother.

We travelled to the funeral by rail, a journey involving several hours and two changes of train. The weather was cold and our carriages unheated, and Mum alternately railed against herself and wept. Lucas and I consumed quantities of the sandwiches we had brought with us (Mum refused to eat anything) and spent our time reading or playing battleships and hangman on scraps of paper. It was not a happy journey.

The funeral itself was conducted in a small parish church by a wild-haired vicar with a beard who looked, I thought, exactly like John the Baptist. He had the appearance and the air of someone who might well have blazed a trail on a diet of locusts and wild honey, and he conducted the service with energy and humour. Our grandmother was then laid to rest in the pretty churchyard, and we all adjourned to the parish hall for tea and cakes (there had been no one to organize a proper wake, much to Mum's distress).

Here things became more interesting, because we encountered relatives whom we had barely heard of (although they all appeared to have heard of us), and for almost the first time in my life, I had a sense of family. I also got the distinct impression that Mum was the black sheep of that family, and that it was unlikely her present condition would do much to redeem her.

But as next of kin to the deceased (my mother had been an only child), Mum was deserving of some sympathy, and having miraculously recovered her composure, she milked the situation to the full.

As I watched her kissing the pale powdery cheeks and embracing the frail bodies of the friends and family members who came up to offer their condolences (why was everyone so *old*?), I was bowled over yet again by Mum's charm; her smile, the tilt of her head, the way she listened to people as though there was no one in the world she would rather be with. These were rare traits, and although they were genuine enough, she was not above using them to her advantage. This, I suspected, was how she tempted willing Lodgers into our damp basement and even more willing lovers into her bed. At her best, my mother was quite simply irresistible.

'There,' she said, after we'd taken our leave and set off on our walk back to the station. 'I think I've managed to stave off the worst of the gossip. At least for the time being. They might even manage to overlook the – well, the baby now.'

'Does it matter?' I asked, for after all, we rarely had any kind of contact with these people.

'It's a good point, Cass. But yes. It does matter. In spite of everything, I mind what people think.'

'Why? Why do you mind?' For quite often it seemed as though my mother couldn't have cared less what people thought of her.

'Because I haven't made much of a success of my life, have I? I haven't done anything particularly clever. I haven't really achieved anything. But if people like me, well, that's something, isn't it?'

'Of course people like you. Everyone likes you. My friends think you're wonderful.'

'Do they really?'

'You know they do. I've told you.'

'I don't deserve it, though, do I?'

'Oh, Mum! Of course you deserve it.'

'At the moment I don't feel as though I deserve anything.'

Once again, the tears were very near the surface. My mother thrived on people and attention, and now that the attention had ceased and we were on our own again, she seemed to wilt like a plucked flower.

'Come on, Mum,' said Lucas, as anxious as I was to get her onto the train in one emotional piece. 'You've done really well today. Keep it up just a bit longer, and we'll soon be home.'

But it was too late. Once again, the tears were pouring

down Mum's cheeks, landing in bright splashes on the red wool of her scarf.

'I miss her,' she sobbed, fumbling in her pocket for a handkerchief. 'I'm going to miss her so much. I know she's not been – herself for some time, but she's my mum. My poor little mum,' she repeated, stumbling on the kerb and clutching at my arm. 'And she'll never see the baby now, will she? My poor baby will have no grandparents at all.'

Somehow, we managed to get her home, steering her on and off trains, mopping her up and patting and soothing her as best we could. By the time we got home we were all exhausted.

Greta had stayed up in her dressing gown to welcome us back, although it was well past midnight.

'Nice-cup-of-tea?' she said, as Mum fell through the front door and into her arms.

And for once, I could have kissed her. Greta might have been a fusspot – she was often infuriating – but she was kind, and most of all, she was one of us; in her own way, far more a member of the family than my late grandmother had ever been.

'Oh, Greta!' I said, as I took off my coat and peeled my gloves from my frozen hands. 'What would we do without you?'

Fifteen

I made the decision to stay at home until the following week, for I was worried about Mum. She was in a bad state, and while to a certain extent this was to be expected after her bereavement, the signs were ominous. She took to her bed, eating little and subsisting on cups of tea, and when she wasn't asleep, she spent her time weeping or simply gazing out of the window, leaving her room only to go to the bathroom.

We had been down this road before. Mum never did things by halves, and her depressions were full-blown and frightening; and while they didn't usually last long, everyone dreaded them. It was these (mercifully rare) occasions that brought it home to all of us how central Mum was to the mood if not the running of the household, for everyone relied on her cheerful good humour, her hospitality, her knack of making people laugh and her sheer kindness.

The house fell suddenly quiet, and we all crept around speaking in whispers as though someone much closer than my grandmother had died. The wireless was silent; there were no noisy recitals on the ironing board; even The Dog, who it seemed could do depression almost as well as Mum, lay outside her bedroom door and whimpered miserably.

'Mum, what can I do to help?' I asked, bringing in yet another cup of tea and setting it down on the bedside table. 'There must be something we can do for you.'

Mum looked at me as though noticing me for the first time.

'Why aren't you back at school, Cass? You shouldn't be here at all.'

'I stayed on to help. I can't leave you like this.'

'But do the school know?'

'Of course they do. Call Me Bill rang and explained.' It had seemed more appropriate to ask an adult to phone on my behalf than to ring the school myself.

'But you can't miss school, Cass. You must go back.'

'I can. I'll be fine. I've got some reading to be getting on with, and I can easily catch up next week.' I paused. 'Mum, shouldn't you see a doctor? Get some – pills or something?'

'If you like.' Mum patted my hand absently. 'Though I'm not sure pills will help.'

Dr Mackenzie, a wholesome no-nonsense Scotsman who knew our family well, was duly summoned, and having run the gauntlet of The Dog – who seemed to have appointed himself Mum's guard dog – he was reassuringly down to earth.

'Now then, Mrs Fitzpatrick—'

'Miss.'

'Miss Fitzpatrick, then. What's all this about?'

Mum shrugged and gave him a wan little-girl smile. Dr Mackenzie sat down on the bed.

'You've lost your mother, and of course you're upset. But you've your new little one to think about. You can't go starving yourself and worrying your family like this.'

'I'm not starving—'

'Cassandra here says you've hardly eaten anything in the past week. Isn't that right, Cassandra?'

As Mum's female next of kin, I had thought it appropriate that I should be present at this interview, and as it turned out this was just as well.

'Just cups of tea,' I said. 'And a bit of toast.'

'A bit of toast? Have you no sense, woman?'

Mum looked startled. She wasn't accustomed to being challenged in this way.

'You may well look shocked.' Dr Mackenzie got out his instruments and took Mum's blood pressure. 'A bit on the low side,' he said. 'You need to eat, and take exercise, and get some fresh air in your lungs. What kind of a bairn are you going to produce if you go on like this?'

'I hadn't thought.' Mum looked down at her hands.

'No. I daresay not. Now, I shall be round tomorrow morning, and I want to find you out of bed and dressed.'

'No pills?' Mum asked.

The doctor patted her shoulder kindly. 'There's no pills for what you're suffering from, my dear. It has to take its time. But while it's doing that, you've a life to get on with.' He stood up and closed his bag. 'A life and a family.'

'Is there anything we ought to be doing for her?' I asked, as I showed Dr Mackenzie out.

'Yes. A good deal less than you're doing now. Wait on her, and she'll never leave that bed of hers. She's not had it easy, your mum, but she needs to get back to normal. To start functioning again. And you can help her do that.'

'Is it all right if I go back to school?'

'Back to school? Of course you should be back at school! You've your own life to lead, lassie. You need your friends, too.'

His kindness brought tears to my eyes, and I suddenly realized how tired I was.

'You're a good daughter, but don't you try to be too good a daughter. It'll not do either of you any good. Away with you to that school of yours. Get back to normal. I'll keep an eye on your mum.'

'Doctor?'

'Yes?'

'When – when's the baby due?'

'Has she not told you?'

'I suppose I just never got round to asking.'

'Oh – about June time I think. Not so long to go now.'

'*June?*'

'Aye. June.' He laughed. 'Don't they teach you anything at school nowadays?'

'Not – that. They told us all about – well, you know – but not how long.'

'Not how long, eh? Then it's a bit of a shock for you?'

I nodded.

'Don't you worry. It'll be all right. Your mum's a strong woman. She'll manage.' He looked at me and smiled. 'And so will you. But you've to remember, this is her bairn, not yours. She's done it all before. You get on with your school-ing and enjoy being young, Cassandra. It doesn't last long, let me tell you. Don't you go taking on your mum's problems. You'll have plenty of your own, soon enough.'

If only he knew that I felt I had quite enough problems as it was. I would have loved to have been able to talk to this good kindly man, and I wondered what it would be like to have a father like him; someone strong and sympathetic; someone who would go out to work every morning carrying a briefcase, and come home with a nice safe pay cheque at the end of the month; someone who would protect me from people like Uncle Rupert and Alex.

After the doctor's visit, Mum made an effort to pull her-self together. She got up and dressed the next day, and made arrangements to return to work the following week. She even baked a cake.

But she was not herself, and I was worried. I knew it made no sense to stay at home, but it also seemed wrong to leave Mum to Lucas and Greta. I thought of the disparate collec-tion of relatives who had attended my grandmother's funeral, and wondered where they all were. Would any of them come to our rescue, if we needed them? I very much doubted it.

I returned to school on the Sunday afternoon by train (no car was necessary as I only had a small suitcase). Call Me Bill drove me to the station and waved me off, and while I felt uneasy at leaving everyone else to cope with Mum's precari-ous mental state, I also felt a guilty sense of relief. After all, Dr Mackenzie had told me to get on with my own life, and so that was what I should do.

Sixteen

The rest of that term passed uneventfully, and I managed to achieve my aim of coming top overall in the end-of-term exams. I returned home for the Easter holidays with an excellent school report and feeling more confident than I had in a long time.

Mum seemed almost back to her normal self, and insisted on organizing the annual Easter egg hunt in the garden, although Lucas and I tried to tell her that we were far too old for such frivolities.

'Nonsense! No one's too old for Easter eggs, and this makes them more fun,' said Mum, undeterred, but she invited some neighbours' children round to join in and salvage our dignity.

Mum's size had increased considerably since half-term, and it was with a kind of horrified fascination that I observed her swollen body and breasts. I had never had any close contact with pregnancy, and hadn't realized that the human body could expand so rapidly and in such an astonishing way. It did nothing to change my feelings about all things sexual, for

I certainly never wanted to look like that. What must it feel like to be *inhabited*; to have someone else conducting their own small separate existence inside you, with no apparent reference to your own? There'd been a time when I had assumed that one day I would be a mother; now, I was absolutely determined it should never happen.

But Mum seemed to be enjoying her pregnancy, and was looking forward keenly to the birth of her baby. Richard had decorated the box room, and courtesy of Greta, who was in her element, the baby had enough knitwear to last it until it started school.

'Won't it be a bit hot?' I asked, fingering shawls and matinee jackets, bonnets and bootees. After all, there had to be a limit to the amount of warm clothing a June baby would require, even in the coolest of British summers.

'Do you think so?' Mum picked up a little jumpsuit knitted in a startling shade of purple. 'Maybe you're right, Cass. Perhaps I should get some cotton things as well.' She put the jumpsuit back in the drawer. 'I've forgotten what they need. It's been a long time.'

Other things Mum appeared to have forgotten included a cot and a pram, although she had purchased a plastic bath, a matching potty and enough nappies for a small army of incontinent infants. Mum's memory wasn't so much bad as selective. The rest of us did our best to help her fill in the gaps, but my knowledge of babies was scanty and Greta's non-existent. Call Me Bill was helpful in the field of fringe pharmaceuticals, and brought home liberal supplies of baby powder and nappy cream, most of them with suspiciously faded labels.

But Lucas showed little interest in the baby. Having recently shed the worst of his spots and caught up with his new bass voice and gangling limbs, he had suddenly become popular. He spent a lot of time in the bathroom doing interesting things to his hair and spraying himself with pungent smells, while the telephone was kept busy with breathy female voices asking to speak to him. He seemed unaware that the journey upon which he was embarking with such enthusiasm was the same one whose benefits – if that's what they could be called – our mother was about to reap. When it came to it, I concluded sadly, everything seemed to come down to sex.

I managed to divert Mum from her prenatal trance long enough to get her to buy me my school summer uniform of, among other things, 'blue checked dresses, four' (Mum sent me back with three), 'white ankle socks, six pairs' (I had four) and 'white tennis dresses, two' ('Whatever do you want with two tennis dresses?' Mum cried. I was grateful that she saw the point of even one tennis dress). And Call Me Bill drove me back to school for the new term.

Looking back, I remember that summer term as a magical time. In the forgiving light of early summer, the main school house seemed to shed its air of menace and looked almost inviting, while the gardens really came into their own. Smooth lawns were edged with a variety of shrubs and shaded by two large cypress trees, and beyond the main garden there was an outdoor swimming pool discreetly concealed behind a high hedge. There was also a large meadow which became a carpet of the kinds of wild flowers so rarely seen these days. Bees and butterflies busied themselves among drifts of cowslips and buttercups, which later gave way to pale purple orchids, scabious, vetch, harebells and a myriad other flowers.

Occasionally, when the weather was unusually hot, we were allowed to have our lessons out of doors, and we would sit on the grass under one of the cypresses, making notes in exercise books propped on our knees, the sound of the teacher's voice interrupted only by the calling of wood pigeons and the distant sound of a cuckoo. To this day, I shall never be able to hear a cuckoo without being taken straight back to the smell of newly mown grass and the sound of Miss Kennedy reading the poetry of Browning: 'God's in his heaven. All's right with the world.'

One evening towards the end of June, I was summoned to Miss Armitage's office to receive news of the birth of my new sister.

'Mother and baby are both doing well,' she told me. 'I'm sure you'd like to speak to your mother. You may use the office telephone when she comes out of hospital next week.'

I left the office unsure of how I should be feeling. Of course I was relieved that Mum was OK, but not especially pleased at the news, and I certainly wasn't looking forward to seeing the new arrival. Was there something wrong with me?

My friends did nothing to help my flagging self-esteem.

'Oh, how wonderful!' cooed Helena. 'You are lucky! A sister, too.'

'I already told you. I didn't want a sister.'

'You'll change your mind when you see her. I'm sure you will.'

'I wouldn't count on it.'

'Oh, Cass. You're such a misery sometimes.'

'On the contrary. I'm usually perfectly cheerful. I just don't happen to want a baby sister. Or any kind of baby, come to that.'

'A new little baby,' said Fern dreamily. 'Oh, Cass! You'll love it. I know you will. How can you not love a new little baby?'

What was wrong with everyone? I wondered crossly. Why did babies render perfectly sensible human beings all gooey and sentimental? After all, babies were only underdeveloped people, and hadn't we all started out like that? I tried to imagine Miss Armitage as a baby, or Call Me Bill. Had Call Me Bill's entrance into the world been greeted with glad cries of 'It's a boy!'? Had people once cooed and gurgled over Miss Armitage? It was hard to imagine. The whole baby thing defeated me. I could see that babies were necessary – that we all had to start somewhere – but why did everyone have to make such a *fuss*?

When I spoke to her on the telephone the following week, Mum was euphoric.

'You should see her, Cass. She's beautiful. She's got lots of hair and big blue eyes, and such tiny little fingers and toes.' It would appear that Mum had gone as daft as everyone else.

'You're not still calling her Octavia, are you?' I asked.

'Of course I am! She's always been Octavia. Why should I change my mind now? You'll come round to it, Cass. She just is an Octavia. Octavia Beatrice, after Mother. I thought of calling her Octavia Cassandra after you, but it was a bit of a mouthful. I hope you don't mind.'

'Don't mention it,' I said, relieved that at least I wouldn't have to share my name.

A few days later, I received in the post a grainy black and white photograph of Mum in her nightdress holding in her arms something tiny and swaddled. It could have been a doll, or even a small animal for all the resemblance it bore to a human being, and I hid the photograph away. If I showed it to my friends, it would be one more thing for them to swoon over, and by now I was thoroughly sick of the whole subject of babies.

End of term came, and Call Me Bill, who in the last year had become quite a member of the family (even to the extent of converting a dusty storeroom into a bedroom for himself), fetched me home in his car.

Mum greeted me in the hallway, holding a swaddled bundle.

'Meet your sister, Cass!'

Obediently, I inspected the bundle. And fell instantly in love.

Of course, I had seen babies before, from a distance, and they really did seem to me to look much the same. I tended to feel that once you'd seen one, you'd more or less seen them all. I acknowledged that their parents could no doubt tell them apart, but was pretty sure that no one else could.

But this baby was different.

'Goodness!' I said, taken aback.

'Yes. Isn't she?' Mum laughed. 'Do you want to hold her?'

I put down my bags and very carefully took the bundle in my arms. The baby stared up into my face with unblinking blue eyes from beneath a shock of dark hair, her tiny mouth pursed as though considering what to make of me, one walnut-sized fist showing above the blanket.

'Iss beautiful baby, no?' Greta was standing beaming beside Mum, as though the baby had been the result of some joint effort involving herself.

'Yes. Oh, yes.' I laid a finger against the baby's cheek, and it was like touching a petal. 'I didn't know babies could be – like this.'

Poor little Octavia Beatrice. Such a big name for such a tiny person. She was to affect our lives in a way none of us could have imagined.

Seventeen

'Cass?' She grips my hand.

'Yes?'

'I'm frightened.'

'Of course you are.' Who wouldn't be?

'It'll be all right, won't it? After all' – a small smile – 'lots of people have done it before. Lots of people have died.'

'Yes. Of course they have.'

'Shakespeare, Queen Victoria, Charlie Chaplin. They've all done it.'

'Yes.'

She moves restlessly.

'Do you believe in Heaven, Cass?'

'I don't know, Mum. I'd like to. I do feel that something of all of us lives on.'

For how could anyone as full of life as Mum cease to exist; simply stop, as though someone had turned off the ignition? Somehow, the idea of no afterlife seems even more implausible than the comforting picture of clouds and angels in the illustrated children's bible I was given as a child. I have often *thought that if death were not so commonplace – if we weren't all in the same boat, heading towards that same unavoidable destination – it would simply be too outrageous to be believable.*

'I've had a good life, really.' She sighs. 'I've been lucky.'

Oh Mum! How can you say that, after all you've been through? But then my mother has never been a complainer. She has known depression and disappointment, loneliness and tragedy, but while I have often seen her weeping, and sometimes desperate, I don't think I have ever heard her complain. At her best, she has been capable of the kind of happiness which is totally infectious, lighting up those around her and dispelling ill-temper in even the most curmudgeonly of companions.

Mum was certainly happy in the months following Octavia's birth. She appeared to achieve a degree of serenity I had never seen before, and the household seemed to settle down as though with a sigh of contentment, not untempered with relief.

The weather that summer was fine, and although we didn't go away (there had rarely been enough money for summer holidays, and Lucas and I had long ceased to expect them), as always we managed to enjoy ourselves. Lucas's new life largely excluded me, not least because my lack of interest in the opposite sex was equalled only by his preoccupation with it, but I was happy simply to be at home. I spent my time walking with The Dog, crying over Thomas Hardy (my latest discovery), and catching up with Myra and some of my other friends.

And then there was Octavia. Her neat round head, her peachy skin, the watchfulness of her navy-blue eyes, the feathery crescents of her lashes when she was asleep – they all combined to fascinate and enchant me, and in my enslaved state I was happy to do for her anything Mum asked. Helena and Fern would have been proud of me, for I changed her nappies, bathed her and took her out for walks, and it was I who was rewarded with her first wobbly smile.

Only one thing about Octavia bothered me. Ridiculous as it might seem, I found myself scrutinizing her for any sign, any clue, which might identify her father, for as things were, I felt as though I only knew half of her; it was almost as though that other half – the unknown half – would remain forever a stranger. There had been a time when I had done the same with my own reflected image, ruling out the features which were Mum's and building up a (probably totally inaccurate) picture of my father from the bits of me which didn't match hers.

Octavia was certainly very like Mum, with the same creamy complexion, and hair which was already showing hints of auburn, but she was a very long baby (Mum was fairly short), and I suspected that her father had probably been tall. A tall stranger with a beard and problems. It certainly wasn't much to go on, and as time went by, I abandoned my researches. I didn't know what Mum planned to tell Octavia, for she certainly seemed to remember more about this baby's conception than she had about mine or Lucas's, but that bridge needn't be crossed for some time yet, so I put the thought to the back of my mind.

Mum's attitude to Octavia was doting but scatty, and I

noticed in her the same haphazard attitude to mothering which Lucas and I had experienced when we were younger. She obviously adored the baby, but was quite happy to leave her care to the rest of us if it suited her. Octavia didn't seem to have any kind of routine, and appeared not to expect any. Mum fed her when she cried, got her up if she wanted to play with her or show her off, and put her back in her crib when she had better things to do. One minute she would be all over the baby, taking her out to visit friends, playing her lullabies on a cracked record (singing along with the inevitable ironing board accompaniment), even taking her to the clinic to be weighed and crowing proudly over her progress. The next, she would be off out ('Cass, look after Octavia would you, there's a dear'), and might not return until late.

It gave me some insight into the way Lucas and I must have been treated as infants, for while I knew that our upbringing had had little structure, I had no idea this had gone as far back as our babyhood. It went some way to explain our indifference to order or routine, and – at least when we were younger – our unquestioning acceptance of the unexpected.

Although I enjoyed looking after Octavia, there were times when I couldn't help feeling taken for granted. But this rarely lasted long, for just as I was beginning to wonder whether Mum was pleased to have me home for my own sake, or more because I provided a free babysitting service, she would bake my favourite cake, or take me out to buy me a new dress she could ill afford, and I would feel valued again. I know this wasn't a deliberate ruse to keep me sweet – Mum was incapable of being that devious – but I did feel as though everything was done more on a whim than with any proper planning. She had a childlike knack of living for the moment, and while this could be infuriating if it required childcare at the drop of a hat, it could also be enormous fun if it involved a trip out or an unexpected treat.

Sometimes I worried about how she would manage when I went back to school. Greta was fine, but she tended to fuss, and while she too adored Octavia, she wasn't what I would call a natural where babies were concerned. Twice she let Octavia roll off the bed onto the floor, and on one occasion she nearly drowned her in the bath. I also caught her apparently trying to feed the baby chocolate.

'Greta! What are you doing?' I caught Greta's hand.

'Chocolate. She like, no?' Greta looked hurt.

'No! I mean, she might like the taste, but she's much too young.'

'She lick,' Greta countered.

'Of course she licked it. She licks everything. That doesn't mean it's good for her.'

'I try.' Greta's eyes filled with tears.

'Of course you tried.' I put my arms round Greta's shoulders. 'You're very kind. You're good to all of us. It's just that – well, perhaps we ought to ask Mum before we give the baby anything new.'

'OK. I ask.' Reluctantly, Greta put away her chocolate.

But as I might have known, Mum was no use at all.

'Chocolate? Of course she can have a little lick of chocolate from time to time. What harm can it do?'

I had no idea what harm chocolate could do to a young

baby; all I knew was that it didn't seem appropriate. But in the event it didn't seem to affect Octavia in the least.

The summer holidays came to an end all too soon, and almost before I knew it, it was time to return to school. Lucas, who had recently passed his driving test, offered to take me in the borrowed van, and while the prospect didn't exactly thrill me, the thought of a journey with Mum plus baby and quite possibly The Dog was even worse, so I accepted the offer.

Although I was much more settled than I had been a year ago, and was looking forward to the new school year, I was apprehensive about leaving home and I knew I would miss Octavia dreadfully.

'You will take care of things, Lucas, won't you?' I said.

'Take care of things? What do you mean?' Lucas was driving much too close to the car in front, but I knew better than to interfere.

'Well, you know. Keep an eye on Mum, make sure the baby's OK, see that Greta doesn't start feeding her apple strudel. That sort of thing.'

Lucas grinned.

'We've managed a whole year without you, Cass. I'm sure we'll cope.'

'But Octavia—'

'Octavia will be fine.' Lucas pulled out to overtake, and I closed my eyes. It seemed to me that much of my time travelling to and from school was spent with my eyes shut. 'After all,' he added, as we regained our side of the road, 'you and I survived, didn't we?'

'Yes, I suppose so.'

But I wasn't convinced. There was something fragile, something almost impermanent about Octavia, and I feared for her. She was so serene, so undemanding, so obliging; she was almost too good to be true. If it didn't sound so corny I would have described her as truly angelic; almost not of this world.

Eighteen

Mum's letters that term were some of the happiest I had received from her. Granted, they were still written on odd scraps of paper – the backs of envelopes, shopping lists, the electricity bill (a red one, needless to say) – but they were busy with news and plans.

She had a new job at the dry cleaner's ('Only part-time, but such fun, Cass.' Only Mum could manage to have fun in a dry cleaner's), the autumn colours were the best she had seen for years, The Dog had learnt to 'die for the Queen' (he was probably just exhausted), and she had found a new Lodger ('Such a good-looking young man, Cass.' Oh dear). As for Octavia, she was full of smiles and Mum swore she could feel a tooth coming through. As Lucas had predicted, life at home was evidently proceeding quite happily without me.

I came home for half-term and was mortified to find that Octavia appeared to have forgotten who I was while Greta was now firmly in place as mother substitute during Mum's frequent absences. In spite of her initial misgivings, Octavia seemed happy to have me look after her, but Greta had become proprietorial and bossy (possibly in retaliation for the chocolate incident), and I had to mind my step if I wasn't to encroach on this new and treasured territory. Lucas's attention was equally divided between the latest girlfriend (a leggy blonde) and consideration of his future (A levels loomed); and Call Me Bill was preoccupied with his new hobby, compiling a slim volume of his own verse. None of us had been aware that Call Me Bill was a closet poet, and when he had coyly submitted some of his poems to our scrutiny, I think we all very much wished that that was where he'd stayed.

I remember reading a poem entitled 'Avalanche', which included such memorable lines as:

A froth and a fever of snow in Geneva,
A tumble of skis on the high Pyrenees

'It's very – original,' I said, as I handed the closely written sheet of paper back to him.

'Yes. Isn't it?' he said happily, replacing his precious creation in its folder. 'I'm so glad you like it, Cass. Especially as you're the artistic one. It means a lot to me.'

I wasn't aware that I had actually said I liked the poem or that I was particularly artistic, but I seemed to have satisfied Call Me Bill, and I was pleased about that. I also felt humbled by his appreciation, and ashamed that Lucas and I had privately giggled over lines where sense had often been sacrificed for the sake of flowery alliteration. After all, who was I (currently struggling to understand the great T.S. Eliot) to judge Call Me Bill's poems?

The new Lodger was indeed good-looking – even beautiful – and it was Lucas who pointed out that he was almost certainly gay.

'Do you think so?' Mum said, when he mentioned it to her.

'Of course he is, Mum. Can't you see? The way he dresses, the way he walks. Apart from anything else, he's too – too domestic to be anything else.'

'Oh, what a waste,' sighed Mum. 'And I've asked him to stay for Christmas, too.'

For my own part, I thought he was the nicest Lodger we'd had in a long time. He had all the characteristics I liked about men without posing any kind of threat. He was fun, intelligent, and wonderful with Octavia, and I felt happier knowing he was around to keep an extra eye on things.

The rest of the term flew by, and almost before I knew it I was home again for Christmas. Octavia had grown, and was if anything even more beautiful, with the beginnings of a head of bright auburn curls, those huge blue eyes and little pink bud of a mouth. The halls were decked, Mum was in festive mood, and there were enough jolly people around (including the gay Lodger) for Mum to feel content. There was even a dusting of snow.

But I had my own preoccupations. This was a big year for me as well as for Lucas, for I had O levels in the summer and mock exams as soon as I returned to school, as well as possible A level subjects to consider. I spent much of the holiday in my room revising, swathed in cardigans and coats (my room had only a small electric heater), eating extra strong mints and drinking coffee.

'Do come and join us,' Mum would say, appearing at my door at regular intervals. 'We see so little of you, and it's *Christmas*.'

She failed to see that my achievements, of which she was so proud, came at a price; I had to work. She seemed to think that my ability was such that all I had to do was simply turn up for examinations and spill the contents of my remarkable brain onto a piece of paper. But then by her own admission, Mum had never passed an exam in her life, and had scant understanding of what was involved.

During that spring term, I had little time to think about home. Mum's brief letters continued to arrive with their snippets of (still cheery) news, but I was absorbed by my work and thoughts of my future.

I did well in my mock exams, and there was talk of aiming for a place at Oxford or Cambridge if my O-level results came up to expectations. I was terribly excited. I had visited Cambridge once, and had been bowled over by the beauty of the older colleges, with their rosy brick and their ancient walkways, their lawns and their quaint old-fashioned courts. I could think of no greater privilege than to be a part of such a place; to form my own small link in that centuries-long chain of tradition and learning. For the first time in my life, I was imagining a life away from the confines of home or school; a life of my choosing; a grown-up life; a life which was *my own*.

When I came home at Easter, Octavia was crawling and pulling herself up on pieces of furniture. I gathered that she was well ahead of the usual milestones, but then as Greta kept pointing out, she was an exceptional child. She was also amazingly self-sufficient for one so small, and would spend happy hours examining picture books (as often as not upside down) or trying to balance one brightly coloured brick on top of another. She rarely cried, and communicated by small kittenish mewings to express happiness or displeasure. Mum maintained that she was musical, and she certainly appeared to enjoy the ironing-board recitals.

'I think *she* really will play the piano,' Mum said, in a rare if oblique reference to my own brief but failed piano-playing career. 'Someone in this family ought to,' she added wistfully.

Poor Mum. The least ambitious of parents, she had always allowed us simply to be ourselves and to develop in our own ways, but she had nonetheless made no secret of the fact that she would have loved one of us to be a musician. Over the years, she had become convinced that she herself could have been a fine pianist if she had had lessons, and that her life would then have turned out very differently.

I returned to school for the summer term and O levels. That June was baking hot, and we sat our exams in the new sports hall (discreetly positioned behind trees so as not to interfere with all that Victorian gloom), whose glass walls and polished floors encased us in a stifling atmosphere, compounded by the blistering heat and the collective anxiety of the hapless candidates inside. We sat at our carefully spaced desks, fanning ourselves with our question papers, exchanging despairing glances under the stern gaze of the invigilator. Would this summer *never* end?

The last day of the exams was marked by torrential thunderstorms, and I can still picture us all as we ran from the sports hall, whooping with joy and relief. Once outside, we dropped our pens and pencils in the mud and danced in the rain, stretching out our arms, lifting up our faces, running our ink-stained fingers through our dripping hair, revelling in the coolness and the wet and the wonderful fresh smell of damp earth and grass. No one tried to stop us as we whirled and pranced and shouted. One girl even threw off her school frock and tore across the lawn half-naked, finishing with a victory roll down a grassy bank into the bushes. The exams were over; the long summer holidays beckoned.

The very next day I was summoned to Miss Armitage's office. I went along, carefree and unsuspecting. I had done nothing wrong, so I had nothing to fear. Perhaps I was to be awarded a prize at the forthcoming speech day, and had been summoned to give her my choice of books. I had already made my decision in anticipation of just such an eventuality; I had recently discovered Elizabeth Gaskell, and would choose as many of her works as the prize money would allow. I was already anticipating weeks of joyous summer reading.

The moment I was admitted to the office, I knew something was wrong. Miss Armitage wasn't sitting in her usual chair, but was pacing in front of her desk, her expression serious.

'I think you'd better sit down, Cassandra.' She pointed to a chair. 'Please, Cassandra. Please sit.'

Wordlessly I sat down. All at once my throat was dry, my heart thumping in my chest, my stomach churning. No girl was ever invited to sit down in Miss Armitage's office. Something truly dreadful must have happened. I felt sick and empty and very afraid, and yet totally aware of everything that was going on around me; of the ticking of the clock in the corner, of the distant calling of a wood pigeon and the laughter of a group of girls passing beneath the window. I noticed that the calendar on the desk still bore yesterday's date and that the sky outside the window had darkened. Perhaps we were due for another storm.

Miss Armitage looked nervous and ill at ease, and for once, she didn't seem to know what to do with her hands. I watched as she laced and unlaced her fingers, fiddling for a moment with the buttons on her blouse, finally folding her hands firmly together as though to prevent them from escaping. She took a couple of steps towards the window, and then turned to face me again. I waited.

At last she spoke.

'I'm afraid I have some bad news,' she said. 'You're going to have to be very brave, Cassandra.'

Obediently, I continued to wait, sitting on my own hands and tucking my feet behind the legs of the chair to stop them from shaking. In spite of my fear, enough of my brain was still functioning for me to know that if I ever had the misfortune to break bad news to anyone, I would tell them straight away. No preamble, no build-up. However bad it was, I would give it to them straight. For nothing could be worse than this waiting.

Miss Armitage cleared her throat.

'It's your sister, Cassandra.'

'Octavia.' My voice seemed to come from a long way away. *Oh, please please, not Octavia!*

Nineteen

'Cass?' Mum's awake again, and I reach for her hand.

'Yes?'

'The pond. I should have had it filled in. It was all my fault.'

Not the pond again. It's years since Mum has mentioned the pond, and while I know she can't have forgotten it – how could any of us ever forget it? – I hoped that at least it had ceased to preoccupy her; that it had left the forefront of her mind and been filed away somewhere where it had come to cause her less pain.

'It wasn't your fault, Mum,' I say now. 'How could it have been your fault? And Octavia was so young. She wasn't even walking. How could you have known that she would be able to get to it on her own?'

'I should have known. I should have. It was my job to keep her safe.' A tear forms in the corner of her eye and leaks into the starched cotton of the pillowcase, and I ache for her.

'Oh Mum. It was such a long time ago. Years ago.' I hesitate. There is no point in saying that it doesn't matter; that *the passage of years has lessened the significance of Octavia's death, yet I can't bear to see Mum suffer yet again for something for which she has already paid so dearly. 'And her life wasn't in vain, was it? She gave us all so much pleasure.'*

'And we loved her.'

'Oh yes. We loved her.' For no one could have had more love in such a short lifetime than my little sister.

'But the pond—'

'Mum, darling mum, you have to forgive yourself for the pond, even though there's nothing to forgive. You have to let it go.'

Of course, in a way, we were all responsible.

Mum had said just after Octavia was born that we should fill in the pond; that it wasn't safe. But we managed to persuade her to leave it, at least until Octavia was walking.

That pond held so many memories for Lucas and me. Frogspawn in the spring (descendants of that first jam jar of tadpoles which Mum had used in her bewildering introduction to the facts of life) and the joy of fishing for newts with a worm tied to a piece of cotton (not forgetting the excitement when they all escaped from the tank in my bedroom in the middle of the night). Best of all, Prissy Deirdre from next door had fallen into that pond not once, but twice, and had emerged drenched and stinking and completely unrecognizable. The second occasion had confirmed all her mother's worst fears about our family, and that was the last we saw of Prissy Deirdre.

So the tragedy wasn't just Mum's fault. Lucas and I had wanted to keep the pond; even Greta had put in a good word for it ('Iss pretty, no?' No. Not really. But we knew what she meant). Besides, who could have anticipated that Octavia would manage to crawl down the back steps and across the lawn and get as far as the bottom of the garden in the time it took for Mum to answer the phone?

I have no idea how I got home that afternoon. I believe someone took me in a car – I have a vague memory of being wrapped in a blanket and of the unfamiliar smell of leather seats – but everything else about that dreadful journey passed in a blur.

The house seemed to be full of people. I remember Dr Mackenzie and some neighbours and Richard, and the gay Lodger making tea, and Call Me Bill ushering people in and out, and Greta (inevitably) weeping. I remember the pale controlled face of poor Lucas, who was being heartbreakingly brave as the Man of the House, and the whimpering of The Dog, who had a sixth sense where disaster was concerned.

And Mum.

Mum was sitting on the floor when I went into her bedroom, her arms locked round her knees, rocking to and fro. Just rocking.

'I don't know what to do. I don't know what to do. I don't know what to do.' Rock, rock, rock. 'I don't know what to do.'

Her face, when she lifted it, was completely drowned in tears, so swollen that I couldn't see her eyes, her hair and clothes were soaked in tears. I had never in my life seen anyone weep the way Mum wept.

'Cass.' She held out her arms to me. 'Oh, Cass! What am I going to do? Whatever am I going to do?'

I knelt down beside her, and we wept and rocked together, holding each other and sobbing into each other's shoulders. There was something primitive and strangely soothing about that rocking. Maybe it was to do with the automatic way mothers rock their babies, or perhaps we both felt that the swaying rhythmic movement would in some way help us to keep ourselves – and each other – alive. For at the time, I felt that if I were to let go of Mum she might simply lie down and never get up again.

Eventually, I persuaded her to sit on the bed, and we stayed there together for some time, holding each other, as dusk dimmed the sky outside and the busy comings and goings downstairs continued. People tiptoed in and out of the room, murmuring and bringing us cups of tea, and Dr Mackenzie returned to check on Mum.

'There there, my lass.' He joined us on the bed. 'My poor poor lass.' He held her hand and stroked it. Then he took a bottle of tablets from his pocket and shook two of them into his palm, offering them to her with a glass of water. 'You take these and try to get some rest.'

Mum took the tablets and pushed her sodden hair out of her eyes.

'Did she suffer, doctor?' Her voice was so low that he had to bend down so that his head was touching hers.

'Only for a wee while,' he said. 'Maybe a minute or two at most.'

I was grateful to him for being truthful; for not trying to patronize Mum with any of that stuff about not suffering at all; words which fool no one, and offer less comfort than the truth.

Mum nodded.

'Thank you,' she said.

Dr Mackenzie got up from the bed.

'Well, I'll be on my way,' he said, 'but I'll be back tomorrow.' He paused in the doorway. 'There's nothing I can say that will comfort you,' he added. 'Nothing at all. But you will get through this. Somehow, you'll get through it.'

He indicated for me to follow him out of the room, and after he had closed the door, he put his hands on my shoulders.

'Now you take care of yourself, Cassandra. Don't take too much responsibility. This is your loss, too, and you need to grieve as well as your mum. Give me a ring if you're worried about anything, or if you just want to talk.'

Yet again, Dr Mackenzie reminded me of the father I never had; his steady masculine presence brought home how much we needed a man – a proper man – in the family, especially at a time like this. I gave a brief thought to that other bereaved parent, Octavia's father, who didn't even know he'd been a father, and just for that moment, I hated him. He might have missed out on knowing his little daughter, but he had also been spared this agony, and I found that hard to forgive.

Downstairs, I found the Lodger making yet more tea, while Greta tried to concoct something for our supper (why? I couldn't imagine any of us ever wanting to eat again). Call Me Bill had had to go back to work to sort out some problem, and Richard had disappeared. Lucas was out walking The Dog. The house seemed to be full of flowers, but otherwise it felt almost normal.

'Where is she?' I asked Greta. 'Where – where is Octavia?'

'I think at hospital.' Greta struggled to open a tin of corned beef, cutting her finger.

'Did you see her?'

Greta paused, a tea towel wrapped round her hand.

'Yes. I see her.'

'What – what did she look like?'

'She look like sleeping,' Greta said. 'Just sleeping.'

'The ambulance men were brilliant.' The Lodger handed me a cup of tea. 'But there was nothing they could do. Oh, Cass. I'm so sorry.' He gave me a hug, and as I clung to him, I heard the sob in his own throat. 'I'm so very, very sorry. She was a very special little human being.'

'Yes.'

I looked round the kitchen. Some of Octavia's clothes were still drying on the clothes horse, and a woolly dog with three legs and a well-chewed tail lay where she had left it on the floor.

How were we ever going to get over this?

Twenty

During the week between Octavia's death and her funeral, life in our house seemed to stand still. Cards and letters and flowers continued to arrive, together with a succession of visitors. Food was prepared (although little was eaten) and gallons of tea were consumed. Laundry and shopping were done and The Dog was taken for walks, but otherwise nothing *happened*. We said little to each other – what was there to say? – and moved around each other carefully, politely, like awkward strangers, although of course it was tragedy that was the real stranger in the house.

Call Me Bill took the week off work to help, although there was little he could do, and the gay Lodger, who was currently between jobs, was a tower of strength. Poor Greta did her best to stem her weeping, aware that to outdo Mum in the weeping stakes would be inappropriate (if not impossible), and Lucas continued to be stoical.

'It's OK to cry, you know,' I said to him one evening, watching his pale still face. 'After all, everyone else seems to be doing it, and she was your sister.'

'I can't, Cass. I just can't.' He turned to me with a hopeless shrug. 'I've even tried sticking pins into myself, but it's as though I've lost all feeling.'

'Oh, Lucas.' I put my arms round him. 'What are we going to do?' I found myself echoing Mum's words.

'I don't know. Nothing seems real any more, does it?' He allowed my embrace but didn't return it. 'It's odd to think that a short time ago she didn't exist. Not at all. Not even as a tiny speck. No one wanted her or expected her. We were all quite happy without her. She just – arrived, and then she died. And now look at us all.' He paused. 'We only had her for a year.'

I had assumed that Mum's reaction would be similar to her behaviour after the death of our grandmother, but being new to the business of bereavement I hadn't realized that death has its own hierarchy, and that for Mum, Octavia's death far outweighed that of her own mother.

Almost overnight, Mum's room became a shrine to Octavia. There were photographs of her on every surface, together with her toys and books, and her small garments had all been carefully laid out on the bed, as though they were waiting for her to wear them again. In the midst of all this sat Mum, grubby and dishevelled, clutching Octavia's comfort blanket and favourite teddy, still rocking and weeping.

'What can we do?' I asked Dr Mackenzie when he called in on the third morning. I had expected him to approach Mum in the kindly but firm manner as he had last time, but he seemed to be treating her with the same kid gloves as the rest of us.

'There's nothing I can do, Cassandra. Not really. I can

only keep an eye on her and give her something to help her sleep. That's all.'

'But you helped her when Grandma died. She took notice of you then.'

He sighed.

'This is different, my dear. The loss of a child is the worst thing that can happen to anyone. You lose your parents and – well, that's sad, but it happens. But not your child. No one expects to outlive their own child.'

'Isn't there anything we can do?'

'You're doing all you can, but strange as it may seem, your mum knows what's best for her. What she's doing may look a bit weird, but she's dealing with it in her own way. It won't always be like this. One day, she'll let go of Octavia's things, and one day – one day – she'll let go of Octavia. But not yet. Not for a long time. The poor lass has quite a journey ahead of her.'

'And – us? What about us?'

For I missed Mum. I missed having her around *for me*. This was the worst thing that had happened to me as well as to Mum, and yet although she responded when I spoke to her, I knew she was a long way away; that I couldn't really reach her. Ever since that first evening when we had clung together, she no longer seemed to need me. She didn't appear to need anyone. She was alone with her pain and her guilt and the ghost of her dead baby.

'Ah, poor Cassandra.' He put his arm around my shoulders. 'I know it must be so hard for you too, but there are people in this house who'd be glad to have you lean on them. Greta, for instance. She's not a strong woman, but so kind.

155

She's longing to comfort you, but doesn't like to say so. And she needs some comfort, too. That little baby seems to have belonged to all of you. You must all help each other.'

That night, I joined Greta on the sofa, and we held each other and wept together. She wasn't the same as Mum, but I think we were able to offer each other something, and Greta had loved Octavia at least as much as I had. Octavia was probably the nearest she'd ever come to having a child of her own, and having no other family, her loss must have been all the worse for that.

Octavia's funeral was held on a perfect June day in our little parish church. We had never been churchgoers, but Mum said she wanted the best for Octavia, and none of us was going to argue with that.

I don't know what I had expected, but I found the sight of Lucas walking down the aisle carrying the tiny white coffin more heartbreaking than anything that had happened in the whole of that awful week. There had been no shortage of volunteers for this last sad task (Call Me Bill and the gay Lodger to name two) but Lucas had insisted. His position in the family dictated that he should be the one to carry Octavia's coffin, and that was what he would do.

The church was packed with people, many of whom I'd never seen before, but I was rapidly learning that the death of a child touches everyone, and that these people needed to be there for themselves as much as for us, even if we were never to see them again. The wispy grey relatives of my grandmother's funeral were mercifully absent – they probably didn't even know what had happened – and for that I was grateful.

The church smelled of cool air and polish and roses, and there was complete silence as Lucas laid down his small burden in front of the chancel. It was as though we were all holding our grief in check, waiting for the permission that only Mum could give. But she remained silent; she probably had no more tears left to weep. So the rest of us had to contain ours as best we could.

I remember envying those people whose cultures allow them to stamp and howl and rage around a grave or funeral pyre; who can express their grief physically, who can embrace and console each other while screaming their outrage to the heavens. It seemed so much more natural than our stiff upper lips and rigid self-control, and the robed ritual and musty prayers of the Church of England.

Octavia was buried in the churchyard. There had never been any question of cremation, for Mum said she found it unthinkable that anything should be done to damage her small body even further. It was far better that she should lie among the ancient gravestones and the yew trees, where we could visit her. I know now that Mum needed a grave to tend; a place where she could go to nurse her grief. I myself have always favoured the gentleness of burial over the violent destruction of cremation, and on more than one occasion have been reminded of the comforting words at the end of Wuthering Heights:

I lingered . . . under that benign sky; watched the moths fluttering among the heath and harebells, listened to the soft wind breathing through the grass, and wondered

how anyone could ever imagine unquiet slumbers for the
sleepers in that quiet earth.

There mightn't have been any heath or harebells in our churchyard; rather the ubiquitous daisies and the brazen faces of dandelions. But I derived some small comfort from the thought of Octavia slumbering – such a deeply peaceful, consoling word – in the gentle environment of grass and trees and sky.

I remember little about the rest of that day. I know people came back to the house with us, and we must have offered them some kind of refreshment, but all I can recall is the feeling of utter exhaustion. Too tired to talk, too tired to cry, too tired even to think, all I wanted was to go to my room and curl up under the blankets in my old familiar bed, and sleep and sleep.

Twenty-one

I didn't go back to school that term. Call Me Bill collected my trunk and the rest of my stuff, and returned with a car full of my belongings together with a box of kind little notes and messages from my friends and teachers. Miss Armitage had already sent me an uncharacteristically warm letter of sympathy, closing with the injunction to 'be brave, but not too brave'. I got the feeling that it wasn't the first occasion upon which she had had to write such a letter to one of her pupils, and I have never forgotten that wise advice.

Grief is a strange thing. There were moments, even days, when I felt almost happy again; when I would read a book or go for a walk or see a friend, and everything would seem normal. Then some little reminder – a baby in a pram or a small head of auburn hair – would set me off again, and it was as though everything had happened only yesterday.

For the first time ever, the summer holidays seemed too long. As we moved from July into August, one drab sultry day merged into the next, the dusty leaves seemed to wilt on the trees and in the hedgerows, and flowers and weeds drooped together in our neglected garden. I think we were all painfully aware of the contrast with the previous August, when the house had been alive with the cries and the new presence of Octavia, but none of us said anything. We were each of us cocooned in our own sadness and our own memories, and while we did our best to help one another, I think that for each of us the journey was a different one.

Mum still spent much of her time in her room, but while she had gradually relinquished Octavia's clothes, she kept the teddy and the blanket in her bed with her. Sometimes I found her sniffing them, as though she were trying to extract from them the last traces of Octavia, and one day towards the end of August, I found her in tears.

'I can't smell her, Cass. Her smell's gone. I can't smell her any more. I shall never smell her again!'

I knew what she meant. I myself had paid covert visits to the bathroom where a tin of Johnson's baby powder was still sitting on the window sill, and had sprinkled it onto my hand and sniffed it, causing the tears to well up yet again as I remembered Octavia's bath times and her warm baby smell.

Why do we do these things? Why do we put ourselves through such painful experiences again and again, when there is no need? Is it simply hanging on, or is there more to it? Could it be that by pouring salt into our wounds we are in some way trying to purge them? Or perhaps we are testing ourselves, just to see if it still hurts as much as it did last time, like poking one's tongue into the gap left by an extracted tooth.

The aloofness which had come over Mum before Octavia's funeral had gone, and she became pathetically dependent and afraid of being left on her own. Each time she heard a door open or close, she would call out, and if any of us left the house she would question us closely as to where we were going and how long we'd be away.

'Where are you going, Cass?' Her voice followed me wherever I went, and I found it increasingly hard to be patient. Of course I needed my family, but I also needed my friends, and some time to myself to sort out my own feelings; to come to terms with what had happened and to think about my future. Because whatever anyone else might do, I had to make plans. I couldn't allow my life to come to a full stop because my sister had died, tragic though that was. Sooner or later, I had to move *on*.

When my exam results arrived I had done even better than anyone had expected, and for a few precious hours things seemed to return to normal as everyone rejoiced with me. Mum was terribly proud, and spent a happy morning with the telephone and her address book, phoning anyone and everyone to tell them how clever I was. Normally I would have found this embarrassing, but I was so pleased that she had found something to be happy about – that she was still capable of happiness – that I would cheerfully have consented to a full-page announcement in a national newspaper if that would have prolonged the atmosphere of celebration.

Lucas's A-level results, on the other hand, were abysmal, but then, as he himself pointed out, he didn't deserve good results since he hadn't done any work. He had recently decided to join the police, and they didn't seem to mind too much about his academic prowess. I suspected then – and still do – that Lucas got in on charm, since that has always been his greatest asset, although when I suggested it I was told very firmly that that was not what the police were looking for. Privately, I thought the police force could do with a bit more charisma to ginger up their image, and Lucas might be just what they needed. No doubt my idea of a policeman's role was naive, but I could see Lucas consoling the victims of burglaries or talking potential suicides off bridges and rooftops, and was quite sure he would be a success. As for Mum, she was so taken with the idea of having a policeman as a son that the failed A levels barely registered with her at all.

'It'll be so *useful*, Cass,' she confided to me, in one of her bewildering twists of logic.

I knew better than to challenge her. If she wanted to dream of a lifetime's immunity from the law, then that was fine by me.

As the end of the holidays drew nearer, I began to feel anxious. There had been no mention of my going back to school; no half-hearted replacing of outgrown uniform or grumbling over the price of hockey sticks. I didn't like to bring the subject up as it seemed heartless to be thinking of leaving home at such a difficult time, but the new term was almost upon me.

'Mum?' I found her sitting in the kitchen, absently brushing The Dog and gazing into space. 'About – well, about school.'

'What about school?' Mum removed a burr from The Dog's tail, and examined it as though it were suddenly of great interest.

'Going back, I suppose. We – I – haven't done anything

about it, and the term starts next week. I need – well, I need new things.'

'New things,' mused Mum. 'What new things?'

'My skirts are terribly short, although Greta's let them down as far as they'll go, and my blouses—'

'You mean boarding school?'

'Well, yes. Of course, boarding school.'

'Oh. I didn't think.'

'What didn't you think, Mum?' I sat down beside her.

'I suppose I didn't think you'd be going back. But you must go back. Of course you must.'

'Yes.'

'If you really want to.'

'Well, yes. In any case, they're expecting me. I can't just not turn up.'

'No, of course you can't.' She gave The Dog a final pat and pushed him away.

'Well then?'

'Well then,' she repeated, and took my hands in hers. 'Oh, Cass. What am I going to do without you?'

'Mum, you've got everyone else, and I'll soon be home again. I'll write lots, and I expect they'll let me phone.'

But I knew. Perhaps in a way I had always known. I wouldn't be going back to boarding school. For even if Mum could bear to part with me – and this seemed doubtful – how could I leave her like this?

'I shouldn't be doing this to you,' Mum said. 'It's all wrong.'

'You're not doing anything to me, Mum.'

'Yes, I am. I'm putting pressure on you. I don't mean to.

I want you to have your own life, of course I do. And I don't want to – hang on to you. It's not fair. Especially with you being so clever.'

I laughed.

'Oh, Mum! What's my being clever got to do with it?'

'Opportunity, I suppose. It's the least I can do, to let you have your opportunities. You could go far, you know, Cass. You could even be a doctor.'

To Mum, being a doctor represented the pinnacle of achievement.

'Mum, I don't want to be a doctor. The thought's never even crossed my mind.'

'Ah, but you could be. If you wanted.'

'Almost as good as being a policeman?' I teased her.

'Even better than being a policeman,' Mum said, giving me one of her increasingly rare smiles.

I got up and walked across to the window. There was already an autumnal light in the sky, and the bushes were festooned with those pretty jewelled spiders' webs which seem to appear towards the end of summer. The grass was thick with dew, and swallows were beginning to line up for their autumn journey. This time of year always reminded me of blackberry-picking and the glossy brown of newly hatched conkers, of sharp pencils and clean white rubbers, and the inviting smell of shiny new exercise books. Most people see spring as the season for new beginnings, but for me it has always been the autumn.

But not this year. This year, I wasn't looking forward to autumn at all.

'I won't go back, Mum,' I said, turning away from the window. 'I'll stay at home with you.'

'Oh, you must go, Cass. Of course you must,' Mum said, but I could see the relief already beginning to dawn in her face, and I knew she wouldn't need much persuading.

For a few moments I was filled with anger. I had been packed off to boarding school with no reference to my feelings and through no fault of my own, and now, when I was really settled, I was being compelled to leave. It wasn't fair. Whatever might or might not have happened, it simply wasn't fair.

But my anger was short-lived. I looked down at Mum, who had aged ten years in the past few weeks; at the empty high chair which was already gathering dust in the corner of the kitchen, and at poor lonely Greta, who had just come in with a basket of clothes to iron, and I sighed.

Of course it wasn't fair, but then life wasn't fair. How could I ever have expected it to be?

Twenty-two

My old school had been the local secondary modern, for in order to remain with my friends when we left our primary school, I had taken pains to ensure that I failed the eleven-plus. I had enjoyed my time there, where the company was convivial, the discipline lax and such talents as I had as yet undiscovered. Now, however, it appeared that I was High School material, and if my education were to continue, I had little choice but to enrol.

The local High School was prestigious, and proud of it. It had a good record of Oxbridge entrants (the honours board in the assembly hall glowed with the collective triumphs of the girls who had passed through its classrooms), and it was very soon made clear to me that in the fullness of time, my own name was expected to appear among them. To this end, pressure was applied at every turn; pressure to work hard, pressure to conform, pressure (it seemed to me) to sacrifice any pleasure I might have found in my studies in the interests of better examination results. And I was not accustomed to pressure. So, before I had been there a term, I switched off.

In vain did my teachers lecture me on wasted talent and the importance of my future. In vain did they talk of present frustration and future regret. I was deaf to them all. If my future really was my own, then presumably it was up to me what I did with it, and as to future regret, well, that too would be *my* problem.

I'm sure that much of my lack of co-operation was due to the effects of Octavia's death (something which my teachers seemed to disregard, although they were all aware of it), but I had always had an obstinate streak too. Apart from Mum's decision to send me away to school (and for that, I had long since forgiven her), I had always been consulted as to what I wanted to do, and I saw no reason why that should change.

At the beginning of my second term Miss Carrington, the headmistress, sent for Mum, but if she had any hopes of getting parental co-operation from that quarter, she didn't know my mother.

'Silly cow,' Mum said, on her return from this interview. 'I see what you mean, Cass. I don't think I'd want to do anything that woman told me, either.' She paused. 'But think about it, Cass. You are clever, and you don't want to waste it.'

This was the nearest Mum came to trying to influence me, and I did think about it. But since Octavia's death, the dreaming spires of academe had lost much of their appeal. I was probably being foolish, but nowadays I found it hard to contemplate any kind of future beyond the life that I had at the moment, and in any case, leaving home seemed an impossibility. Mum needed me, of that I was certain, but I was becoming increasingly aware that I also needed her and the familiarity of home. It wasn't just the loss of Octavia itself which had made me insecure; it was the realization that nothing could be relied upon any more; that you could wake up one morning expecting everything to be as usual, and go to bed the same evening with your world in tatters.

Mum, finally acknowledging that all of us were suffering to some degree, was wonderfully kind to me, and it seemed that once more we had slipped back into our original roles; she was the mother, and I very much the child. I think it probably did her good to realize how much she was still needed, and it may well have been some small help to her on her long road to recovery. There were still occasions when she would cling to me, but as the months went by, there were reassuring glimpses of the old mum, and I began to hope that perhaps there might eventually be life after Octavia for all of us.

Meanwhile, we had a fresh diversion, for just after Christmas (and I shan't even attempt to describe that first aching Christmas following Octavia's death), there occurred an unexpected development in our household when, quite out of the blue, Call Me Bill took Mum aside, presented her with flowers, and made her a proposal of marriage.

While obviously shocked, Mum also appeared to be both touched and entertained by this unexpected offer, and quite at a loss as to how she should deal with it.

'Just imagine,' she said, when she told Lucas and me about it. 'Just imagine Call Me Bill proposing! Proposing to *me*! Me and Call Me Bill *married*!'

Lucas and I tried to imagine, but neither of us could manage it. Call Me Bill married was enough of a challenge in itself; Call Me Bill married to Mum was something that not even our lively imaginations could begin to address. Apart from anything else, Lucas and I had long since decided that Call Me Bill wasn't interested in sex, and the thought of Call Me Bill in bed with my worldly wise mother must surely be out of the question. Perhaps he was planning a celibate relationship; one of friendship and mutual support. But if that was the case, how would he cope with Mum when she returned to her normal philanderings?

'He's probably sorry for me,' said Mum.

'Mum, everyone's sorry for you at the moment, but they don't all come round with offers of marriage,' I said.

'True. But what on earth shall I say to him?'

'You mean you haven't given him an answer?'

'I said I'd think about it.'

'That was a bit of a cop-out,' Lucas remarked.

'Well, I couldn't just turn him down, could I? It would have been so unkind.'

'So you're not planning to turn him down,' Lucas said.

'Of course I am!'

'Well, then. The sooner you tell him, the better. It's even more unkind to leave him in suspense.'

'I suppose so.' Mum sighed. 'I didn't think Call Me Bill was the marrying kind,' she went on. 'I suppose this'll change everything. He'll be upset and move out, and nothing will be the same.'

'Perhaps he could marry Greta?' I suggested, but without much hope.

'Greta's certainly not the marrying kind,' Mum said.

'It would seem,' said Lucas, 'that no one in this house is the marrying kind.'

'So. What are you going to say to him?' I asked.

'Well, I shall say how honoured I am, and grateful. That sort of thing. And then I shall say I hope we can still remain friends and—'

'Oh, for goodness' sake, cut to the chase, Mum,' Lucas said.

'All right. I shall tell him – I shall say I'm, well, I'm—'

'Not the marrying kind,' we finished for her.

'Something like that.'

'You'd better get on with it, Mum. He's been waiting nearly twenty-four hours,' I said. 'Better get it over with.'

In the event, Call Me Bill took Mum's decision with the kind of stoicism we had come to associate with him. Lucas and I privately thought he might even have been relieved. It was more than possible that he'd thought he was doing the right (rather than the sensible) thing in offering marriage to Mum; that her vulnerability had finally got to him, virtue had temporarily triumphed over common sense, and by now he could well be regretting his actions. Whatever his motives, Mum needn't have worried about his future plans. It appeared that Call Me Bill had no intention of moving out of the house, and nothing was going to change. And if Lucas and I noticed a new lightness in Mum's step, and a lift in her mood, we knew better than to mention it. If she had received a boost from Call Me Bill's proposal, then that was all to the good.

'What iss happen?' Greta wanted to know, sensing that

something was being withheld from her. 'Something iss happen. I know this.'

I hesitated. Should I tell her? It wasn't really my news to tell, and yet Greta was one of the family. It didn't seem fair to keep secrets from her.

'Call Me Bill asked Mum to marry him,' I told her.

'Oh,' Greta's face fell.

'Don't worry,' I patted her shoulder. 'She's said no, and he's taken it very well.'

For a moment, Greta didn't seem to know what to say, but I noticed that the tear which had been threatening to fall had disappeared.

'It's OK to be pleased,' I assured her. 'I'm pleased, too. So's Lucas. There's been enough change round here recently. I think we're all much better off as we are.'

Still Greta hesitated, then she smiled at me.

'Nice-cup-of-tea?' She had obviously decided to return to safer and more familiar territory.

'Nice-cup-of-tea would be lovely, Greta,' I told her.

Even after all these years, when I think of Greta, I always picture her in her flowered pinny presiding over our ancient blue-and-white teapot. She still never touched tea herself, but it was Greta's tea which fuelled our family in times of crisis and which gave me my life-long tea habit.

Twenty-three

*It is now almost dark, and the unlit room fades to mono-
chrome as I continue my vigil by my mother's bed. I hear the
supper trolley rattle past the door, but it doesn't stop. There
will be no more suppers for Mum, for she can no longer eat.
She exists on sips of tea and water, and the occasional tea-
spoonful of the brandy I have brought for her. I am
exhausted and hungry and I could do with a shower and a
change of clothes, but I daren't leave her. Mum saw me into
the world; it seems only right that I should see her out of it
and do all I can to ease her journey.*

*Lucas visits, in a hurry. Lucas is always in a hurry. He has
an important job and a demanding wife, and he is afraid of
death. I don't really blame him. He brings grapes she can't
eat, and the wrong sort of flowers; garage flowers, wrapped
in crackly cellophane. But she seems pleased. Mum has always
adored presents, and never seems to mind if they are not what
she wants.*

A young nurse comes in to check on her.
'She looks very peaceful,' she whispers to me.

'I'm not dead yet,' retorts Mum, making the nurse start.

'Oh, dear. I didn't mean to upset her.'

'I'm not deaf, either.'

'That wasn't very kind,' I say, when the nurse has gone. 'She's doing her best.'

'I know.' Pause. Her breathing's a bit more laboured now, and it's an effort for her to speak. 'I'm sorry.'

Mum's eyes close, but her hands start to move over the bedspread. Her right hand rocks rhythmically back and forth, and I recognize Beethoven's Moonlight Sonata.

'Sing it for me, Cass.'

So I hum, and Mum plays, and it all seems perfectly natural. I remember all the other works mum has played over the years on the ironing board, her ancient record player belting out the music.

'I could have been really good, you know, Cass.' The Moonlight Sonata comes to an abrupt halt, and she gives a little hopeless gesture with her hands. 'Really good. If only I'd had the lessons.'

'I know, Mum. I know.'

Oh God, if there is a God, make it all right for her. Be there to welcome her when she arrives, and fill her heaven with suitable men, dependable Lodgers and a Steinway grand for her to have her piano lessons on. And look after her. Please look after her. Because my mother has never been much good at looking after herself.

In February, Mum quite suddenly returned to her ironing-board recitals. She played sad, pensive pieces – pieces she had played after her mother died – but we all took it as a good sign. Greta, who had been heroically doing all the ironing in the aftermath of Octavia's death, must have been particularly relieved, for between recitals Mum managed to get quite a lot of it done. For myself, I took it as another indication that we might eventually return to normality, and I was ridiculously cheered. To anyone outside the family, ironing-board recitals must have seemed – and I'm sure on occasion, were – quite absurd, but to us, they were part of life and very much a part of Mum.

A few weeks later, the gay Lodger left to set up house with his partner (at least, that is what we assumed; he had always been very discreet about his private life). While we mourned his going – he had been a wonderful support over the past months, and a good friend to our family – finding a replacement gave Mum something to focus on.

'We've had an application from a woman, Cass,' she told me. 'Imagine! A woman Lodger!'

I couldn't see the problem myself, although our Lodgers had always been men. A woman might make a nice change. But Mum would have none of it, and adjusted her advertisement accordingly.

Unusually, we had several applicants, and Mum settled on a hunky Charlton Heston look-alike with a Ph.D. in bats.

'Bats!' Mum cried gaily. 'Now isn't that interesting, Cass?'

I had never found bats especially interesting, and suspected that it was the Charlton Heston aspect rather than the bats which had appealed to Mum. But provided he didn't bring his bats with him, if he was going to help reawaken her interest in the opposite sex, then I certainly wasn't going to argue.

The bat-loving Lodger appeared to bring Mum a new

lease of life. They stayed up late into the night talking, they went for long walks together (ostensibly looking for bats, but even I knew that bats are in short supply at two o'clock in the afternoon), and from the covert padding of feet on floorboards and the opening and closing of bedroom doors in the middle of the night, no doubt engaged in other activities as well.

If Call Me Bill was hurt by Mum's activities so soon after his proposal, he didn't show it, and the rest of us were relieved that yet another aspect of Mum's life appeared to be returning to normal.

'Do you think we ought to talk to her about – well, about birth control?' Lucas asked me, when this had been going on for about a fortnight. 'We don't want another – another—'

'Octavia?' I said.

'Well, yes. I mean Octavia was lovely, but I just couldn't bear to risk going through all that again.' It was almost the first time Lucas had referred to his own feelings about Octavia's death, and I was touched.

'You're right. I'll speak to her.'

When I mentioned our conversation to Mum, she didn't appear to mind at all.

'Oh, Cass! There are these dear little pills you can take now, which take care of all that. Isn't it wonderful?' She rummaged in her bag and brought out a small pink packet. 'One pill for each day, and bob's your uncle!'

'Are you sure?' This sounded to me a bit too good to be true.

'Quite sure.' Mum beamed at me. 'Dr Mackenzie gave them to me ages ago. Wasn't that kind?'

'You won't forget to take them?'

'Of course I won't forget to take them. Now stop fussing, Cass, and run along. I've got a lot to do.'

Not for the first time, I thanked God for Dr Mackenzie. Meanwhile, at school, I continued to plod. I listened in class, did my homework and generally toed the line, but I put no effort into anything I did. In a less able child this would have passed unnoticed, but it continued to frustrate my teachers, who all knew I could do so much better. The only teacher who seemed to understand at all was Mrs Harvey, the kindly woman who taught us English.

'What's this all about, Cass?' she said one day, when I had stayed behind to help her tidy up the classroom. 'You have outstanding O levels and an excellent brain. You could go such a long way if you wanted to. What are you planning to do with your life?'

'I don't know.' I put down the blackboard rubber and dusted my hands on my skirt. 'I honestly don't know. I did know, once, but now life's so – so muddled, I'm not sure of anything any more.'

'In what way, muddled?'

'Mum, Octavia—'

'Octavia?'

'My little sister. She – she—'

'Yes, I know. It must have turned your world upside down.' She sat down on the edge of her desk. 'And your mother?'

'Mum needs me. Us. She needs us all to be together. I couldn't leave her even if I wanted to.'

'And do you want to?'

'No. Well, sometimes I suppose I do, but I feel – safer at home.'

'And you think that by producing mediocre work – and it is mediocre, Cass – you're guaranteeing yourself a permanent place at home?'

'Maybe.'

'If you work hard and do well, you'll still have a choice. Just a wider choice than the one you'll have if you carry on as you're doing at the moment. You can still choose to stay at home if that's what you really want, but you can also go to university if you change your mind.'

'I'm not so sure about that. Does anyone in this place really have a choice? It's just – *assumed* that we'll all go to university if we get good A levels. No one even bothers to ask us if it's what we want.' I slammed the lid of my desk shut. 'Well, not me. I'm not going to be pushed around.'

'I can see that.' Mrs Harvey sighed. 'But don't cut off your nose to spite your face, Cass. It would be such a waste.'

'Perhaps.'

'And it's not too late, you know. You could easily catch up.'

'I'll be fine,' I said. 'Don't worry about me.'

'But I do worry about you, Cass. You're a lovely girl with a really bright future ahead of you, there for the taking. And no,' she said, seeing that I was about to interrupt, 'I don't just mean university. You could do anything you wanted if you wanted it enough. Anything.'

'Well, at the moment I just want to be left alone,' I said unkindly.

'That's your choice, too. And you have the right to make

it,' she said, ignoring my rudeness. 'But think about it. And if you ever want a chat – about work or jobs or anything at all – I'd be more than happy to help.' She stood up and picked up her briefcase. 'You know where to find me.'

Of course, I should have taken Mrs Harvey up on her offer. After all, I had nothing to lose, and probably a great deal to gain from talking to someone outside the family who was willing to listen; someone who obviously liked me (no one had ever called me a lovely girl before) and cared about my welfare. Looking back now, I think I was probably quite depressed, for while Mum was still supportive, she was obviously beginning to feel a bit better and expected the same to apply to everyone else. That we all dealt with Octavia's death in our own ways and at our own pace didn't seem to occur to her; there was light at the end of her tunnel, and she assumed it was the same for the rest of us.

However, she was still often overcome by great waves of grief and crushing fits of weeping, when she would once more take to her bed for a day at a time, berating herself for that moment of inattention which had contributed to Octavia's death, and mourning the loss of her little daughter. But she would recover from these bouts quite quickly – especially since the arrival of the new Lodger – and often failed to notice that the spirits of the rest of the household didn't necessarily keep pace with her own. I resented the Lodger; not so much because of Mum's relationship with him, but because I feared he was taking her attention away from me.

Spring gave way to summer, and the first painful anniversary of Octavia's death. At Mum's suggestion, we marked the occasion with a party in her memory, but instead of being the celebration of her life which Mum had envisaged, it turned into a maudlin all-night binge, at which Mum got hopelessly drunk and eventually passed out draped over the ironing-board where she had been giving a tearful rendition of 'Rock-a-Bye Baby'.

'It was too soon,' I panted, as Lucas and I hauled her unconscious body up the stairs to her room. We could have done with Charlton Heston, but he had mysteriously disappeared. Call Me Bill had long since taken himself off to bed, tutting with disapproval. Sundry guests were lying in unhelpful heaps all over the house. 'We should never have let her do it. I mean, a *party*, for goodness' sake! Whatever can she have been thinking of?'

'No one,' said Lucas grimly, hitching Mum's legs over his shoulder, 'stops Mum when she's decided to do something. You of all people should know that.' He too was very drunk, and being drunk always made him disagreeable.

I put Mum to bed in her clothes, too exhausted to be bothered with trying to undress her. I felt lonely and miserable and hopeless. It had been altogether a horrible day; I had just received my exam results, which were every bit as bad as I deserved, and I had a splitting headache from a disgusting vodka mixture of Lucas's.

Returning to the kitchen, I found the gay ex-Lodger making coffee, and fell weeping into his arms.

'Everything's awful, I've got no one to talk to and I'm an utter failure,' I sobbed into his shoulder. 'Whatever am I going to do with my life?'

Twenty-four

At the beginning of my final school year, the pressure to pull my academic socks up was really on, so in order to get my teachers off my back, I told them I was going to be a nurse.

I should explain that in my particular educational establishment, there only ever appeared to be three career options. If you were in the A stream, you went to university; and if you were in the B stream, you either went to teachers' training college or you became a nurse. Since both professions were supposed to be vocations, it seemed strange (not to say convenient) to me that those who were under-equipped for the academic life should be automatically assumed to have a calling in one or other of these directions. Since I felt that by this stage I had had enough of teachers and their profession to last me several lifetimes, I opted for nursing.

I don't think that at the time I had any real intention of carrying this through – apart from anything else, I still wasn't ready to contemplate leaving home – but the reaction of the teaching staff, who did everything in their power to dissuade me, proved irresistible.

Mum, needless to say, gave me her full backing.

'A nurse!' she said dreamily. 'How worthwhile. You a nurse, and Lucas a policeman! Oh, Cass! I'm so proud of you both!'

Dear Mum. Her reasoning, as ever, was flawless. How could anyone fail, with a nurse and a policeman in the family? Crime and disease would be forever kept at bay, and she need never worry again. Within twenty-four hours, she had us both promoted, and was happily anticipating her role as mother to a Chief Detective Inspector and a Hospital Matron. Never mind that Lucas was at the very bottom of his career ladder (with his lowly qualifications, there were to be no short cuts for Lucas) and I was still at school; in Mum's eyes, we were both consummate successes. And Lucas had a uniform. Mum had always had great respect for uniforms, and even I had to admit that Lucas looked rather fetching in his.

But if I thought that getting into a nursing school was going to be easy, I was badly mistaken. Many of the better hospitals had waiting lists, with no chance of getting a place for at least two years, and the two interviews I did have went badly.

'Why do you want to be a nurse, Miss Fitzpatrick?' asked the tightly upholstered, hatchet-faced matron of the first hospital I went to.

Such an obvious question, you would have thought, but it hadn't occurred to me to prepare an appropriate answer.

'Well, I couldn't really think of anything else,' I confessed. 'And' – remembering Mum – 'it's so worthwhile, isn't it?'

'Is it?' Her penetrating gaze seemed to pin me to my chair like a helpless insect.

'Well, yes. I mean, looking after sick people . . .' My voice trailed away uncertainly.

'Nurses certainly look after sick people,' my tormentor continued, in the kind of tone one might use to a very small, very stupid child. 'But I think you'll find there's a little more to it than that. You obviously haven't given the idea a great deal of thought, have you? I expect you imagined that you'd just put on a pretty uniform and float about doing good works?' She folded her hands together on the desk and waited.

This was almost exactly what I'd thought, and I blushed.

'Hm. I thought as much.'

By this stage, all I wanted was to escape into the fresh air, away from this stuffy office and this awful woman.

'I'd still like to be a nurse,' I said feebly.

The matron pursed her lips and consulted a sheet of paper on the desk in front of her. I recognized the school's headed writing paper, and my heart sank.

'Your head teacher doesn't seem to think you are particularly suited to the job of nursing, and I'm inclined to agree with her.' She rose from her chair, indicating my dismissal. 'You will be hearing from us in due course.'

I escaped into the sunny street outside, seething with anger; anger at myself, anger at that horrible woman, but most of all anger at Miss Carrington who, for reasons best known to herself, seemed hell-bent on sabotaging any chances I might have of (to use her own words) 'making something of myself'.

For my second interview, I was better prepared. I read everything about nursing I could lay my hands on, from the life of Florence Nightingale (who turned out to be more pioneering battleaxe than ministering angel) to the present day, garnering in the process enough information to fill a fairly hefty manual.

But the second matron appeared to be no more impressed than the first.

'Miss Fitzpatrick, you seem to have swallowed an encyclopaedia,' she observed. 'Just tell me what it is about nursing that appeals to *you*?'

I was ready for this, too.

'I'd like to be at the cutting edge of modern hospital care. I'd like to contribute to the standard of that care, and make a difference,' I spouted recklessly, aware that I sounded more like a government white paper than a candidate at an interview, but somehow unable to stop. 'I'd like to—'

'Hold on, Miss Fitzpatrick.' The matron held up her hand, sparing my further efforts. 'I simply want to know what it is you think you have to offer us. Personal qualities, for example. What personal qualities do you have which might make you a suitable applicant?'

'I think I'm kind,' I said desperately.

'That's certainly a start.'

'And – and my sister died.' I burst into tears.

I have no idea what made me say that, but perhaps I detected beneath that starched bosom and stern expression a hint of the sympathy I still craved. The matron didn't look in the least surprised at my outburst, but I detected a softening of her features as she leant forward and handed me a spotless handkerchief.

'Tell me about it,' she said.

I started talking, and once I'd started, I found I couldn't stop. I told her about Octavia, about the terrible day when she had died and about leaving boarding school. I told her about Mum and our unusual family set-up, and I told her about the pressures I had received from school and the real reasons I had applied to be a nurse. I was sure I'd scuppered any chances I might have, but I no longer cared. I was carried along on a tide of words and emotion, and by the time I'd finished, I felt better than I had in a long time.

There was a long pause.

'I see.' The matron straightened the papers on her desk, and looked at me over her spectacles.

'Miss Fitzpatrick, do you think you are ready to be a nurse, even if it is what you want? Do you think you can deal with the problems of others when you have recently had so many of your own?'

'I don't know. I hadn't thought about it.'

'Well, do. Do think about it. Nurses have a great deal to cope with. They see people in pain, people dying, and they can't always make everything better. They have to be strong. Not hard-hearted, but emotionally tough. I think at the moment you are too fragile to take on a job which will drain you both physically and mentally.'

'So that's – it,' I said, feeling more disappointed than I would have imagined.

'Not necessarily.' She smiled at me. 'I like you, Miss Fitzpatrick. You are sensitive and honest and intelligent, and it may surprise you to know that I think that, given the right circumstances, you might be a good nurse. But not yet. Not for a while.' She paused, as though assessing my reaction. 'Take your A levels – you're going to need them, even for nursing – and come and see me again, and we'll have another talk.'

'But the waiting list is so long,' I wailed. 'It'll be years, even if you decide to accept me.'

'I have ways of opening doors,' she said, 'to the right candidates. I can't promise we'll take you next year, but if things have settled down at home, and you're feeling stronger, well, we'll see. That's all I can say at the moment. I'd like to give you a chance, but I can't make any promises. Fair enough?'

'Fair enough.' I summoned up a smile. 'And thank you.'

'Oh, Cass! You've been crying! What's that dreadful woman done, to make you cry?' Mum, who had travelled up with me for the interview, was waiting for me outside the door.

'Mum, you haven't even met her. She's actually rather nice,' I said.

'Poor Cass,' Mum appeared not to have heard me. 'Doesn't she want you?'

'Perhaps. But not yet.'

We proceeded to walk together back down the corridor.

'Not yet? What can she be thinking of?' cried Mum. 'The woman must be mad.' She sniffed. 'Anyway, there are plenty of other jobs you can do. You don't need to be a nurse. Just look at them,' she added, as we passed a group of nurses. 'Look at them, with their black-stockinged stalks of legs and their smug little nurse faces! I think you're well out of it, myself.'

'Well, you've certainly changed your tune.' I couldn't help laughing. Mistress of the volte face, Mum could execute a speedier change of direction than anyone I knew. 'And you haven't let me explain. She was actually very kind, but she thinks I need more time. She's prepared to see me again next year. I think she's probably right,' I added. 'And I'd like to come here. It feels – right.'

'Oh.' Mum's anger subsided as quickly as it had arisen, but I felt sorry for her, for I knew she was disappointed, for herself as well as for me. She had been looking forward to telling people about my new vocation, and now she would have to wait.

As we took our seats on the train for the journey home, I gave Mum an edited account of my interview, and she seemed to accept it.

'You could try somewhere else, Cass,' she said. 'There are plenty of other hospitals.'

'I know. But I like St Martha's, it's one of the best and it's in London' (I had set my heart on London). 'And the matron was right. Perhaps I do need a bit more time. I could even have changed my mind again by next year.'

'I suppose so.'

'Don't look so sad, Mum. I'll get a job sooner or later, and I promise I'll do my very best to make sure it's one which requires a uniform!'

'Am I that pathetic?' Mum asked.

'No. Not pathetic at all. I know you want the best for me,

and you've never tried to push me. You're the best sort of mother to have.'

'Are you sure?'

I thought of my peers, many of whom were threatened or bribed into getting the best grades; whose parents' aim seemed equally divided between trying to relive their lives through their children and boasting about the academic achievements of their brilliant offspring. And then I thought of Mum, who had praised and encouraged me every step of the way, however good or lowly my achievements, and whose unconditional pride in me had come to mean so much.

I gave her a hug.

'Quite sure,' I told her.

As our train drew out of the station, and we passed the terraces of grim, sooty houses with their defiant lines of bright washing flapping in their cluttered back gardens, my spirits lifted. A woman picked up a screaming child and carried him indoors, a black and white cat sat washing itself in a patch of sunlight, an old man filled a bucket from a heap of coal.

I was determined that one day – one day quite soon – I would be back.

Twenty-five

I was by now nearly eighteen, an age at which clothes and make-up and, above all, boys might be expected to feature prominently in my life, but while I certainly liked nice clothes, and even occasionally wore make-up, my interest in the opposite sex remained non-existent.

Not so my classmates, whose conversation was now dominated by the fascinating subject of who was going out with whom, what they had been up to and, most pressing of all, whether or not they had *gone the whole way*. One girl who had certainly gone the whole way was the hapless Pamela Adams, who started to put on a suspicious amount of weight, was observed by our PE teacher, interviewed (with her parents) by Miss Carrington, and left in tears. We never saw Pamela again. The Sixties may well have been swinging, but not yet for us, and certainly not in our school.

My only experience of boys my own age (apart from Lucas and his friends, and my disastrous encounter with Alex) had been the challenging ordeal of a term of ballroom dancing classes, in the lower sixth form, with the boys from the Grammar School. These were entirely voluntary, taking place after school, and I was persuaded by my friends (and much against my better judgement) to give them a try.

The classes would commence with a ritual that could have been a precursor of the car boot sale, with a touch of the cattle market thrown in. The girls huddled self-consciously on one side of the school hall, while the boys regarded them critically from the other. Then the more streetwise of the boys would swoop, carrying off the beautiful, the confident and the downright sexy for a faltering hour of quicksteps and waltzes, with more than a smattering of flirtation thrown in, while the luckless remainder would trail across and pick up the remnants: the shy, the plump, the spotty or the downright plain.

I don't think that I was unattractive. Photographs of me at that age show a serious-looking girl with wide-apart eyes, a ponytail of dark hair and a nice if hesitant smile. I was reasonably slim, had as much bosom as I felt I needed, and my legs, as I recall, were quite respectable. But I was always one of the last to be chosen, and the humiliation stayed with me for a long time.

I wasn't normally shy. In our household, where people came and went and strangers were often entertained as a matter of course, I had long been accustomed to meeting – and getting on with – new people. But this was different. Here, I was being judged according to a whole new set of criteria, and the experience was disconcerting, to say the least.

Oh, the agony of standing there waiting, of undergoing the scrutiny of the equally wretched also-rans among our male counterparts, and praying the desperate prayer of the wallflower: don't let me be chosen last. Oh, please don't let me be the last!

Thanks to the presence of a short fat girl named Alice, and an equally unfortunate classmate with a squint and a speech impediment, I never was the very last, but on more than one occasion, I came dangerously close.

'Why do we do this?' I whispered to Alice on one occasion, as we stood together awaiting our fate.

Alice shook her head miserably.

'My mother wanted me to come,' she said. 'She says it will give me confidence.'

'And has it?' I asked curiously, wondering what sort of mother Alice must have. At least my mother had had nothing to do with my own decision.

Alice shook her head.

'I hate it,' she admitted. 'But I don't want to let Mum down. Besides,' she added, 'she collects me late on Tuesdays because of my sister's violin lesson, and there's nothing else to do.'

I could think of plenty of other things to do, which begged the question of why wasn't I doing any of them, but I think there must have been something in me that was refusing to be beaten. I'd signed up for the dancing, not the boys, and I wasn't going to give up simply because of a few minutes of blushing discomfort.

In fact I felt I could have enjoyed the classes, given the right partner, but that partner rarely came my way, and so I had to put up with fumbling fingers and equally fumbling apologies as we made our uncertain way round the dance floor. By the end of the hour, I don't know which were more bruised; my feelings or my feet.

After half-term, however, I was picked by a boy who if not good-looking was certainly quite pleasant, and what was more, he could dance. We both learnt fast, and after two sessions we were selected to show the rest of the class our tango. Miss Mason (PE teacher turned dance instructor) was obviously impressed.

'Very good, Cass. Excellent – er, what's your name?'

'Daniel, Miss.'

'Yes. Well done, Daniel.'

My friends were also impressed, but not so Daniel's colleagues. He had to put up with their mincing imitations all the way home, he later told me, and acquired the new nickname of 'Dancing Danny'.

'I don't mind, though,' he said, as we waltzed carefully round the room. 'It's worth it, to – to dance with you.'

'Thank you.' I was trying to concentrate on the music (one-two-three, one-two-three).

'Can I – could I walk you home?'

'But I only live ten minutes away.' The point of being walked home completely passed me by. Whatever did he want to walk me home for, especially as he lived in the opposite direction?

'I – I like you,' Daniel said lamely, as we swept round a corner (one-two-three).

'Oh. OK, then.'

Daniel smiled and blushed and we got out of step. Whatever was the matter with him? I thought crossly, as I tried to put things to rights (one-two-three). We were here to dance, not to have this kind of silly conversation.

For the next three weeks, Daniel walked me home, but I found our walks awkward and uncomfortable, since without the dancing, it appeared that we had little to say to each other. I soon realized that Daniel's interest in me went beyond my prowess as a dance partner, and on several occasions he tried to take my hand (I solved this problem by thrusting my hands into my pockets, pleading cold fingers and chilblains).

'How do you tell a boy you don't like him?' I asked Mum, our willing source of information on such subjects.

'Oh, Cass! Have you got a boyfriend? How sweet!'

'No,' I explained patiently. 'I haven't got a boyfriend and I don't want one. That's the whole point.'

'Well.' Mum sat down on her bed. 'What's he said to you?'

'Nothing really. He just walks me home after dancing and tries to hold hands.'

'And you really don't like him?'

'He's OK I suppose.'

'Good-looking?'

'Not bad.'

'Well then.'

'What do you mean, well then?'

'When I was your age, I always used to think that any boyfriend was better than none,' Mum said. 'Someone to go out with, do things with. You know.'

'No. I don't know.' I was beginning to get cross. I had my own friends to go out with. I didn't need a boy in order to have fun. 'And I don't suppose you ever had to go out with anyone you didn't fancy, did you?'

'Well, no. That's true.' Mum's face took on a dreamy expression. 'I was rather lucky, as it happens.'

'And you liked boys.'

'Oh, I certainly liked boys.'

'Well, I don't like boys. I've never liked boys. I probably never shall.'

'Don't be ridiculous, Cass!'

But I couldn't see that there was anything ridiculous about the way I felt. Since I certainly didn't want to get married and had never been especially keen on the idea of having children, there didn't seem to be any need for me to have anything to do with men at all, other than on a casual basis. I had always rather liked the idea of a future where I had a place of my own; a small flat or cottage somewhere, with my own things in it; a place where everything stayed where I had put it, any guests came by invitation (my invitation), and when the phone rang, I would know it was for me.

It wasn't that I disliked men. I was fond of Call Me Bill, and had formed comfortable relationships with some of our Lodgers. Many of the men who passed through our house – friends, visitors, and what Mum liked to call her Special Friends – were pleasant enough. But I didn't want a man of my own. In my experience, if you excluded Call Me Bill and the gay Lodger, men were on the whole poor helpless creatures, who forgot birthdays and couldn't find their socks.

In the end, Mum was of little help when it came to the question of how to discourage Dancing Danny, so I withdrew from the dancing classes pleading a sprained ankle (the ankle also got me out of games, so something good had come out of the experience, even though I had to remember to hobble for three weeks).

Nearly a year later, I was still as indifferent to boys as I had ever been, and if I felt the occasional stirrings of interest when confronted by a nice smile or an appraising pair of eyes, I quickly stifled them. As for Mum, she wisely let me be. I know now that she hoped I would train as a nurse and go on to fall in love with a doctor, and reasoned that if I were to get involved with someone while I was still at school, neither of these eventualities might take place.

Twenty-six

August 1965

My final school year passed uneventfully. I did just enough work to gain the A levels required by the nursing school while ensuring that they fell comfortably short of the standard I would need to gain a place at a decent university. And to my delight, after a further interview and some uncomfortably searching questions from the matron, I was offered a place at St Martha's for the following November. Matron said that while she was still concerned that I might find the whole experience harder than I imagined, she thought that I'd matured since she had last seen me, and had 'managed to come to terms with the family bereavement'.

I had once heard Dr Mackenzie tell Mum that the pain of bereavement never goes away, but that over time, it changes from a wound into a scar. This seemed and still seems to me the best description of a pain which is in many ways beyond description; a mental pain which is also physical, tearing at the solar plexus, the very centre of one's body. I remember during those first months after Octavia's death Mum doubling up over her own pain, clutching it to her, almost nursing it, curling herself round it and rocking it as though it had a soul of its own.

There had been no party to commemorate the second anniversary of Octavia's death; even Mum realized that this had not been a good idea, and that something sombre and reflective might be more appropriate. So this time, we had all trooped down to the churchyard with armfuls of roses from the garden and scattered them on her grave. It was a beautiful June day; the best kind, with a blue and white sky and air alive with the sound of birdsong; the kind of day which can so easily exaggerate emotions and rekindle joy or grief.

After the scattering, no one seemed to know what to do. Had we been religious, we would no doubt have prayed, but as it was we just stood in silence, covertly watching each other, waiting for a cue from Mum as to what was to happen next. Beneath my lowered eyelids, all I could see was feet: Mum's unsuitable high-heeled shoes, already sinking into the wet grass, and the childish round-toed shoes favoured by Greta; the crisp turn-ups of Call Me Bill's trousers and Richard's ancient brogues neatly laced with string. Lucas's shoes were black and highly polished as Mum had requested that he should come in his uniform, and the more sensible among us had come in stout shoes or boots. In Lucas's *Scouting for Boys*, a book over which he and I used to howl with mirth, we had read that one could tell a lot about a person from his footwear, and for once I could see it might well have a point.

I am ashamed to say that my thoughts were preoccupied

not so much with Octavia but with the unwelcome presence of the Charlton Heston Lodger, whose attendance both Lucas and I thought quite inappropriate. After all, he had arrived after Octavia's death, and any feelings he had were inevitably centred around Mum. I noted with satisfaction that when he placed a protective arm around her shoulders, she shook it off and moved away from him. Perhaps she too felt that while this relative newcomer might be accepted into her bed, he was not welcome at the graveside of the baby he had never known.

But that was back in June, and now it was August, a month I was accustomed to look forward to as the one time in the whole year when I could please myself. This year, however, was different, and while I was still glorying in my new freedom from the world of school and examinations, I realized that I couldn't just sit around at home doing nothing for the next three months, so I took a job at the local cinema as an usherette.

At first I was rather pleased with myself. For the first time in my life, I had regular money of my own (Mum's attempts at distributing pocket money, although doubtless well meant, had been sporadic and unreliable), the work was undemanding, and I had a torch to read by. But by the time I had seen *Seven Brides for Seven Brothers* twenty-nine times and sold enough ice cream to put me off the stuff for life, I thought I would go mad, especially as it was very soon made clear to me that reading books by torchlight was not in the job description.

'Give it up and do something else,' advised Mum, whose easy-come easy-go attitude to the world of work seemed to have done her little harm. But I liked to think that I was made of sterner stuff and so I stuck it out, much to the entertainment of Lucas and his friends, who regularly heckled me from the back row between their amorous gropings. I have never felt quite the same about the cinema since, and am always particularly nice to the usherettes.

Meanwhile, I was eagerly looking forward to November. The doubts which had been sown as to my suitability as a nurse had only served to fuel my enthusiasm, and while a year ago I had never even considered nursing as a career, now I couldn't believe that I had ever thought of doing anything else. I knew I was intelligent, I believed that I was caring, and while I liked to think that I had taken on board the matron's warnings of the pressures of hard work and emotional stress, I was in no doubt that I could cope with them when they arose. As for leaving home, London was only an hour and a half away by train, and there was always the telephone. Mum was still preoccupied with Charlton Heston, Lucas was living at home, and Greta and Call Me Bill were there to help hold the family together. They would hardly notice that I was gone. As I stood for long hours in the darkened cinema, with nothing but my thoughts and the noise and dazzle of yet another all-too-familiar film to occupy my mind, I built up such a delightful fantasy of my new life that I am surprised I could have been so gullible as to believe in it.

The reality, when it came to it, was of course totally different.

For a start, I and the others in my group were stationed in a nurses' home some distance from the hospital for eight weeks of classroom training. I had to share a bedroom with a girl called Angela, who looked as though she had come straight off the set of a *Carry On* film; all long legs and pouting lips and fluttering mascara. Angela and I disliked each other on sight, and this made for a difficult few weeks.

Then there was the Home Sister, a redoubtable woman of the old school, whose mission in life seemed to be to ensure that military discipline was maintained at all times, and that during the hours of darkness we were kept in and anyone of the opposite sex was kept out. This last group included Lucas, who came to visit me, and Angela's father (at least, she said he was her father but he looked a great deal too young and glamorous to be anyone's father – in this, I was on the side of the Home Sister).

Those eight weeks seemed interminable. The drone of the tutor's voice induced in me a kind of torpor, and the only relief came from our brief forays into the practical room, where we practised our hospital corners and bandaged one another's arms and legs, and the one afternoon a week when we were allowed onto the hospital wards, where we felt more like spare parts than proper nurses.

And, to my surprise, I was homesick. It was the first time I had been away from home since Octavia's death, and I felt suddenly vulnerable and insecure. Octavia had died while I was at St Andrew's, and in some part of my mind there was the illogical thought that if I had been at home, it might never have happened; that my presence at home was necessary in order to keep everyone safe. I knew this made no sense, and that it was more about my needs than those of my family, but I couldn't get away from it. I worried and fretted if I hadn't heard from home, and when Mum's letters did come, they were as irregular and scatty as the ones I had received at boarding school, and all the more poignant for that, for they reminded me of a time when our family was still untouched by tragedy. As for phone calls, the evening queue for the only pay phone was long, and I rarely had more than a few minutes to talk.

'You're all right, are you, Mum?' I would ask. 'You're sure you're all OK?'

'Of course we're OK,' Mum would reply, sounding amazingly cheery, and she would grab hold of the nearest person to endorse her reassurance (on one occasion, the only family member available was The Dog, and I was subjected to a costly minute of snufflings and lickings which offered no consolation whatsoever). 'Have you seen any operations yet?'

'No, Mum. I keep telling you. I shan't see operations for ages. I'm still in school, remember?'

'Oh yes.' She sounded disappointed. A nurse who hadn't seen any operations obviously didn't really count.

'But I shall. We have to. We all have to do a spell in theatre.' I hesitated, trying to think of something which would interest her. 'We did see a brain in a bucket,' I offered.

'A brain in a bucket! Fancy!'

The brain in question had been brought in to illustrate a session on the nervous system. It looked grey and pickled and very dead, and yet all I could think of was that that brain represented a *whole person*; all of someone's life and thoughts and memories were in that bucket, together with their talents and abilities, their sadnesses and their triumphs. When it came to it, I reflected, only your brain was really *you*; other parts of the body were mere trappings in comparison with that amazing organ. I found the whole experience quite unnerving, and while the other girls appeared to be torn equally between disgust and hilarity, I found my encounter with the bucket and its grisly contents very sobering.

Twenty-seven

Mum is asleep now, drifting on a gentle tide of morphine, gradually bobbing away from me. Before long, she will be out of reach. She will have embarked on that part of her journey where I can't be with her. Soon, I shall no longer be able to talk to her.

I'm glad that she is at peace, but at the same time I want to say to her: 'Don't go! Stay a little longer! Please don't leave me. I'll be lost without you.'

Another memory. I am about five years old, and have become separated from my family in a London park. Everything seems enormous – huge trees, vast expanses of grass, a lake as big as the sea. I feel very tiny and very lost and absolutely terrified. What if they never find me? What if I have to stay here all night? What if the swans come and get me ('They can break a man's arm, you know,' my mother had helpfully informed me only minutes before). And worst of all, what if I get carried away by a Stranger?

They eventually find me, filthy and sobbing, hiding under a bush only yards from where I last saw them. Mummy! Oh, *the joy of being folded into that familiar bosom, petted and soothed, and comforted with strawberry ice cream in a cone.*

Drifting in and out of sleep, I wonder in my wakeful moments whether in some strange way her mind and mine might join together in our separate states of unconsciousness; whether her sleep can merge with my own, and she can find some comfort in the companionship of my dreams. For these dreams – tiny little vignettes now – are all about my mother. I see her running down a hill on a bright summer's day, arms outflung, laughing; decorating a cake for my birthday, the letters melting into each other, the C of my name running down the side of the cake; weeping over the intransigence of a particularly difficult Lodger.

And appearing, totally out of the blue, at visiting time, sitting by the bed of a patient in what was only my second week as a proper signed-up member of the nursing staff on my first ward.

'Mum! What on earth are you doing here?' I hissed, looking around to see if anyone had noticed her.

'I had to come up and see you, Cass. In your uniform.' She beamed. 'I thought it would be a lovely surprise for you. You don't have to take any notice of me,' she added. 'Just you carry on. I shan't be any bother.'

I hesitated. On the one hand, Mum looked much like any other visitor, and might well pass as one provided she behaved herself. On the other, try as she might to make it otherwise, 'bother' of some kind or another tended to accompany Mum wherever she went.

'What about your job?' I asked her. 'Shouldn't you be at work?'

'Oh, that!' Mum laughed. 'I phoned in with the flu. And don't look so disapproving, Cass. This is important. I couldn't let you down, could I?'

If being let down involved not being visited by Mum at work, I felt I could have coped with it all too easily, but I knew that she would never understand. To Mum, not coming to see me in my new uniform would have been the same as not coming to see me in the school nativity play when I was five.

'You will be good?' I pleaded, aware of the ward sister watching me from behind her desk.

'Good as gold,' Mum promised. 'This lady hasn't any visitors, so I can keep her company. She comes from Bromsgrove,' she added, turning to her new friend. 'I had a cousin who lived in Bromsgrove,' she told her. 'Now isn't that a coincidence?'

It was also, as far as I knew, untrue, but if Mum did nothing worse than enliven someone's dull afternoon with fictitious tales of her past, I wasn't going to stop her, so I returned to my work. When Mum left at the end of visiting time, I breathed a sigh of relief. She had made her inspection, and that, as far as I was concerned, was that.

But I had underestimated Mum, for two weeks later, she was back.

'Mum, you can't keep doing this,' I muttered, making as though to straighten a pillow. 'Or if you must come, you could at least warn me.'

'That would spoil the surprise,' Mum said.

'I don't want surprises.'

'Don't be so ungrateful, Cass. I don't know what's got into you.'

'What's got into me,' I said, 'is that I have just started on a busy surgical ward with a dragon of a sister, and I want to make a good impression. Having my mother following me around does not make a good impression.'

'Nurse Fitzpatrick! I thought I told you to do the temperatures!' The booming voice of the dragon interrupted our little dialogue.

'Temperatures!' murmured Mum, pink with pride. 'Fancy!'

These visits of Mum's – always unannounced but always at visiting times, and on one occasion, she even came accompanied by a friend – continued sporadically until the day when she was found feeding grapes and chocolate to a patient who was supposed to be fasting in preparation for an operation.

'Who is that woman?' demanded the sister. 'She's a blessed nuisance. I'm sure I've seen her before.'

But none of the other staff knew, and I certainly wasn't going to say that the blessed nuisance had anything to do with me. To Mum's credit, she allowed herself to be soundly reprimanded and escorted off the ward without so much as a glance in my direction, although she did make her feelings clear when we met for tea afterwards.

'I think it's disgraceful, starving a poor old woman like that. She hadn't even had any breakfast!'

And try as I might to explain why this was necessary, Mum simply couldn't see it. If someone was hungry, then it was her duty to feed them, just as it was her duty to house the homeless (increasingly, I suspected, in my room, since I was no longer around to defend it).

But in those early months, there were other and worse surprises than Mum's visits. I learnt, among other things, that the decibels generated by a trolley's worth of gleaming metal bedpans cascading onto the floor rivalled the kind of sound one might expect if a high-speed jet ploughed into an iron foundry; that a carelessly spilt pint of blood could make a bed – not to mention its hapless occupant – resemble a battle-field; and that an apparently sick and frail little old lady could, when confused, throw an amazingly powerful punch (I had the bruises to prove it).

I also learnt, for the first time in my life, what it felt like to be totally exhausted – physically as well as mentally.

'How do you do it?' I asked Angela, who was preparing for yet another night out on the town (I was becoming quite attached to Angela, possibly because we no longer had to share a room). 'Where do you get the energy?'

'Priorities, Cass. Priorities.' Angela applied another layer of mascara to her bat-black lashes. 'After a day in the sluice, a girl needs to remind herself what it's like to have a good time.' She applied a generous dose of lacquer to her hair. 'It wouldn't do you any harm to come with me.'

'No thanks.' I was lying on her bed, watching her get ready. 'A hot bath and bed for me.'

'You're old before your time, Cassandra.' She shook her sleek peroxide head at me and bent to squeeze her feet into a pair of needle-sharp stilettos. 'What you need is a bit of fun.'

'Am I so boring?' I asked her.

'Not boring.' Angela shrugged her bare shoulders into a faux fur coat borrowed for the occasion. 'It's just that you never seem to let your hair down. You always look so – serious. You don't go to parties or out on dates—'

'I went to that party last week!'

'Yes. And stood in a corner looking miserable. That nice boy tried to chat you up, and you behaved as though he was trying to abduct you.' She gave a final twirl in front of the mirror and grinned at me. 'I wouldn't have minded being chatted up by him, I can tell you.'

After Angela had left on a waft of cheap perfume, I returned to my own room and thought about what she had said. It was true that I didn't like parties. All that getting-to-know-you small talk, usually conducted against a background of ear-splitting music; embarrassed shuffles round a smoky dance floor followed by the fighting-off of unwanted advances; the solitary walk home, leaving my friends still part of that vibrating, hormone-charged, inebriated mass of partying humanity.

Later on, lying in the bath, gazing at the twin humps of my breasts, ribcage, hip bones, knees and toes, rising like pale hillocks from the steamy water, I acknowledged for the first time my fear of the opposite sex. Hitherto, I had rationalized my feelings, putting them down to disinterest rather than anything stronger; thinking that I was independent-minded enough to plan – even to want – a future without the encumbrance of husband and children. But now at last I saw what had been staring me in the face for some time.

I was afraid of men.

Twenty-eight

I suppose I must have imagined that Uncle Rupert had, if not ceased to exist, then at least been expunged from our lives. After that day when Mum had unceremoniously thrown him out of our house, I had assumed that she'd also thrown him out of her life. It never for a moment occurred to me that she might have kept in touch with him.

But of course I should have known better.

Incoming calls were received by the payphones situated on each floor of the nurses' home, and if no one felt like making the pilgrimage to the end of the corridor, they often went unanswered. But on this occasion, I had a feeling that the call might be for me, and so it was I who answered it.

'Oh, Cass!' Mum sounded breathless. 'I'm so glad it's you. Something awful's happened.'

'What? What's happened? Is it Lucas?'

'No. Not Lucas.'

'Well, who? Who then?'

'Uncle Rupert.'

'*What?*'

'Uncle Rupert.'

'Uncle Rupert.' My voice sounded very faint, drowned out by the thumping of my heartbeats, and I felt the blood rush to my face.

'Yes. He's in prison.' There was a catch in her voice. 'Oh, Cass. I didn't want to have to tell you, but there's no one else I can talk to about it.'

'And what exactly do you expect me to do?' I began to feel seriously angry. 'Feel sorry for him? Bake him a nice Victoria sponge with a chisel in it? If that disgusting old man's ended up in prison, then it's probably high time, and no more than he deserves.'

'I know it's terrible, Cass. I know that. But in a way he can't help it. That's the way he is. He's just, well—'

'Hang on a minute. Are you telling me that he's done something like – like what he did to me – again? Are you saying he was *free* to do it again? Is that what's happened?'

'Well, yes. I mean, he hasn't actually harmed anyone. Not really.'

'Oh, sure. Just paraded around naked, or showed his disgusting appendage to some poor innocent schoolgirl. Nothing to worry about, then. No harm done.'

'Something like that. He was in this park, and—'

'Mum, I don't want to hear about it. I really, really don't want to hear about it.'

'No. Of course you don't. I'm sorry.'

'That's OK.' My anger evaporated as quickly as it had arisen. I was never able to stay cross with Mum for long, and now I took pity on her. 'Look, Mum. I know you were fond of him. I know he's your family. But you've got to understand

209

that this has come as quite a shock to me. I thought he'd – disappeared a long time ago. I'd no idea you were still in touch with him.'

'Well, I wasn't. Not really. Just – just the odd Christmas card. That's all.'

Only my mother would send Christmas cards to the man who had abused her daughter, not to mention her hospitality. Only my mother had this extraordinary capacity for forgiveness. Only my mother could be so naive, so trusting, so *stupid*.

'*Mum!*'

'I know. I know, Cass. I've been so silly. But I really thought he'd change. He promised me, when I sent him away. He said he'd get help.'

'Where did you send him?' My curiosity got the better of me. 'Where's he been all this time?'

'He's got this cousin in Northumberland. He's a vicar or something. It sounded – safe.'

I knew very little about either Northumberland or vicars, but they sounded as though they might offer something in the way of security, if not actual redemption. But apparently not.

'And I had to tell you, Cass, in case it gets into the newspapers.'

'*The newspapers?* Is that likely?' I asked.

'You never know. The press seem to like – that sort of thing.'

'You're – you're not going to visit him, are you?'

Was there the tiniest hesitation, before Mum replied? It would be just like her to battle her way halfway across England to visit her fallen relation.

'No. I don't think so.'

'Thank goodness for that.'

'But – but would you mind if I wrote to him, Cass?'

'Why ask me? It's nothing to do with me.'

'It is. You know it is. If you don't want me to, I won't.'

'Oh, no. You're not doing this to me, Mum. I'm not taking responsibility for what you do or don't do. This has to be your decision.'

'But I wouldn't want to upset you, Cass.'

'Mum, you *are* upsetting me. This phone call's upsetting me. I didn't ever want to hear – *that man's* name again, and now here it is, out of the blue, and you're asking my permission to write him comforting little notes in prison!'

'Perhaps I'll just not tell you. How would that be?' Mum said, after a moment.

'OK. Don't tell me. But the thought of you even thinking about him after all this time – well – it's horrible. I don't want to talk about him or think about him ever again. You do whatever you have to do, but please leave me out of it.'

'I'm so sorry, Cass.'

'Yes.'

'Shall I ring off now?'

'Perhaps you'd better.'

'Goodbye, then.'

'Goodbye.'

When I'd returned to my room, I wondered if I hadn't been a bit hard on Mum. I sat down on my bed and tried to unscramble my thoughts. Sheets of paper with my notes on the digestive system surrounded me (we were supposed to be revising for a test), and I shoved them to one side. My own digestive system was making threatening noises, and for a moment I thought I was about to be revisited by the rather unappetizing hospital supper I had just eaten. I took some deep breaths to steady it, then went over to the washbasin and splashed my face with cold water.

I must pull myself together and stop overreacting. Nothing had changed; I was perfectly safe, and Uncle Rupert was well out of reach in his prison cell. I wondered whether they'd allow him to continue inventing things, and whether there was anyone to bring him his tobacco and aniseed balls. My emotions were a mixture of anger and fear and icy contempt, but I felt no pity whatsoever. I like to think that I am, as a rule, a sympathetic person, who tries to see the best in people, but I could see no best at all in Uncle Rupert. To this day, I think he is the only person I have ever thoroughly loathed, and while years later I was able to reach a degree of understanding, if not actual forgiveness, I have been unable to summon up any real feelings of compassion.

'Are you OK, Cass?' Angela asked me at breakfast a few mornings later. 'You look as though you've seen a ghost.'

'I suppose in a way I have. Well, heard about one, anyway.' I buttered a piece of leathery toast.

'That sounds intriguing.'

'Not intriguing. Rather disgusting, actually.'

'Do you want to talk about it?'

'No. Not really. If I don't talk about it, maybe it'll go away.'

It could well be that it might have helped me if I had been able to talk about it. Not at breakfast, perhaps, but at some other more appropriate time. When Angela managed to relieve her brain of its usual preoccupations with men and clothes and make-up, she could be a surprisingly good listener, and had I been able to unburden myself even a little, it might have made all the difference.

But hindsight is a wonderful thing, and my anxiety didn't last for long. Besides, at that time I was still unaware that the legacy bequeathed to me by Uncle Rupert went a lot deeper than an unpleasant phone call, some shocking memories and a few broken nights' sleep.

Twenty-nine

Despite my mother's undoubted courage during her illness, she has not been an easy patient. Unaccustomed to being told how to behave, she did not take easily to her role as a patient, and couldn't see why she had to fit into a routine; why she was only allowed visitors at certain times, and why she wasn't allowed to smoke in bed.

'But Mum,' I tried to explain. 'It's dangerous. Can't you see that? You might fall asleep with a cigarette in your hand and set fire to yourself.'

'I never have before,' she replied.

'You've never smoked in bed before. In fact, come to that, you've hardly ever smoked at all.'

'I've hardly ever needed to. It's very stressful, this whole dying business. I just felt I needed a cigarette. What's the harm in that?'

So on several occasions, we closed the door and opened a window, and Mum smoked while I listened out for the brisk footsteps which heralded the approach of authority. When we were eventually caught out, it goes without saying that I was the one who made all the apologies, while Mum sat, cigarette in hand, mutinous and unrepentant.

The half-finished packet of cigarettes is in her locker still, hidden from prying eyes inside a toffee bag. But Mum won't be smoking any more cigarettes now, and idly I wonder what will happen to them. They will probably be handed over to me later, when she is gone, together with her other belongings. I have always hated these collections of patients' 'personal effects'; the last pathetic remnants of people's lives; the toilet articles, the handfuls of coins, the half-eaten packets of sweets or chocolate, the get-well cards which failed to bring about the hoped-for miracle.

I wept over the contents of the first bedside locker I had to clear out after its owner had died; all those little reminders of a life once lived and the small treats brought in by a family who hadn't yet come to terms with the prospect of an inevitable outcome. I remember that there were, among other things, an old newspaper with the crossword half-completed, a home-made card from a grandchild, a freshly ironed pair of pyjamas, some sweet papers, a wristwatch. What would the family do with them? I wondered. What was a newly widowed woman expected to do with a worn shaving brush and a pair of spectacles?

It was the staff nurse, a kindly woman with more understanding than I probably deserved, who took me aside and helped me see that it wasn't so much that I hadn't confronted death before, but rather that I had, and I realized she was right. Octavia's death, something which I thought I had managed to put behind me, was still very much a part of me, and as we talked, I was able to tell her about our hopelessness when we were confronted by the toys and clothes and all the other baby paraphernalia that had remained after my little sister's death.

But on the whole, I was enjoying my new career. It was exhausting and demanding, but never boring, and I developed a new respect for the courage and humour of my fellow human beings. True, not everyone suffered their ordeal in saintly silence, and there was always that tiny minority of patients who expected to be given the majority of the attention, but it was all part of the job, and if I occasionally had to retire to the sluice to take a few deep breaths (in those days, junior nurses spent a great deal of their time in the sluice), there was usually someone around to commiserate.

And so I moved from a surgical ward to the Outpatients' Department, with a couple of weeks off for lectures and study (this time a welcome break) and then on to a spell of night duty.

Working at night was like being in a different world; a world of dim lights and murmured voices and soft footsteps. There were no meals to give out, no blanket baths or dressings to administer, none of the routine maintenance of the day shift. Doctors appeared when they were needed, their hurried evacuation of their beds evident in uncombed hair or a glimpse of pyjamas under a white coat. Any rushed activity heralded a new admission or an emergency, and in the case of the latter I did my best to keep my head down. With my lack of experience, I felt I would be of little use in the event of a cardiac arrest, and while I had been trained in the arts of resuscitation, I was in no hurry to try them out on a real patient. Clarrie – the reassuringly unrealistic and limbless rubber patient we practised on in the classroom – was one thing. I was happy enough to empty my lungs into her recumbent body, or thump new life into her imagined heart. A genuine emergency was something else altogether. Fortunately, on these occasions it was usually made clear that I was surplus to requirements, and I would be relegated to 'keep an eye on the rest of the ward' while the serious business took place behind drawn curtains.

Mum's impromptu visits had ceased some time ago (no doubt the novelty had worn off), and her contact was sporadic. But when the time came for the third anniversary of Octavia's death, I received an excited phone call.

'I thought we'd all go and see *The Sound of Music*, Cass. How does that sound?'

'*The Sound of Music*. Well, it's certainly a thought,' I said carefully, wondering where on earth the inspiration for this extraordinary idea had come from.

'Yes. Octavia would have loved it' – would she? – 'and we can all go out for tea afterwards.'

'Who's we?'

'Oh, everyone. Greta – she'll love the mountains, won't she? – and of course Call Me Bill, and we'll pay for Richard, and—'

'OK, Mum. I get the picture.'

'You don't sound very excited.'

'Well, it's not easy. Getting the time off may be a problem, for a start. And how do you know it will be on?'

'I saw it advertised, that's what gave me the idea. It's such a happy family film, Cass. It'll help to cheer us all up.' She

paused. 'And last year wasn't – well, it wasn't very successful, was it? I'm determined that this year will be better.'

I agreed that almost anything had to be better than last
year, and a visit to the cinema was certainly a novel idea. I
myself had already seen *The Sound of Music* twice, and Mum
to my certain knowledge three times, but it was a nice story
and the songs were tuneful and cheery. Maybe Mum was
right. It could just be that *The Sound of Music* was what we
all needed.

But in the event, it proved to be far from what Mum
needed.

We started off happily enough as we trooped into the
cinema with our bags of sweets and settled ourselves in
the back row. Greta wept at the sight of the mountains,
but then that was to be expected, and Call Me Bill dozed
off a couple of times, which was probably to be expected too
(Call Me Bill was not what you would call a romantic). But
Mum seemed to be enjoying herself, tapping her feet as
Julie Andrews sang and danced her way across the Alpine
meadows, and humming along to 'I Am Sixteen Going on
Seventeen' (much to the annoyance of the people in front of
us). So far so good. But as the film progressed, I noticed that
she was becoming quieter. When 'Raindrops on Roses' came
round for the second time, I was aware of vague snifflings,
and by the time we had reached 'The Lonely Goatherd', she
was beside herself.

'What on earth's the matter, Mum?' I whispered, reaching for her hand in the darkened cinema. 'You said yourself,
this is a happy film.'

'They're – all – alive,' sobbed Mum. 'All. *All alive.*'

'Of course they are. It wouldn't be a happy film if they weren't!' I squeezed her hand. 'Shh, Mum. We're going to disturb everyone else.'

But it was too late. Mum was sunk in misery, impervious to the shushings and the fierce glances of those around us, and in the end I had to take her out, with the rest of our party in reluctant attendance. We emerged into pouring rain (for which we had come totally unequipped), and hurried Mum into the nearest cafe, where we sat her down behind a potted palm and ordered strong coffee.

'Now, what's all this about?' I asked her, stirring sugar into her coffee and pushing the cup into her hand. 'Come on. Drink this up and tell us what's the matter.'

'They're all alive,' Mum said again, between sobs. 'Beautiful alive children. We should never have gone to the cinema. It was a silly idea.' She took a sip of her coffee and added more sugar.

'But we could hardly have gone to see a film about dead children,' I reasoned, beginning to get her drift. 'That wouldn't have been a very jolly thing to do.'

'No. But I didn't realize,' Mum said. 'I just didn't realize.'

Poor Mum. How could she have known – how could any of us have known? – that the joyous singing and dancing of all those merry, healthy children, with their bright smiling faces and their unlikely abundance of musical talent, would be for Mum a dreadful reminder of what could never be for Octavia? Never mind that Octavia was unlikely ever to have danced or yodelled on a flower-spangled mountainside; but if she had lived, at least the possibility – however remote – wouldn't have been so cruelly snatched away.

After an uncomfortable half-hour, in the course of which we tried to cheer ourselves up with scones and cream and fruit cake (Lucas seemed to be the only person with any appetite), we escorted Mum home, where I helped her up to her room.

'Oh, Cass!' She sat down on her bed and ran her fingers through her hair. 'I thought I was over it. Over the worst of it, anyway. But I'm not, am I?'

'Poor Mum.' I sat down beside her and took her hand. I noticed that there were grey streaks in the auburn of her hair, and that new lines were forming round her eyes and mouth. 'You know you're not over it. You'll never really be over it. But these waves will become less frequent, and you'll be more – more used to it.'

'Will I?' The face turned towards mine was childlike and hopeful, as though I might have the answer; as though I might be able to make everything all right again.

'I think so. Of course, I don't know. Nobody knows. But that's the way it seems to be with most people.'

'Is that the way it is for you, Cass?'

'Well, it's different for me. She was my sister, and although that's awful, it's not the same as losing your own child, is it?'

'That's the trouble.' Mum sighed. 'There's no one to share it with. No – father.'

It was the first time since her pregnancy that Mum had mentioned Octavia's father, and I was surprised. Perhaps it had taken Octavia's death and the long journey which followed it for her to realize that another parent would have made a difference; there would have been someone else to share her bereavement in the way that only a parent can, someone who would have fully understood how she felt.

It was natural that Mum should be upset on Octavia's anniversary, but I was worried about her. Would she be all right when I returned to London the next morning? Of course Greta would keep an eye on her; and Call Me Bill, although never exactly warm, was kind and dependable. But Lucas was out a lot, preoccupied with his job and a very dishy WPC from his department, and the Charlton Heston Lodger had departed some weeks ago after an unseemly row about scrambled eggs (I never did quite get to the bottom of that) and had not yet been replaced. As far as I knew, there was no new man on the scene; no one to offer the kind of support which Mum seemed to find so essential for her emotional survival.

'You will look after Mum, won't you?' I said to Lucas that night, when Mum had gone to sleep.

'Don't I always?' Lucas leant against a kitchen worktop, drinking beer out of a can.

'Up to a point. But you're – well, you've got other interests.'

'You mean Gracie.' Lucas grinned. 'Aren't I allowed a life?'

'Of course you're allowed a life,' I said, thinking that Gracie seemed an oddly inappropriate name for a policewoman. 'I'm just asking you to look out for her, that's all.'

'It's all right for you, Cass.' Lucas put down his can and wiped his mouth on the back of his hand. 'You're never here.'

'That's not fair. I come home whenever I can.'

'Whenever you want, more like.'

'And I suppose you stay at home out of the goodness of your heart, do you? Not by any chance because it's cheap and convenient and Greta does all your laundry?'

'Probably a bit of both,' said Lucas peaceably. One of the infuriating things about Lucas is that he would never have a proper row. 'But don't worry, Cass. You know Mum. She'll be OK. And of course I'll look after her.'

'And keep me posted?'

'And keep you posted.'

But in spite of his reassurances, I felt uneasy, and when I said goodbye to Mum the next day she was still in bed, with The Dog curled at her side (never a good sign, for The Dog had not improved with age, and these days he was arthritic and not a little smelly; he occupied the bottom of the barrel where Mum's sleeping companions were concerned).

'Bye, Mum.' I kissed her cheek. 'I'm off now.'

'Goodbye, Cass.' She returned my kiss, absently fondling The Dog's ears. 'You will – you will come home again soon, won't you?'

'As soon as I can,' I promised. 'I'll come home as soon as I possibly can.'

Thirty

It was with a sense of relief tinged with guilt that I returned to London after my emotional sojourn at home. At the hospital I had my friends and my work. I had my own little world, removed from the emotional problems of home, and if my social life was unexciting, then I had only myself to blame. Here in London I could truly be myself, and while I wasn't always happy – is anyone? – my lifestyle and my choices were my own. For the first time in my life, I was beginning to feel like an independent adult, no longer defined as a daughter or even a sister. Homesickness had become a thing of the past, and while I loved my home and family, I could envisage a time in the not too distant future when I would no longer necessarily depend on them.

The situation on the boyfriend front was not improving. By now I had been out with several men, one or two of whom I had liked a lot, but I was unable to progress towards anything approaching intimacy. As soon as someone tried to kiss me or even put an arm around me, my body seemed to freeze, and with it any inclination on my part to take the relationship further. I became adept at sidestepping physical contact, and if anyone tried to kiss me, I found that gazing down at the floor often proved discouragement enough.

Of course, medical students had a reputation – Lucas had cheerily reminded me of that before I had even left home – and I found that many of them more than lived up to it. I very quickly learnt not to accept invitations back to student rooms 'for coffee' (at least one prospective seducer didn't even possess a kettle), and endeavoured to stay in mixed company at all times. The result of course was that I was usually summarily dumped after a couple of dates, and would return once again to the uncoupled state.

'What's wrong with you, Cass?' Angela asked, after I had been dropped by two men in rapid succession (by this time Angela had sampled more 'coffee' than could possibly have been good for her).

'Nothing's wrong with me. I just like being single,' I replied, trying to sound convincing.

'No one likes being single,' Angela said. 'We aren't made to be single.'

'Maybe I am.'

'Of course you're not. Come on, Cass. You're an attractive girl. You're young. You've got it all. What are you afraid of?'

'Lots of people prefer to be single,' I persisted. 'Some of the ward sisters, for a start.'

Angela snorted.

'Only the old ones, poor old trouts. Probably all lost their men in the war. In their day, I don't suppose there were enough men to go around. Nowadays, there are plenty of spare men.' She grinned at me. 'We're lucky, Cass. It's a good time to be young.'

She was right, of course. In a way, our generation had it all. Far removed from such world events as the Vietnam War (of which, I'm ashamed to say, I knew very little), we had opportunities undreamed of by previous generations, and looking back, I think I managed to be happy much of the time. I had all the Beatles records, I had even come to enjoy dancing (especially as nowadays it was no longer necessary to have any contact with one's partner; in fact sometimes one didn't even need a partner at all) and I had the right sort of legs for a miniskirt. I just wouldn't be needing the pill.

But part of me wanted a boyfriend. I wanted someone who was special to *me*; someone who was mine, if only temporarily; someone who would take me out on my birthday and send me flowers on Valentine's Day. The annual Nurses' Ball loomed, and I had no one to go with, while most of my friends had their partners already lined up and Angela appeared to have at least three candidates to choose from.

But in the event, there was to be no Nurses' Ball for me, partner or no partner, for three days before it was to take place, I received a phone call.

'Cass?' Lucas's voice sounded strained. He rarely phoned me, and I immediately sensed trouble.

'It's Mum, isn't it?' I said, after a moment.

'Well, yes.'

'Tell me, then. Don't keep me waiting.' What had Mum been up to now? A broken love affair? A bent Lodger? Or, worse, another unplanned pregnancy?

'She's depressed. She's been really bad since Octavia's

anniversary, and she doesn't seem to be coming out of it. I don't know what to do.'

'But she can't be! I spoke to her two days ago, and she sounded fine. Why didn't she tell me? Why didn't you tell me?'

'I thought she'd come out of it. After all, she usually does. And besides, she didn't want you worried. She's so proud of you, Cass. You and your nursing. She said she didn't want to – to disturb you, I think she said. So we thought we'd wait—'

'We?'

'Greta and I. After all, Greta's very good with her, and she's at home all day, and—'

'But you should have told me! Of course you should. You had no right to keep something like this from me, Lucas. She's my mother, too. I need to know!'

'Do you? Do you really?'

I felt a sudden surge of resentment and anger; anger with Mum for failing to cope, anger with Lucas for being right, because of course I didn't need to know about Mum's problems, but also anger with myself for even having such thoughts.

'You want me to come home.' It was a statement rather than a question.

'Would you, Cass? Just for a few days? You're so good with her, and you're – you're—'

'A woman?' I said helpfully.

'Well, yes. She doesn't talk to me the way she does to you. You seem to understand each other.'

'Does she want me to come home?'

'Of course she doesn't. Mum thinks you're totally indispensable, and that countless lives will be lost if you desert your post for more than a day.' He paused. 'But she'll be delighted to see you, I can promise you that. And I know you'll make a difference. I wouldn't ask if I wasn't desperate, but I've tried everything, and I simply can't get through to her. Greta's out of her depth, and as for that new doctor, well, he's useless.'

Not for the first time I thought nostalgically of Dr Mackenzie, who had been so efficient at dealing with Mum. But that good man was now enjoying a well-earned retirement, and his replacement – a spotty young man with the bedside manner of a shy teenager – would most certainly be unable to handle her.

Managing the time off proved easier than I had anticipated, and within hours I had packed a bag and was on the train home.

The scene which met me was not encouraging, but I wasn't surprised, since it was always this way when Mum had one of her depressions. While she rarely actually did any housework herself or made any attempt to keep things in order, without her the whole place seemed to wilt. It was as though it required her spirit, her good cheer, to energize everyone else into making an effort. Now, the house was dusty and neglected, Call Me Bill was apparently away visiting a friend (how could he, at a time like this?) and Richard was at the kitchen table drinking coffee and reading the *Daily Sketch*. Greta was sitting beside him, knitting something long and shapeless in an unpleasant shade of green.

'Where is she?' I asked, after the formalities were over.

'Iss in bed.' Greta gave me a hug. 'Iss not well,' she added unnecessarily. 'I take you up, yes?'

'That won't be necessary.' I was annoyed with Greta, who was becoming lazy. She had enjoyed our hospitality for years now, making very little financial contribution. The least she could do now was to keep things in some sort of order even if she'd given up trying to cope with Mum herself.

I was hit by a wall of stale air as I entered Mum's room, and when my eyes because accustomed to the gloom (the curtains were drawn) I could see her curled up like a child under the covers with The Dog lying across her feet.

'Cass!' She sat up and held out her arms to me. 'What a lovely surprise!'

'Hello, Mum.' I kissed her, then went over to the window and drew back the curtains.

'Oh, don't.' Mum held her hands up to her eyes. 'It's too bright!'

'No, it's not. It's a beautiful day, and this room is disgustingly hot and stuffy.' I flung open a window, then came back and sat down on the bed. 'That's better. Now, what's all this about?'

Mum shivered and drew the covers up to her chin.

'You're being all hearty and firm,' she said reproachfully.

'Well, someone's got to be hearty and firm.' I pushed The Dog off the bed, and he slunk off into the corner, whimpering with indignation. 'Have you seen the doctor?'

'Oh, him! He's quite useless. He wouldn't give me any pills, so I told him to go away. He said that in that case he had patients who really needed him, and I haven't seen him since.'

'I'm not surprised,' I said, revising my opinion of the youthful GP.

'Well, he could have called back. To see how I was.'

'But you told him to go away!'

'I didn't mean it. I was just – testing.'

'Mum, it's no good playing silly games with the doctor. He hasn't the time even if you have. Look . . .' I stood up. 'I'll go and run you a nice bath, and we can talk while you're having it.'

'But I don't want a bath.'

'Mum, you need a bath. No arguing. Then I can change the sheets on this bed and give it a good airing.'

'Is this the way you treat your patients?'

'Oh, I'm much worse with my patients.'

I ran a deep bath, and poured into it the contents of several nearly empty bottles and jars, producing a great deal of foam and an interesting but not unpleasant-smelling cloud of steam.

'Ugh.' Mum hovered in the doorway. 'What's that smell?'

'Essence of Roses, Jasmine Garden, Lemon Soufflé and Eastern Delight,' I read out the labels on the bottles. 'Who thinks up these ridiculous names? Now, in you get.'

I closed the door and whipped off her nightie. Obediently she stepped into the warm water. I noticed that she had lost weight.

'Mmm. Not bad.' Mum lay back in the bath, and there was a shadow of a smile. A sea of foam trembled up to her chin, and the sunlight filtering through the bathroom window caught the red of her hair. She looked like a tousled film star.

I reflected that it would take more than a bout of depression to cause Mum to lose her looks.

'Now talk to me.' I sat down on the bathroom stool.

'It's Octavia.'

'Of course it's Octavia. But what's brought this on now?'

'I didn't know anniversaries would be this bad,' Mum said. 'I thought this time would be better. I wanted to celebrate her, remember her, but not – not feel like this.'

I knew what she meant. We could go on trying to tell ourselves that an anniversary was just another day, but the time of year, the June sunshine, the roses in the garden – they would always be a poignant reminder of that awful day three years ago. How could they not be?

'Maybe one day we'll be able to celebrate her,' I said gently. 'But it's only been three years, Mum.'

'Oh, Cass. What am I going to do?' Her eyes filled with tears. 'Whatever shall I do?'

'You'll just go on, Mum. As you have been doing. And there'll be good days and bad, and eventually there will be more and more of the good days. Then one day you'll be able to look back and remember Octavia and smile. And be glad you had her.'

'Are you glad, Cass? Are you glad we had her?'

'Yes. Oh yes.' Funnily enough it was a question I had never asked myself, but now I found myself replying without hesitation. The baby who had been neither planned nor wanted had become central to our family, and although we no longer had her with us, her place in the family was assured for as long as we were around to remember her. 'How could

I ever regret knowing her, having her for my sister? She was – she was just perfect,' I finished lamely.

'She was, wasn't she?' Mum seemed pleased.

'Of course she was. And now she can never be anything else. A perfect, happy baby.'

When Lucas got home from work that evening, he was impressed to find Mum sitting up in bed between clean sheets, eating supper off a tray. I probably should have persuaded her to get dressed and come downstairs, but I reckoned that the bath was victory enough for one afternoon.

'I knew you'd be able to do it, Cass,' he said. 'I knew we could depend on you.'

But for how long, I wondered some time later, as I took The Dog out for his late-night pee, lingering beneath the huge silent arc of a star-studded sky, smelling the scent of damp grass and flowers. For how long would I have to continue to take responsibility for my family? For my mother?

The winking lights of an aeroplane crossed slowly over-head; The Dog, mission accomplished, whined and licked my hand; Greta called from the back door that she had made me a cup of cocoa and it was getting cold.

I sighed, and turned back towards the house.

Thirty-one

'Has she come yet?' My mother's voice is as faint as the whisper of dried leaves, yet it startles me, for these are the first words she has spoken for hours.

'No. Not yet. But she will. She will come.' I take Mum's hand and stroke it. I thought she had forgotten, but once again, I have underestimated my mother. 'She's on her way. She'll be here as soon as she can.'

Mum nods, and closes her eyes again. She doesn't have to say who she means and I don't have to ask, but I'm relieved that I know now what it is – who it is – that Mum's been waiting for. But please, please let it be soon, for even Mum can't hang on indefinitely.

It's strange how, at the end, people so often seem to have control over the timing of their death. Some, like Mum, wait for a particular person to come before they can finally let go, while others will hang on until a person close to them has gone home, or perhaps merely left the room for a few minutes, and thus spare those closest to them their last moments. Or maybe they simply want to die in privacy, claiming the *last prerogative which is truly theirs, for dying can be an undignified business as well as a lonely one.*

Outside the door, the ward is slowly coming to life after the relative peace of the night. A telephone rings, there is the brisk sound of daytime footsteps, laughter, the rumble of a trolley. An orderly brings in a cup of tea, then remembers, and makes to leave the room.

'Please?' I hold out my hand. My mouth is dry, my head aches and I am groggy from lack of sleep. 'Is it OK if I have it?'

'Sorry. Of course.' She places the cup on the locker. 'Can I get you anything else? A piece of toast?'

'No thanks. Tea will be fine.'

Dark brown, stewed hospital tea. But this morning, it tastes like nectar, and I drink it gratefully, watching as the new day washes the colour back into the room; the pale green of the walls and the darker tiles of the floor, the white sheets, the blue of my skirt. Lucas's flowers – red and white and yellow, a horrible combination – are in a vase on the locker, already wilting from the stuffiness of the central heating, and outside the window the maple leaves continue to drift and swirl on their downward journey.

Mum is sleeping again, her breathing shallow, one hand twitching slightly outside the covers. Even now, it seems odd to see her within the narrow confines of a single bed. I doubt whether my mother has occupied a single bed since she was a child, and it must seem strange to her, too.

I wanted her to be allowed to die in her own bed and in her own home. I wanted to look after her myself. It didn't have to be like this, I told her.

But Mum had been adamant.

'You've your own life to lead, Cass. The least I can do is to die in hospital. Tidily. After all, lots of other people do, so it can't be that bad. You can visit me,' she had added, as though this were a novel idea. 'You can come and see me in hospital. I've been enough trouble to you over the years. Quite enough trouble.'

But has she really been so much trouble? Or could it be that my need to take care of her has been at least as great as her need to be taken care of? I may not have seen it at the time, but I didn't have to keep running home to her. She certainly never asked me to. And she would have coped. For in a way, Mum has always been on her own, and even if she hadn't had Lucas and me, she would have got by somehow.

But in the first two years of my nursing training, I must have made at least half a dozen mercy dashes home, including the case of the thieving Lodger (who I'm pleased to say ended up behind bars), Greta's appendicitis, another of Mum's depressions and the death of The Dog.

The Dog had become increasingly decrepit over the years, and must have been quite an age, although given the circumstances under which we had acquired him, there was no way of knowing exactly how old he was. Various organs were beginning to fail, his hearing and eyesight were poor, and his bodily functions unreliable. The vet, a no-nonsense man who Mum said would have been better suited to working in an abattoir, recommended that we have him put down.

But of course Mum would have none of it. After the difficult time The Dog had had, it was only fair to 'let him die peacefully at home', as she put it.

'But Mum, he will die peacefully at home,' I told her, when she relayed this piece of information over the telephone. 'I'm sure the vet will come to the house to do it. He won't have to go anywhere. You could give him his favourite meal first,' I added, trying to soften the blow.

'You've become very hard, Cass,' Mum said, after a pause pregnant with disapproval. 'It must be this nursing business.'

Given that Mum was still enormously proud of me and my 'nursing business', this seemed hardly fair, but I let it pass.

'Not hard, Mum. Kind. I'm trying to be kind.'

'Hmm.'

'Well, what's the point of telling me about him if you don't want to hear what I think?' I asked, exasperated.

'I thought you'd be sympathetic.'

'I am sympathetic. But he's a *dog*, Mum. He's had a good innings. We've given him a fantastic life, and now I think it's time to let him go.'

But Mum refused to listen, and when a month later The Dog, on one of his increasingly rare forays into the outside world, wandered blindly into the road and was knocked down and killed, she was understandably upset.

'You'll have to come home to deal with him, Cass,' she told me, when she phoned to break the news. 'After all, you're a nurse.'

'Being a nurse doesn't qualify me to bury dogs any more than anyone else. Can't Lucas do it?'

'Lucas is away on a course. Call Me Bill says dead bodies make him sick and Greta won't stop crying. The Lodger doesn't like dogs,' she added, as though an affection for dogs were a prerequisite for anyone thinking of burying one.

'Where is he?'

'At his German class I think.'

'Not the Lodger. The Dog.'

'He's in the cupboard under the stairs.'

'Ah.' The cupboard under the stairs was warm and stuffy. Time was not on my side.

'Can you put him outside, or at least somewhere a bit cooler?'

'No one wants to pick him up. He's a horrible mess, Cass. The man wrapped him in a blanket so we wouldn't have to look.'

'What man?'

'The man who ran him over. He was awfully nice. It wasn't his fault. He was just going down to the village to buy some paint stripper, and his wife—'

'Mum, I don't need to know the domestic arrangements of this person.'

'All right. But you will come, won't you? I think you owe it to The Dog. Even if you won't do it for me,' she added.

After the hours of walks and grooming and bathing which I had lavished on this very spoilt and fortunate animal, I didn't feel I owed him anything, but I had loved him as much as anyone, and perhaps I ought to put in an appearance.

Fortunately the death of The Dog coincided with a week's legitimate annual leave. It would also get me out of a date with Neil, a charming young junior doctor with melting brown eyes and large capable hands, and the kind of bedside manner which would make being ill a positive treat. However, he also had something of a reputation, and, I suspected, another kind of bedside manner which I was all too eager to avoid.

'Ah, little Cassandra,' he sighed, when I told him I had to go home. 'Excuses, excuses.'

'It's not an excuse. It's an emergency.'

'Emergency, excuse, whatever you say. But this is the third time you've stood me up. A man can only hang around for so long.'

For a moment I hesitated. I imagined those eyes gazing into someone else's, those hands holding a hand that wasn't mine, and the thought was not pleasing. Then I thought of the distinct possibility of being invited back to his place for coffee (and I was sure that Neil had made a great deal of coffee in his time), and my mind was made up.

'I'm sorry. I have to go home. My – my mother needs me.'

When I arrived home the following morning, the house seemed very quiet without the hoarse barking which usually greeted my arrival, and I was overcome with sadness.

'Oh, Cass. There you are,' Mum said as though I'd just popped in from next door. She kissed my cheek, and I couldn't help noticing that, considering the circumstances, she appeared remarkably cheerful. Occasions such as this tended to generate either deep gloom or wild celebration where Mum was concerned, and it was with sinking spirits that I sensed a party coming on.

'I thought we'd have a party,' she continued, as though reading my thoughts. 'The Dog never had a party while he was alive. I think we should give him one now.'

'A party.' I dropped my case on the kitchen floor and sat down. 'What does everyone else think?'

'Oh, I haven't told them yet. You're the first to know.' She beamed, as though this were a truly splendid piece of news. 'I've got it all planned. I thought we'd have the burial first, and then we can all come back to the house for food and drink. We can ask the neighbours, of course, and Lucas will want to bring Gracie, and Greta's got a friend over from Switzerland, and—'

'I thought Lucas was on a course.'

'Oh, didn't I tell you? It was cancelled.'

'No. You didn't tell me.' So I needn't have come home after all. I swallowed my irritation. 'Who's digging the hole?'

'The hole?'

'Yes, the hole. For The Dog.'

'I hadn't thought.'

'Well, it's not going to be me,' I said. 'If I've got to – to deal with the body, the least you can do is organize someone else to do the digging. I'm tired, Mum,' I added. 'I've just had a gruelling spell of night duty. Grave-digging duties are not part of the deal.'

Late that afternoon, the noisome and very unpleasant remains of The Dog (had he really only been in the cupboard for twenty-four hours?) were interred in a deep hole under the cherry tree (the hole courtesy of a very disgruntled Lucas, who felt that he was being shown up in front of the lovely Gracie). Tears were shed, Richard gave an interesting rendition of the last post on his ukulele (yes, it is possible, just, but I doubt whether anyone else would have recognized it), a bright wreath of marigolds was laid, and we all repaired to the house for the party. There seemed to be a lot of guests; people I'd never met in my life before, and quite a few old friends. How on earth had Mum managed to assemble them in such a short time?

She had certainly done The Dog proud. His framed photograph formed the centrepiece on the dining-room table, and around it there was enough food to feed a small army. As ever, the drink flowed, and Lucas, having recovered from his post-burial sulk, made his vodka mixture, so everyone got riotously drunk.

'What we need,' mumbled Mum, as she lay on the floor with her head in my lap some time after midnight, 'what we need is – is – is—'

'What do we need, Mum?' I stroked her hair, reflecting through a haze of alcohol that whatever might be said about Mum, she certainly knew how to throw a good party.

'What we need is—' – she waved a hand vaguely in the air – 'is one of those things – you know – woof woof.' She giggled.

'You mean a dog?'

'That's the one. We need a dog. Clever Cass. A dog. A new dog. That's what we need.'

It seemed a bit soon to be replacing The Dog when we had only just come to terms with his loss, but even after she'd had time to sleep on the idea and recovered from her hangover, Mum was adamant. After all, as she explained to us, there was an open tin of dog food in the fridge. It would be a shame to waste it. Besides, a new dog would cheer us up, and would take our minds off the old one. She said that it would be best if she went to choose the new dog on her own; that way, she would have no one to blame but herself if Things Went Wrong.

Thus two days later, she set off to the rescue centre, and returned in triumph, a small bouncy black and white hearthrug frolicking at her feet. Its eyes were entirely obscured, and it seemed to be lacking something. It took me a few minutes to realize exactly what.

'Mum, do we really need a dog with three legs?' I asked.

'He doesn't mind,' Mum said gaily. 'He's used to it. Apparently he lost it ages ago. And look at it this way, Cass. He'll have only three legs whether we have him or not, so he might as well live on three legs here. And he won't need so much exercise, will he?'

'Won't he?'

'Of course not. He's got one less leg to exercise, hasn't he?'

'Where are his eyes?' I couldn't even tell which end of the hearthrug was which.

'Under here somewhere.' Mum poked about in the matted fur. 'There we are! Lovely brown eyes! We'll give him a nice bath, and he'll come up as good as new.'

Her new friend did not enjoy his nice bath, and Mum emerged some time later soaked to the skin and sporting several nasty scratches, but with her enthusiasm still intact.

'Here we are,' she said. 'Doesn't he look lovely?'

Lovely was hardly the word, but we all agreed. When Mum was in this kind of mood, we would do anything to keep her there. Besides, she now had something to look after, and Mum was never happier than when she felt needed.

We looked at each other and gave a collective sigh. New Dog had joined the family.

Thirty-two

I returned to London reassured. New Dog had settled in happily (although personally I had yet to understand what Mum saw in him), Mum was in her element ('There might be someone who could make him a new leg, Cass. Or perhaps even a little wheel?'), and things were more or less back to normal.

At the hospital, things were not back to normal. The bad news was that Matron summoned me and kindly but firmly informed me that since I had had far more than the permitted amount of leave, I would be taking my final exams four months after everyone else.

These tidings were not entirely unexpected, but I was nonetheless disappointed. I had hoped that I might scrape by – just – but what with my numerous visits home on compassionate leave, and a nasty bout of glandular fever in my first year, my luck had run out. In a few months' time I would have to bear the humiliation of seeing my colleagues promoted to the role of staff nurse, while I remained a humble student.

The good news (if you could call it that) was that the

dashing Neil seemed intent on waiting for me to change my mind about going out with him, and to that end had endured a whole week without the pleasures of female company (or so he informed me).

'Come out with me, Cass.' He cornered me on the ward, where I was writing up some notes. 'Just one little date. And then if you really don't like me, I promise I'll leave you alone.'

'I never said I didn't like you.'

'Well, then.'

'It's not as simple as that.'

'Of course it's simple.' He drew a chair up to the desk and sat down beside me. 'Look at me, Cass. Look me in the eye, and tell me you really don't want to go out with me.'

'Well . . .'

'Great. That's settled, then. Tonight? Shall we go out together tonight?'

'I don't know. I've got things to do. I've got to—'

'Wash your hair?'

'Well, yes. Among other things.'

'I like your hair just the way it is.'

As most of my hair was invisible under my cap, I couldn't help laughing, and Neil seemed pleased.

'You've got a sense of humour,' he said with satisfaction. 'I like a girl with a sense of humour. So that's fixed, then? You'll come out with me?'

Still I hesitated. Rationally, I could think of lots of reasons to go out with Neil. He was attractive, caring and kind, and if he had something of a reputation, well, I was a big girl. Surely I could look after myself, couldn't I? By now I had dealt with cardiac arrests and haemorrhages and all manner of emergencies; I had run the gauntlet of the great Professor Armstrong-Phillips, whose tantrums in the operating theatre would put any self-respecting toddler to shame; I had on occasion even been briefly in charge of a busy ward. What was a night out with a young doctor in comparison with any of these? So I agreed, feeling that since I had neither a valid excuse nor the ability to tell a convincing lie, I didn't have a lot of choice.

But that first date proved my misgivings to be quite unfounded. We had dinner in a little bistro in South Kensington, all checked tablecloths and candles in wine bottles and real French waiters, and we found plenty to talk about. Neil was the perfect gentleman, there was no mention of going back to his place for coffee, and he saw me home with a chaste kiss on the cheek. It was the first time I had felt completely relaxed on a date, and I was both happy and relieved. I felt as though I had finally broken through some invisible barrier. Maybe from now on things would start to improve.

After two more similar dates, I decided that I was in love. I found myself singing as I walked down the street, lying awake at night just basking in the warm feeling of being loved (or so I thought), and daydreaming as I went about my duties. I felt wildly happy and more alive than I could ever remember feeling before.

'What's the matter with you, Cass?' Mum asked suspiciously, when I phoned to ask how things were at home. 'Something's up. I can tell.'

'Nothing's up. I'm fine.'

'I know – you're in love! That's what it is.' Mum had a

nose for this kind of thing. 'Oh, Cass! How wonderful! Is he a doctor?'

'Well, yes. As a matter of fact he is.'

'What's his name?'

'His name's Neil.'

'Have you been to bed with him yet?'

'I'm not prepared to say,' I replied primly.

'Oh, come on, Cass. You and I don't have any secrets from each other.'

It was true that Mum certainly didn't seem to have any secrets from me (or, come to that, from anyone else) but that was her choice. I decided that my love life was going to be just that. Mine. I wasn't going to allow it to become public property the way hers was. I could just see news spreading round the household and among Mum's friends like celebratory wildfire. For some time now, Mum had been making it clear that she thought it high time that I divested myself of my virginity (she had lost her own so long ago, she told me, that she couldn't remember the occasion or even the man in question). A doctor, as she explained now, would be just the person to do it with, since 'doctors know all about that sort of thing'.

'Mum, I don't want to talk about it,' I said now.

'Oh, Cass.' She sighed. 'Who would have thought you'd grow into such a prude?'

I thought of my friends, most of whom also went to considerable lengths to conceal their sexual exploits from their parents, but for reasons quite different from my own, and wondered for the hundredth time what it would be like to have a normal mother; one who would wait up at night for me, to demand 'What time do you call this?', or warn me against the perils I might incur from involvement with the opposite sex. But of course, I would never know.

'If there's anything important to tell you, then I will,' I said.

'You don't have to get married,' Mum continued, as though I hadn't spoken. 'I've never had a lot of time for marriage, myself,' she added (what a surprise). 'Living together is just fine.'

'Mum, I've only known him three weeks. Give me a break.'

'You could bring him home for the weekend. We'd all love to meet him. Or I could come up to London.'

'No, Mum. *No*.'

'Why? Are you ashamed of me?'

'Of course I'm not ashamed of you. It's just that it's too soon. It's not such a big deal. Not yet, anyway. Now can we let the subject drop, please?'

But in the event, Mum never did get to meet Neil.

By the time we reached our fourth date, Neil was obviously ready to raise the stakes and invited me back to his rooms for a meal.

'It'll be more cosy there. We've never really had time on our own, Cass,' he said.

'Yes we have!'

'No. I mean really on our own. I don't call eating in a crowded restaurant being on our own.'

Why did I feel this frisson of fear? Why wasn't I jumping at the chance of spending an evening in the company of a man with whom I imagined myself to be in love?

'Come on, Cass. I'm not such a bad cook, although I'll admit the facilities aren't up to much.'

'It's not the cooking.'

'Well what, then? What is it? Don't you trust me?'

'Of course I trust you.' I smiled at him. 'And OK, I'd love to come. Thank you.'

Neil's room in the doctors' quarters was cramped, and the kitchen in which he was operating to produce our meal even smaller. I made myself at home, as instructed, while he beavered away amid clouds of steam and the odd muttered curse. I was plied with wine and peanuts but my offers of help were refused, and since there didn't seem to be room for more than one cook to turn round, never mind do anything useful, I occupied myself by examining Neil's collection of books (mainly medical) and browsing through a copy of the *British Medical Journal* (full of dense earnest print and long words, illustrated with graphic photos of tumours and suppurating skin lesions).

We ate our meal off trays on our laps, and Neil opened a second bottle of wine. I was by now feeling pleasantly euphoric and relaxed (notwithstanding Mum's parties, I wasn't normally much of a drinker), and I was beginning to wonder what on earth I had been worrying about. The food was certainly edible, Neil was in excellent form, and I knew I was looking good in my new miniskirt and blouse.

'Come and sit beside me on the bed,' Neil said, when he had cleared away our trays. 'It's much more comfortable.'

Obediently, I did as I was told, and then, as he put an arm round my shoulders, I lay back against the pillows beside him. The Beatles thrummed from the record player ('she loves

246

you, yea, yea, yea'. Oh yes, I thought. I do. *I do*), Neil's after-shave smelled deliciously masculine and the feel of his cheek against mine was strong and protective. I gave a little sigh.

'Enjoying yourself?' Neil asked, shifting slightly beside me.

'Mm. Yes.' The room tilted slightly and then righted itself. A poster appeared to be sliding slowly down the wall, and the books in the bookcase jiggled and blurred. I smiled, and moved closer into Neil's willing arms.

'That's better,' Neil murmured. 'I was beginning to think you didn't fancy me.'

'What do you mean?'

'Well, you've always jumped like a startled rabbit when I've touched you, and done that ducking thing with your head when I tried to kiss you. You're a cool customer, little Cassandra. I'll say that for you.' He kissed the top of my head. 'And I reckon I've been a very good boy.'

'Of course you're a good boy.' Another poster seemed to be joining its partner on their journey down the wall. I was certainly feeling very strange.

'But being good is fine, as far as it goes,' Neil murmured, placing a hand somewhere in the region of my midriff. 'I'd like to go a bit further.' The hand began to meander slowly upwards in the direction of my bosom. 'Just a tiny, tiny bit further.'

His voice was soft and caressing, like that of a parent soothing an anxious child. The posters, which seemed miraculously to have regained their former positions, now began to tilt slowly sideways, and the narrow bed swayed beneath us.

'A bit further? What do you mean?' I held on to the edge of the bed in an effort to steady it.

'I think you know what I mean.' The hand paused for a moment, and then continued on its travels upwards. 'Come on, little Cassandra. You know you want it as much as I do.'

'Want what?'

At this stage I have to say it must have seemed that I was quite extraordinarily stupid, but I was very drunk, and the civilized nature of the evening's proceedings had persuaded me that Neil's reputation was entirely undeserved. As ever, he had behaved impeccably, and I felt that he had been the innocent victim of vicious gossip from people who ought to know better. As for my own feelings, these had always been emotional rather than physical. I certainly longed for Neil, but my longing was of the children's fairy-story variety; all hearts and flowers, being gently wooed, and then perhaps carried away into the sunset like Snow White.

Of course I knew that Neil probably wanted more, but so far he had seemed so sensitive to my finer feelings that I think I had managed to persuade myself he might be prepared to wait. After all, this was love, and if he was in love with me (and why wouldn't he be?) then his feelings could be helped to transcend anything as basic as sex. If sex were ever to come into our relationship it would be in the fullness of time and when I was ready. I certainly wasn't ready yet.

So when the wandering hand, having found its way between the buttons of my blouse, finally arrived at my left breast and grasped it firmly by the nipple, I was taken completely by surprise.

'*No!*' I gripped his wrist and pulled his hand away. 'What do you think you're doing?'

'What do *you* think I'm doing?' Undeterred, the hand made its way back.

'No. Please. Please, don't!' I pulled away from him and tried to sit up.

'What on earth's the matter with you, Cass? Anyone would think I was trying to rape you!'

'Just – don't. I don't want you to – to do that.' My feet found the floor, and I stooped down and tried to put my shoes on. The room was still spinning gently and my head was pounding, but I was thinking perfectly clearly and all I wanted was to get away as quickly as I could.

'Well, you little prick-teaser!'

'I'm not!' Tears stung my eyelids. 'That's a horrible thing to say!'

'Is it?' Neil's voice was cold. 'I think you've just been leading me on all this time, Cass. I suppose you thought it was a bit of fun. You probably even told your friends, I shouldn't wonder. Had a laugh at my expense.'

'That's not fair!'

'No. *You*'re not being fair. I've taken you out, I've tried to understand this – problem you seem to have. And all the time you were just stringing me along.' Neil swung his legs off the bed and stood up.

'It wasn't like that.' By now I was weeping. 'Please try to understand.'

'Oh, I understand all right. I understand perfectly. Just let me warn you, Cass. This game you're playing is a very dangerous one, and could land you in serious trouble. Not everyone's as nice as I am.'

'Well, I don't think you're being nice at all.' I hunted for my bag, trying to see through a blur of tears.

'I don't suppose you do.' Neil watched me as I struggled into my coat. 'I'm sure you'll understand if I don't see you home.'

It took me several weeks to get over Neil. I think he really was my first love, and while first loves are often insubstantial things, helped along by a combination of youthful imagination, optimism and a sturdy pair of rose-tinted spectacles, their passing can be very hard to bear.

Worse still, though, was the realization that my problem with men really was here to stay.

Thirty-three

Six months later, I took my final examinations; and after what seemed an interminable wait, received the news that I had passed. I was now a State Registered Nurse, with a shiny badge and a royal-blue uniform to prove it.

Within days, Mum paid a visit to inspect me, but this time with my reluctant permission, and with promises not to embarrass me or – more importantly – give food to the patients. Her proud gaze followed me for an entire afternoon, and while her behaviour was beyond reproach ('I'm afraid I'm not allowed to feed you,' I heard her whisper to an elderly man, as though he were an animal in the zoo), I found her presence discomfiting.

'Why don't you go and get yourself a cup of tea in the canteen?' I asked her at one point.

'Oh no. I don't want to miss a minute of this. There might be an emergency, Cass. I'd hate to miss seeing you dealing with an emergency.'

Fortunately, there were no emergencies, and the afternoon passed without incident. But while I was of course grateful for the interest Mum took in my promotion, I was also relieved to hear that there wouldn't be a repeat performance.

'It's difficult to get away nowadays. New Dog needs me,' she explained, after we'd had some supper together before she caught the train home. 'I can't leave him for long. The others – well, they don't understand him.'

I don't know exactly when I realized that I was suffering from depression. I suppose because I had always considered myself to be a reasonably sanguine person, it never occurred to me that I should fall prey to any kind of mental problem. Certainly, life had had its ups and downs, but then that was the same for everyone, and if I was occasionally sad or fed up, then I knew that sooner or later I would snap out of it and return to normal.

Of course I had long been accustomed to Mum's depressions. These were unmistakable, tending to strike suddenly out of a clear blue sky, plunging her into the depths of weeping despair, paralysing her mentally and physically and dragging everyone within her vicinity down with her. Then, just as she seemed to reach rock bottom, and we were wondering whether she was ever going to return to normal (although 'Mum' and 'normal' were not words I was accustomed to use in conjunction), she would bounce back as though nothing had happened.

My own depression was different, creeping up on me over several weeks, and so gradually that for a while I didn't realize what was happening. I was tired, certainly, but then I had been working hard. I wasn't sleeping, but I had suffered from bouts of insomnia before. I had no boyfriend, but that was nothing new, and since the unfortunate episode with Neil, I had long since managed to persuade myself that I was better off without one. And if life seemed flat and colourless, then that was probably because, what with work and the drab London winter, there didn't seem to be a lot to look forward to.

The bouts of weeping were something else. I have never cried easily, but now I found myself bursting into tears at the slightest provocation. Rudeness from a patient, a phone call from home, the prospect of an extra-long shift – any of these could induce in me a wave of despair quite disproportionate to the significance of what had triggered it. I began to dread waking in the morning, while getting up, washing and dressing – once activities carried out without a thought – now became at best chores, and at worst, almost insuperable obstacles. I know Mum suspected that something was wrong, and of course I could have told her how I felt. But what was there to tell? Nothing awful had happened, I wasn't ill, and life on the whole should have been good.

Eventually, the decision as to what to do was taken out of my hands.

'Nurse Fitzpatrick, you need help.' My ward sister, a tough woman of the old school but one with a surprisingly soft centre, took me aside.

'I'm fine,' I lied. 'Just a bit tired.'

'We're all a bit tired. It's the nature of the job.' She tilted her head, appraising me as though I were one of her patients. 'You're not yourself. You're forgetting things, making silly little mistakes, and there's obviously something the matter. Do you want to tell me about it?'

'There's nothing to tell. Really.'

'Nothing to tell, or nothing to tell me?'

I shook my head, unable to speak.

'I think you should go and see Dr Burns. Just for a chat. Take the rest of the day off, and go to his surgery this evening. I need healthy staff on my ward, and at the moment you're not really up to the job. Get yourself sorted, and then come back to me and we'll have another talk.'

Dr Burns was the medical officer in charge of our health. I don't believe student nurses have such things these days, but we were fortunate, and while the hospital worked us hard, they also looked after us well.

Some hours later, I was weeping helplessly in Dr Burns's surgery.

'I'm fine. Really I am.' I fumbled for my handkerchief.

'So I see.' He regarded me with kindly amusement over his half-rimmed spectacles, then passed me a box of Kleenex.

'I just – just—'

'Feel a bit low?'

I nodded.

'And when did you pass your exams?'

'Eight months ago.' I blew my nose.

'Did you want to be a staff nurse?'

'Of course I did! I mean, I do.'

'Are you sure?'

'Well, yes. Yes, of course.'

Dr Burns steepled his fingers and leant back in his chair.

'It's a big step from being a student. More responsibility. More demands. More people to look after.'

'What do you mean?'

'I know a bit about your history, Nurse Fitzpatrick.

You've maybe had more than your share of responsibility, one way and another. From what you've told me in the past, it seems to me that you've spent much of your life looking after other people. It could just be that there's a part of you saying enough's enough. That it's time to start taking care of number one.'

'Are you suggesting I give up?' I was incredulous. It had never for a moment occurred to me that I shouldn't continue my nursing career.

'No. Not necessarily.' Dr Burns sat forward in his chair once more. 'I'm just wondering whether nursing is the right career for you. Whether it's something you really should be doing.'

'Of course it is!'

'Is it?' He opened a folder with my name on it and perused the sheaf of notes inside. 'You've had a lot of time off, one way and another.'

'But I had permission! I always had permission. I've had family problems as well as being ill.'

'I know all that. Nurse Fitzpatrick – Cassandra. No one's criticizing you. I believe your conduct has been exemplary. But Matron's recently had a word with me—'

'She had no right!'

'She has every right. She's in charge of the nursing staff, and not much gets past her, believe me. I can't tell her what passes between us. Between you and me. That's confidential. But she's within her rights – in fact it's her duty – to tell me if she has concerns about her nurses.'

'Oh.'

'She has no problems with your work, but she is concerned about how you're coping.'

'Then why didn't she say something to me?'

'I believe she was going to suggest you came to talk things over with me, but it seems you beat her to it.'

'I don't know what to do.' I took another Kleenex.

'I know you don't. That's what I'm here for.' Dr Burns regarded me thoughtfully. 'I'd like you to take a bit of time off.'

'But I've had masses of time off! I can't have any more. I want – I want—'

'What do you want, Cassandra?'

'I want to go home.'

I burst into tears again, thinking how feeble that sounded, and wondering what on earth had made me say it. A few hours ago, nothing could have been further from my thoughts, but now the thought of home, the very word *home*, made me ache with longing. The warmth of our big untidy kitchen, Greta's brews of too-strong tea ('builders' tea' Mum called it), my own familiar bedroom (provided there was no one else in it), Lucas's amused banter, and of course Mum herself – suddenly I felt I needed them all as never before.

'Then that's what you shall do.' Dr Burns took up his pen and wrote something in my notes.

'What, *now*? I can't. The ward's busy, and two people are off with flu, and—'

'And I suppose they can't possibly run the ward without you.'

'Well, yes of course they can, but—'

'No buts. You've just said it yourself. You're not indispensable. I'm not asking you, Cassandra. I'm telling you.' He put down his pen and smiled at me. 'You need to go home, get some rest, do a bit of thinking. I'm signing you off for a month.'

'*A month?*'

'Yes. A month. I'm prescribing some tablets for you. Some mild antidepressants. Get some rest, some fresh air. Relax for a bit. I'll see you when you get back, and we'll take it from there.'

'And what about Matron?'

'I'll tell Matron. Just let the ward know what's happening, and off you go. I don't want to see you for another four weeks. All right?'

'All right.'

I left the room feeling numb but oddly relieved. I couldn't remember when anyone had last taken responsibility for my welfare; made important decisions on my behalf; *taken care* of me.

As I changed out of my uniform later that evening it was with an enormous sense of relief, as though I were shedding an ill-fitting skin. But it never crossed my mind that there was any possibility that I might have worn it for the last time.

Thirty-four

February 1970

I spent the first three days at home crying. The relief – the utter relief – of being able finally to let go; to be rid of the constraints of my job, of maintaining a stiff upper lip and avoiding the watchful of eye of Sister was indescribable. I don't think I had fully realized how low I had been until I was able to give full vent to my unhappiness with the blessed release of being free to weep whenever and wherever I wanted to.

Mum's reaction was at first ambivalent. On the one hand, while she was deeply distressed on my behalf, she was also bewildered. For some years now I had been the strong one – the person upon whom she could rely for help and support when she needed it – and for me to disintegrate like this must have been hard for her to deal with. On the other hand, Mum loved looking after people, and once she had got used to the idea that this time it was I who needed her, she was in her element. She rushed up and down stairs with trays and cups of tea, she made all my favourite dishes, she even offered to read aloud to me. Entertained by this idea, I accepted her offer, and we spent a weepy afternoon together while she read me selected excerpts from *Little Women*, one of my favourite childhood books.

To her very great credit, Mum didn't ask any questions until I'd been home nearly a week. A veteran of the battle against depression (albeit her battles had been very different from mine) she knew better than to look for glib answers or easy diagnoses, and she wisely waited until I was ready before expecting me to do any talking.

'I do love you, you know, Cass,' she said unexpectedly one morning, as she brought me breakfast in bed.

'I know you do, Mum.'

'Whatever you do,' she added.

'Yes.'

'And – the nursing thing.'

'Yes?'

'I shan't – I shan't be disappointed if you don't go back.'

How I blessed Mum for that, for while I had given very little thought to my future, I knew what it must have cost her to, as it were, give me permission to turn my back on a profession of which she was so proud.

'I don't know what I'm going to do, Mum,' I said now. 'I don't feel ready to make any decisions.'

'Of course you don't.' She sat down on the bed and stroked my arm. 'You must stay at home as long as you want. There's no hurry.'

'I've got another three weeks before I have to go back. I may be feeling better by then.'

Mum seemed to hesitate, plucking at the bedspread, gazing towards the open window.

'I'm – I'm sorry I haven't been a better mother. I – well, I didn't really know how. And then somehow it was too late.'

'I suppose it's like that for everyone,' I said. 'After all, no one tells you how to do it, do they?'

'No. I suppose not.'

'In any case, you've been a brilliant mother.'

'Do you really mean it?'

'Of course I mean it. I wouldn't have you any other way.'

'You're sure?'

'Quite sure.' I sat up and gave her a hug. 'Besides, you're *my* mother. How could I possibly want any other?'

She nodded, satisfied for the time being.

'But I don't know what to do to help you, Cass.'

'I don't want you to do anything. Just be there, Mum. Just get on with things as normal. I have to sort this out for myself, but if I know I have your support whatever – well, whatever happens, then it'll make it that much easier.'

The rest of the household were equally supportive, and Greta would happily (if that's the word) have wept along with me if Mum had permitted it.

'No, Greta,' she said, as Greta reached for her handkerchief. 'This isn't your depression. It's Cass's. You can't just cash in on it like this. Go and make yourself useful.'

So poor Greta, unable to show her solidarity in the way she knew best, made a reproachful retreat to the kitchen.

Lucas, who was still besotted with Gracie, was abstracted but kind; Call Me Bill bought me flowers; and two ex-Lodgers called in to ask after me. In fact, the only person who thoroughly resented my presence was New Dog. New Dog and I had never really got on, I suspect because he recognized in me a rival for Mum's attention. Now that my victory was beyond doubt, he spent his time sulking in corners or snarling unpleasantly at me from behind doors. In the end, even Mum lost patience with him.

'New Dog! *Basket!*' she yelled at him, and New Dog was so astonished at this unaccustomed treatment that he stayed in his bed for a whole day.

But after a week or so, New Dog and I came to some sort of understanding, and we took to going for long walks together in the fields behind the house, New Dog hobbling with astonishing speed on his three legs and rolling in cow-pats, while I brooded on the meaning of life and what I was going to do with mine.

As the weeks went by, my depression began to lift. Without the pressure of work and the expectations of other people, I felt the knot of anxiety that had taken up residence in my stomach begin to relax and dissolve, and I began to experience moments of happiness once more. Spring was on the way, and here in the country I was able to appreciate it to the full. On fine days, New Dog and I took our walks to the accompaniment of skylarks and blackbirds, blackthorn blossomed in the hedgerows, and the woods were taking on the faintest tinge of green. Greta had started her spring cleaning – an annual ritual which she undertook alone since no one else was interested – and Mum was talking of getting a new job (a sure sign that the year was under way).

I had forgotten how much I missed home, and began to wonder what had been the attraction of London and my independent life there. The familiar routine, from the sound of Greta's feet on the creaky staircase as she went down in the morning to put the kettle on to New Dog's last trot round the garden at night – all these things had been woven into the fabric of my life for so long that I found myself settling back in as though I had never been away.

When the time came to go back to London to see Dr Burns, I was overcome by panic. I don't know what it was that I was so afraid of – after all, it had been made clear to me that I wouldn't have to do anything I didn't want to; that no pressure would be brought to bear upon me – but suddenly the very thought of getting on the train for that now familiar journey, of walking through the doors of the hospital, of all those busy purposeful people, was almost unbearable.

Seeing my anxiety, Mum insisted on coming with me.

'It's all right, Cass,' she said, reading my thoughts. 'I won't talk to anyone. I'll just keep you company on the train. I won't even come into the hospital if you don't want me.' Then her eyes lit up. 'I tell you what,' she added triumphantly, 'I'll bring New Dog with me, then I can't possibly go in with you, can I? New Dog and I can have a nice walk in the park, and we can meet up afterwards and you can tell me how you got on.'

In the event, this proved to be an inspirational idea, for New Dog (who had been bathed and blow-dried by Greta before we left, and was now fluffy and sweet-smelling) kept everyone in our carriage entertained all the way to London. It would seem that having only three legs had its advantages, and New Dog, who could be very charming when it suited him, was not above exploiting his handicap to the full. In the hour and a half it took us to reach our destination, he sat on at least three different laps and was fed a variety of sandwiches and biscuits.

Three hours later, we were on our way home again.

'I'm sorry, Mum,' I said to her, as the train pulled out of the station. 'I'm so so sorry.'

'Don't be.' Mum's efforts to conceal her disappointment were heroic. 'If it's not right for you, then it's not right at all.'

I thought of the kindness of Dr Burns and especially of the final words of Matron.

'I took a gamble when I took you on, Nurse Fitzpatrick. I think we both knew that. You've given us a lot, and I hope we've done the same for you, but I think you need time at home and perhaps a change of direction.' She had smiled at me, closing my file. 'Maybe one day – one day – we'll see you back here again.'

But I think we both knew that that was not to be. I had made my last journey to St Martha's.

Thirty-five

The door opens and Greta comes in, bearing a huge basket of fruit topped with a shiny yellow ribbon.

'Iss all right I come?' she whispers, approaching the bed tentatively, her eyes already filling with tears.

Poor Greta. She has aged immeasurably since Mum's illness, and I worry about what will become of her when the inevitable happens.

'Of course it's all right.' I give her a hug. 'But she's asleep at the moment.'

Greta puts her basket of fruit on the locker and takes a chair.

'She has pain?' she asks.

'Yes. Some pain. But they're giving her stronger injections now.'

I pray that Mum's eyes remain closed, for she finds Greta's visits upsetting. Greta longs to help, but there is nothing she can do, and the distress this causes them both does nobody any good.

'How's the dog?' I ask her now. The dog – Last Dog (per-

haps Mum knew something we didn't) – is an animal after Mum's own heart. He has never learnt to follow even the simplest instructions, and conducts his life with no reference whatsoever to the feelings of those who care for him. Mum adores him. Greta, however, does not.

'Dog iss very bad,' Greta says. 'He take cheese and pork pie.'

'Oh dear. Does he miss Mum?'

'Last Dog miss nobody.'

'Oh well. At least that's one thing less to worry about.'

'Your mum, she like the fruit, yes?'

'I'm sure she will.' Mum hasn't been able to eat anything for days, but it's no good telling Greta that.

For some time, we sit together in silence, listening to the tiny shallow sounds of Mum's breathing and watching the blue and gold of another beautiful autumn day in the world outside the window. I am too exhausted for conversation, and I suspect that Greta is feeling much the same.

After a while, Greta gets to her feet.

'I go. Yes?'

'Well, it's lovely to see you, Greta, but there's not really much you can do.'

'You tell her I come?'

'Of course I'll tell her.' I summon up a smile. 'Look after yourself.'

'Poor Greta,' Mum whispers, when Greta's left the room. 'Couldn't – couldn't talk to her.'

'I'm sure she'd understand.' I squeeze her hand. 'I didn't know you were awake.'

'Disappointed. Hoped it might be – you know.'

'She's on her way. She'll be here soon,' I say, praying that I'm right.

Mum nods and sighs again.

'I'll wait, then.'

Poor Mum. I think she's ready to let go, but she can't. I didn't think she'd live through the night, but I had underestimated her. Mum has unfinished business.

I undo the cellophane wrapped round the basket of fruit (not so useless after all) and help myself to a banana.

I'd now been home for three months, and while much better, I still had no idea what I wanted to do. I had become a regular visitor to the labour exchange, but jobs were in short supply locally, and I had no transport to travel further afield. I was entitled to the dole (what a dreadful word that is, sounding as it does like the tolling of a bell at a wake), but missed my monthly pay cheque and the self-respect that came with it.

In the end, I applied for – and was given – a job in a small local art gallery. The elderly proprietor, who had the unlikely name of Humphrey Hazelwood, was a man of great charm and kindness, and we immediately hit it off.

'I'm afraid you may find the work a little dull after all the excitement of hospital life,' he told me at my interview.

'I think a dull job is just what I need at the moment,' I said. 'Although I'm sure I shan't find it dull,' I added, afraid of offending him.

The gallery was housed in a half-timbered building in the High Street: sandwiched between an even older tea shop and an estate agent. It was a building of uneven wooden floors, low beams and narrow doorways, with a treacherous little staircase up to the first floor. In many ways it was totally unsuited to its purpose, since the windows let in little daylight, and despite strategically placed lighting, customers frequently had to be escorted out into the street to inspect their prospective purchases. But this being England, such inconveniences were generally considered to add to the gallery's charm, and if it would never make its owner rich, then it almost certainly afforded him a comfortable living.

The job itself was interesting without being demanding, involving meeting artists and customers, helping to hang pictures, answering the phone and doing a little typing, and it proved to be exactly what I needed.

'General dogsbody,' Lucas remarked unkindly, when I told him what I was doing.

'If you like. But it's a job.'

'If you say so.' Lucas had never quite understood how I could turn my back on a career for which I had trained so hard, and had done his utmost to make me change my mind.

'I do say so. Lucas, I need a break, and this is relaxing while still being work.'

And it was true. It was wonderful to have so little responsibility, to meet people without being expected to save their lives, and yet still to be able to have an intelligent conversation. The pressure was finally off, and I was enjoying it.

Mum seemed reasonably happy with my choice, and I heard her telling friends that I was 'working in the art world'. She herself was going through an energetic phase, and to that end had decided to train as a postwoman ('Lots of exercise, Cass. And you meet so many interesting people').

I hoped she wouldn't be disappointed, for many people were out when the post arrived, and the rest were unlikely to have the time to exchange pleasantries with the person who delivered it. She had hoped to be allowed to take New Dog with her. After all, as she explained, many of the customers had dogs, so why shouldn't she. Besides, New Dog would fend off the ankle nippers and hand-biters who plagued the lives of those who delivered the post. But the Post Office wasn't having any of it, so New Dog had to stay at home with Greta.

I remember that summer as one of the more peaceful periods of my life. While I wasn't deliriously happy, neither was I discontented. I was enjoying being at home, and had met up again with some of my friends, including Myra, whom I hadn't seen since our schooldays. Myra was now a hairdresser, with a tiny flat of her own and a shaggy boyfriend who favoured beads and kaftans. She was refreshing company, for she didn't hassle me about my future or reproach me for my past, nor did she question me on the delicate subject of my love-life. I was warmly invited to join her and the beaded boyfriend on some of their outings, and found myself having fun. It was a long time since I had had any fun.

The seventh anniversary of Octavia's death passed without incident. Since the disastrous expedition to *The Sound of Music*, Mum had stopped trying to turn it into an Event, so after taking flowers to the grave, we went out for a quiet family meal.

'It does get easier. Just a bit,' Mum admitted, over her prawn cocktail. 'But it never goes away. It's always – there. Part of me.'

'Part of all of us,' I said.

'Perhaps I should have had another.'

'Another what?'

'Baby. Another baby. After all, we'd all got used to having one around, hadn't we?'

Lucas and I exchanged glances.

'Mum, Octavia wasn't like a dog. You can't just go and replace a baby. If you'd had ten more babies, they still wouldn't have been Octavia.'

'Then I shall have to leave the babies to you and Lucas,' Mum said, spooning up that nasty pink sauce which always comes with prawn cocktails.

Summer gave way to autumn, and once more the leaves began to turn and the swallows lined up on the electricity wires outside our house in preparation for their journey south. I had now been home for seven months, and still hadn't made any long-term plans. Next year, I would be twenty-four. *Twenty-four*. Mum had had Lucas by the time she was twenty-four, and while she was hardly a shining example of how to lead a life, it could never be said that hers had been without interest.

Thirty-six

I had never been especially good at art, nor had I been particularly interested. After achieving a reasonable O level in the subject, I had simply forgotten about it. But working in the gallery aroused at first my interest and then my enthusiasm. Talking to the artists, studying the different styles and mediums in which they executed their work and discussing the pictures with our customers became increasingly absorbing, and, perhaps inevitably, the question arose: I wonder if *I* could do that?

At first the answer was a resounding no. There was no earthly reason why my minimal talents should have developed, since I had neither practised nor applied them, and in any case, where and how should I begin? In the end, I discussed the matter with Humphrey, who suggested I should have some lessons. One of our artists, Edward, held evening classes, and was prepared to take me on at a discounted rate (money was still tight).

I opted for watercolours rather than oils, and my first few paintings were poor smudged little efforts. I knew in my head what I was trying to achieve, but transferring the images onto paper was a different matter. Soon, however, I began to get the hang of it, and before long I was thoroughly hooked. The gentle wash of colour over paper, the blurring of water and trees onto a background, the suggestions of light or shade, stillness or movement, the hint of a house or boat or the pale petals of a flower – all these I found deeply satisfying. I enjoyed the flowing movements of my wrist as I painted and the subtlety of the colours as I mixed them on my palette.

'You know, that's not half bad,' Edward told me, after I'd been learning for about six weeks. 'I think you could be good at this, Cass.'

I glowed with pride, and like a child who has been praised at school, I couldn't wait to get home and tell my mother.

'Why, that's great, Cass. Maybe one day you'll be a famous artist' – Mum specialized in imagining short cuts to fame and fortune – 'with pictures in a London gallery and your paintings on postcards. No one in the family's ever been good at art before. I wonder where you get it from?'

I refrained from the obvious suggestion that my artistic talents might have come from my father, since Mum disliked discussions of this kind, preferring to assume that she alone was responsible for the genetic input of her offspring. For myself, I cared little about the provenance of my new-found talent. It was enough that I had discovered it.

After a while, I brought my paints home and began working in my bedroom. It was a light, south-facing room with views over the garden and the countryside beyond. I still have some of my early attempts at portraying that garden, those trees, the fleeting cloudscapes and the jigsaw puzzle coats of the black and white cows in the fields beyond. Looking at them now, they seem amateurish and clumsy, but at the time I was delighted with them, and Mum proudly framed one for the sitting-room wall. It is in her house to this day.

After I had been painting for about six months, Humphrey suggested I might like to try to sell one or two of my pictures. We could hang them in the gallery, he said, and see what happened.

I was enormously excited. While I found great satisfaction in my painting, it had never occurred to me that anyone might like to buy my work. The idea of hanging one of my pictures in the gallery was exciting enough on its own; the thought that someone might actually want to pay for it – to live with it on their walls and make it part of their home – was beyond anything I could have hoped for.

I sold my first painting for £2, and I can still recall the pride with which I stuck the red SOLD sticker onto the frame, then went to share my news with Humphrey.

'Well, that's wonderful Cass. Very well done.' He gave me a hug. 'You know, a long time ago, I had a go at painting, but I was no good at it at all.'

'Really?' I was surprised. For some reason I had assumed that Humphrey must have started off as an artist himself.

'Really.' He laughed at my expression. 'It was disappointing, I have to confess. I can't imagine anything more satisfying than being able to create something beautiful; something which will give pleasure to other people.' His voice was wistful. 'But that was a long time ago. I accepted that it wasn't for me, so instead I learnt a bit about the art world, and went on to start up this little business. If I can't be an artist myself, then I think that what I do is the next best thing. I see myself as a kind of mediator between the creator and the purchaser.'

'You're very good at it,' I ventured, thinking of the encouragement he gave his artists and his knack of matching the right picture to its new owner (not to mention that owner's budget).

'I think the key to a satisfying life is finding something you're good at, whatever that may be, however unexpected, and going ahead and doing it.' Humphrey fumbled in his pocket for his pipe and tobacco. 'That's what I did, and while it'll never make me rich, I've had a lot of fun. So many people drift into moulds or jobs that don't fit them, and spend their working lives being miserable. And there's no need. There's a job out there for almost anyone if they look for it. One doesn't always get it right first time.'

'Is this little talk aimed at me?' I asked, after a moment.

'Take it whichever way you like, Cass.' Humphrey struck a match and lit his pipe, the smell of tobacco clouding his small office. 'I know you've been floundering a bit, but it often takes a while to find what it is you want to do in life, and sometimes that also means finding out what you *don't* want to do. You obviously enjoyed a lot of your nursing, but in the end it wasn't what you wanted to do for the rest of your life. Nothing wrong with that. And your experience will stand you in good stead.'

I thought then, and have often thought since, that I would love to have had a father like Humphrey, who in many ways reminded me of dear Dr Mackenzie all those years ago. While my fatherless state wasn't something I dwelt on a great deal, working for Humphrey brought home to me again what it might have been like to have had a father to love and support me; someone strong and wise; someone who would love me unconditionally; someone safe. I knew Humphrey had two daughters, and just for a moment, I envied them.

Over the next six months, I sold several more paintings, and as my confidence developed, so did my ability. I took to going out on my day off, taking my paints and easel and a packet of sandwiches, and spending the day painting some of the marvellous scenery of the surrounding countryside. New Dog often accompanied me, and was happy to explore the hedges and ditches or simply lie in the sun while I painted. Often walkers would come and look over my shoulder and comment on my work, and while it puzzled me that I was as it were fair game, and not apparently entitled to any privacy, I didn't mind. Their remarks on the whole were kind, and I gained at least one new customer.

Mum continued to be supportive, but was also bewildered by my solitary pursuit. Unable herself to manage more than an hour or so on her own without seeking company or reaching for the telephone, she couldn't understand that I was happy to spend whole days by myself.

'You must get so lonely, Cass,' she said, on more than one occasion. 'It doesn't seem natural.'

'It's perfectly natural to me,' I said. 'I enjoy my own company.'

'And still no boyfriend,' she continued (this was a recurring theme, and unlikely to go away). 'When I was your age—'

'I know, Mum. I know what you were up to when you

were my age. You've told me often enough. But I'm different.'

'Perhaps you're a slow developer.'

'Mum, I've had one career, and I'm embarking on another.
No one could call that slow.'

'You know what I mean.'

'Men,' I sighed.

'Yes. Men.'

And of course she was right. Most of my friends had
boyfriends and several were now married. Even the uncon-
ventional Myra was currently assessing the beaded boyfriend
as husband material. I knew that by spending much of my
leisure time alone and refusing the rare party invitations that
came my way I was avoiding the issue, but I didn't know
what else to do. The incident with Neil had distressed and
frightened me, and while I knew that my reaction had been
out of all proportion to what had happened, I also knew that
I couldn't face risking a repeat performance.

And so I drifted along reasonably contentedly. My pictures continued to sell steadily, Humphrey gave me more
responsibility at the gallery, and life at home was, if not exciting, then too comfortable for me to wish to seek any change.
Lodgers came and went, Call Me Bill suffered increasingly
with an arthritic hip, and Lucas and Gracie got married.

It took some time for Mum to come round to the idea of
a wedding in the family.

'A wedding? Lucas and Gracie want a *white wedding*?
Whatever for?' she asked me.

'It's traditional, I suppose. It's what people do.'

'It's not what we do.'

'No. Probably not. But you're lucky, Mum. All you have to do is wear a hat and behave nicely. I've got to be a bridesmaid.'

In the event, the wedding went off very well. Gracie looked beautiful (looking beautiful was what Gracie did best), Lucas was dashing in his morning suit, and I wilted in my hideous peach frock. As for Mum, she behaved better than I'd expected, and if her enormous lime-green hat upstaged that of the bride's mother, then, as she pointed out, it certainly wasn't deliberate. The flirting at the reception, on the other hand, almost certainly was deliberate, but if one or two eyebrows were raised, then Gracie's family were going to have to get used to Mum. It was going to take more than a nice, conventional daughter-in-law to change the habits of a lifetime.

After the wedding, Mum seemed downhearted.

'I've lost him, Cass. I've lost Lucas,' she told me sadly.

'Of course you haven't.'

'They say you lose a son. When he gets married.'

'That's nonsense. You'll never lose Lucas. He's just moved on, Mum. That's what people do when they marry.'

But while I tried to reassure her, I felt that Lucas had drifted away from me, too. Some of the closeness we had always shared had gone, and Lucas had lost some of his sparkle and become ever so slightly dull. He and I no longer seemed to be on quite the same wavelength or laugh at the same things, and it was hard not to blame Gracie, who, while pleasant enough, appeared to have little sense of humour. It must have been hard for Gracie, too. Her background was so very different from ours that I'm sure she must have felt the difference between our two families as keenly as we did.

I had been working at the gallery for several years when we received some news which was to affect us all.

'Cass, I've just had a letter. From a solicitor.' Mum seemed agitated, and looked as though she'd been crying. 'And – and I don't know how to tell you this.'

'Quickly,' I suggested, with the now familiar feeling that I was about to be the recipient of bad news.

'It's Uncle Rupert. He's – he's died.'

'Oh.'

'Poor man.' She hesitated. 'He must have died all alone.'

'I'm sorry.' What else could I say? Mum was obviously upset, and I was sorry about that if nothing else. Uncle Rupert had been released from prison some two years ago, but Mum hadn't told me where he was living and I hadn't wanted to know.

'It seems he had quite a lot of money.'

'Did he?' We'd always been led to believe that Uncle Rupert was entirely without funds. Where had it been hiding all these years?

'Yes. And – oh Cass! – he's left it all to you!'

Thirty-seven

'How could he. *How could he!*' After the initial shock, I was overcome by blinding rage.

'But Cass! All that money—'

'To hell with the money! I couldn't give a damn about the money!' I turned on her. 'Mum, can't you see? *Can't you see what he's done?*'

'No. What has he done?' Mum looked bewildered.

'He's escaped, that's what he's done. He's escaped, and he's paid me off, or thinks he has. How dare he! *How dare he!*'

'But Cass, I don't understand.'

'Of course you don't understand. You never really did understand, did you? He was a wicked, evil, dirty old man, and now he's got away with it.'

'How can you say he's got away with it? He spent all that time in prison, and now he's dead. I can't see that he's got away with anything. And he's tried to make it up to you—'

'No! No, he hasn't. He's *bought* me; he's paid me off; cleared his nasty little debt. Good old Uncle Rupert. What a brilliant move. He'll never have to face the music now, will he?'

'But Cass, he's *dead*. How can he face the music when he's dead? And all that time in prison—'

'Yes. All that time in prison, and I'm sure he richly deserved it. But that was nothing to do with me. That happened when he did it to someone else. That was when he was *caught*. How many other times were there when he *wasn't* caught? You tell me that. How many other girls' lives has he cocked up?'

'But Cass, I never knew. I thought – I thought you'd got over all that a long time ago. It was years ago. You never said anything. Why didn't you tell me?'

'What was the point? What on earth would have been the point? You couldn't have done anything about it, could you?'

'I was furious with him at the time. You know I was. And I did throw him out of the house.'

'You threw him out of the house! Well, big deal. You could hardly have kept him here, could you, unless you were prepared to risk his raping me. Lucas too – why not? – while he was about it. Perhaps you would have preferred that. Perhaps you would have been happy to let him stay, if I hadn't made such a fuss.'

'Cass! That's not fair!'

'Isn't it? Think about it, Mum. You left him alone with me, knowing what he was, not even warning me. You risked my safety and you risked – you risked my life!'

'Oh, don't be ridiculous, Cass. Uncle Rupert may have been many things, but he wasn't a murderer.'

'I'm not talking about murder. I'm talking about *my life*. What he did to it. How he's – spoiled it.'

'Now you're being melodramatic. How can Uncle Rupert have spoiled your life? You have a good life. You're successful and I thought – I thought you were happy.'

'But there's something missing, isn't there?' I was beginning to enjoy myself in the way that one does when one's so angry that suddenly it seems as though there are no holds barred. And while I knew I was being cruel, I couldn't seem to stop. 'You're the one who's always bringing it up so you ought to know the answer. What is it that's missing from my life, Mum? Come on. It's hardly a difficult question.'

'Well, you haven't got a boyfriend—'

'Right. I haven't got a boyfriend. And why do you think that is?'

'I've no idea. You always told me you weren't bothered about men, and I assumed you were telling the truth.'

'Of course I'm bothered about men! I'm a normal woman, believe it or not. It's just that I can't face – I can't face the physical thing. And it's all because of Uncle Rupert. It's what he did to me; what he left me with. It's all his fault. And no amount of money can make up for that.' I burst into tears and fled from the room.

In my own bedroom I sat on the bed, sick and shaking. I had stopped weeping, but I was overwhelmed by a feeling which I can only describe as shock. Because until that minute, until that conversation with Mum, right up until the moment those words came out of my mouth I had never really known what was wrong with me.

It wasn't as though Uncle Rupert had been constantly on

my mind. In fact I had hardly given him a thought in years. But now I realized that he must have been lurking there all the time, somewhere in that part of the brain which conveniently files away the distasteful or the plain abhorrent; not so much Uncle Rupert himself, but the feelings of fear and revulsion I had had when he came into my room all those years ago. It was something which had cast a shadow over my life for so long that I must have long since learnt to live with it, never thinking to question it, accepting it – albeit reluctantly – as part of what I was.

Now, it dawned on me for the first time that there was probably nothing wrong with *me* at all; that I could have had a normal adolescence and early adulthood and enjoyed normal healthy relationships. I could have partied my way through my nursing years like all my friends; I could have gone out with boys and fallen in and out of love the way everyone else seemed to (I had had plenty of opportunities), and without all that angst, all that neurosis, I could have had so much more *fun*. As it was, my trust and my innocence had been stolen from me, and something which should have been precious and special had been spoiled long before I'd had a chance to exercise my own choice and judgement. It was all such a terrible waste.

And now here I was, twenty-seven years old and living at home. I hadn't been out with a man in years, and my family and friends had already written me off as, if not yet a spinster, then a likely candidate for a cosy little place on the shelf.

Looking back now, I know I was being unfair; unfair to Mum, certainly, and perhaps even a little unfair to Uncle Rupert. I had always been naturally shy, and I couldn't blame him for that, and maybe I could have sought some kind of help. But in those days, people still tended to accept themselves and their lots as faits accomplis, without question and certainly without having recourse to anyone else. Hitherto, it had never occurred to me that the basis for my problem lay anywhere but within myself.

But now, at last, I had someone else to blame, and I felt literally sick with rage; a rage which was entirely impotent since there was no longer anyone upon whom I could justly vent it. Uncle Rupert was dead; the only possible target for my anger now was poor Mum.

For a week or so we avoided the subject of Uncle Rupert altogether. I was still feeling too upset and Mum was no doubt reluctant to incur another of my outbursts. Eventually, however, we had to face the problem of what to do about my unwelcome inheritance.

'It would be a shame to turn it down, Cass,' Mum said. 'Can't you forget where it came from and just enjoy it?'

'No. No I can't. I want nothing – *nothing* – from Uncle Rupert.'

'You could share it with Lucas,' she said, after a moment. 'He and Gracie are always short of money.'

I thought of Lucas and Gracie, who after much 'trying' (that expression always amuses me; it makes the whole business seem such terribly hard work) were expecting their first child.

'I don't know. It's still Uncle Rupert's money.' I hesitated. I had never had much money, and in spite of myself, I was tempted. 'In any case, where did it all come from?'

'I've no idea. He never talked about money, and since he

was always saying how hard up he was I assumed he hadn't got any.'

'Did he ever pay you anything towards rent and things?' Mum looked uncomfortable.

'Well, he did help sometimes.'

'You mean he didn't give you anything.' How typical of Mum, to house someone like Uncle Rupert, to feed him and look after him, expecting nothing in return. Typical, too, that there wasn't a hint of resentment at the revelation of Uncle Rupert's hidden assets.

'That doesn't matter, Cass. It's all in the past. I was happy to do it until – until he went.'

'What about his funeral?' I asked, with the sinking feeling that we might be expected to put in an appearance at his wake.

'All over. He died a month ago, and I only found out when I got this letter.' She sighed. 'I'm so sorry, Cass. So sorry about – well, about everything. I never realized how badly you still felt about him; how much he'd hurt you. And of course, you were right. I should never have let him live with us. He'd only been in trouble once before, and I really thought he could change. He made me a promise, and I trusted him. I don't blame you for being angry. You have every right. I just – I just never thought.'

Poor Mum. How could I stay angry with her? In some ways so worldly-wise, but in others, such an innocent; of course she'd believed Uncle Rupert when he'd promised to reform. She looked for – and usually found – the best in everybody. In Mum's eyes, even Uncle Rupert was capable of redemption.

'I know,' I said, with sudden inspiration. '*You* have Uncle Rupert's money. You've certainly earned it, and if it's mine, then presumably I can give it to whoever I like.'

'Oh no. I couldn't possibly. It's out of the question.'

'Then – then we'll share it.'

'We?'

'Yes. You, me and Lucas. I won't feel so bad about it if we share it, and heaven knows, we could all do with it.'

In the end, that was what we did. And while for some time afterwards I felt uncomfortable about the source of my inheritance, it was true that the money would be useful. I would be able to buy my own little studio; something I had dreamed of for years. Gracie would have free rein to plan her frilly little nursery, while Lucas would be able to replace his car, which for some time had kept going on a wing and a prayer, and Mum . . .

'Mum? What will you do with your money?' I asked some weeks later, when everything had been arranged.

'I'm going to travel,' Mum said grandly.

'Travel? Travel where?'

'Oh, anywhere. I'll just take off, and see what happens.'

'Is that wise?'

'Of course it's not wise.' She patted my cheek. 'I can't wait. I'm going to have such fun!'

'That's what I was afraid of.'

But Mum was no longer listening.

Thirty-eight

My mother is sleeping again, her hands making tiny flutter-ing movements, and I wonder whether she is dreaming of flying.

'I fly in my dreams, you know, Cass,' she once told me.

'How?'

'Breast stroke. You've no idea how difficult it is to get off the ground. Doing breaststroke.'

'I can imagine.'

'Yes. You have to work at it with your arms, and then when your legs leave the ground, you have to kick like mad.'

'Goodness. It sounds exhausting.'

'Oh, it is. But so exciting, too, Cass. Except that no one seems to notice in dreams. Sometimes I call down to them "Look at me!", but no one ever does. They just get on with what they're doing, as though people fly all the time. It's so disappointing.'

'It must be.'

'Much more fun than aeroplanes. You don't really feel as though you're flying, in an aeroplane.'

'I understand what you mean.'

But Mum's disdain for aeroplanes was forgotten as she anticipated setting off on her travels, and she could hardly contain her excitement.

'Imagine, Cass! Just flying off like that. I can't wait!'

'But won't you be lonely, going off on your own?'

'Oh, I'll find people. I always find someone to talk to.'

'And where, Mum? Where are you going to fly to?'

'I don't care. Anywhere. Somewhere sunny, with sea. An island, perhaps.' She was ironing her holiday clothes – an eclectic selection of cotton skirts and blouses, some of them dating back to our early childhood – between skippy little Chopin waltzes.

'Most people,' I said, 'choose their destination before planning their wardrobe. Shouldn't you at least pick a country to start from? You don't have to stay there if you don't like it.'

'You're right. Let's choose a place. Help me, Cass.'

So we got out the atlas (which, needless to say, was wildly out of date, but as Mum pointed out, sun and sea and islands don't move around even if empires do), and after some discussion, settled on the Greek islands.

'Little white houses and blue sea,' said Mum, who had once received a postcard from Crete. 'Perfect.'

'And you can move from one to another,' I said. 'They look quite close to each other, and there are bound to be boats sailing between them.'

'Yes. And there's Athens, with all those statues and pillars and things. Do you think they speak English?'

'Bound to,' I assured her.

'I'll take a phrase book, in case.'

'Good idea.'

'And I can speak a little French.'

'That might be useful,' I said, although even my imagination had trouble envisaging my mother trying to make her way round Greece in schoolgirl French.

A fortnight later, Lucas and I took Mum to the airport.

'I hope she'll be OK,' Lucas said, when we'd waved her off. 'I hope she doesn't do anything silly.'

'Of course she'll do something silly. This is our mother we're talking about. But she'll find people to bale her out – she always does – and if the worst comes to the worst, I can always fly out and rescue her.' I lowered myself into Lucas's new and very posh car. 'But it's going to be very strange without her.'

This was certainly true, for without Mum, the whole household wilted. It was like the occasions when she had one of her famous depressions; the spirit of the house seemed to die. Everyone went about their business as usual, but – to use Mum's favourite word – the *fun* seemed to have gone out of everything. Greta went round looking tragic, the ready tears even nearer the surface than usual; Call Me Bill grumbled because he had to iron his own shirts (Greta refused); and the Lodger, a peevish little man with no sense of humour, complained that there didn't seem to be anyone in charge (there wasn't). Richard popped in from time to time 'to cheer us up' with recitals on his ukulele (these proved counterproductive);

and as for New Dog (not so new now, with arthritis and an increasingly unreliable temper), he took it upon himself to guard Mum's bedroom, lying in the doorway and growling at anyone who came near him. He allowed me to step over him to change the sheets and give the room an airing, but he bit Greta's ankle when she tried to gain access.

'New Dog iss nasty cross animal,' she complained, when I escorted her to the doctor for a tetanus injection. 'Time he put down, I think.'

'I wouldn't if I were you,' I told her. 'Mum would never forgive you.'

In any case, I was fond of New Dog, and I was also sorry for him. Mum was his friend and his rescuer, his protector and his companion. As far as he was concerned, she had always been there, and he was quite naturally upset and confused by her sudden disappearance.

Over the weeks, we received a series of postcards from various parts of Greece. Some of these were of the cheery wish-you-were-here variety (although I very much doubt that she wished any of us were there; we would only have spoiled her fun); others were wistful and occasionally even homesick. But on the whole she appeared to be enjoying herself. She had, she told us, met 'lots of interesting people', she knew several phrases of Greek, and was now adept at Greek dancing.

'What is she doing?' Lucas asked, when he called in to hear news of her progress. 'There's only so much time you can spend doing holiday things. What is she actually *doing* out there? Does she plan to stay there forever, or what?'

'I've no idea. I hope not.' New Dog wasn't the only one who was missing Mum.

'Well, I think she's being very irresponsible.'

'Oh Lucas, Mum's always been irresponsible. In any case, doesn't she deserve a break? She's never really had a holiday before, and we're managing OK without her. And it's hardly affecting you. You don't even live here any more.'

'That's not the point. Besides, the baby's due in six weeks. Doesn't she care about her new grandchild?'

I imagined that few things were further from Mum's mind than Gracie's baby, but I decided not to say anything. Lucas wouldn't understand.

Meanwhile, I had been spending my own inheritance. I had found a small attic bedsit with lots of light and stunning views. It was exactly what I'd had in mind as a studio, and while it was hardly big enough to live in all the time, there was a gas ring, a shared bathroom, and room for a narrow bed. I painted it white, put up blinds rather than curtains and furnished it from a second-hand shop in the village. The effect was clean and simple and airy, and best of all, it was mine. Greta approved of it, Call Me Bill brought me a bottle of wine to celebrate, and Gracie disliked it on sight. I knew I'd done the right thing.

Mum returned after an absence of eight weeks, unannounced and unexpected, brown and cheerful and full of news, the most interesting of which was that she had blown all her money.

'What, all of it?' I asked. 'You've spent *all* your money?'

'Every penny.' Mum opened a bottle of ouzo which she'd brought home with her, and poured everyone a glass, while

New Dog bounced and wagged at her feet in a frenzy of delighted welcome.

'But Mum, that was your chance to save something for – well, for—'

'Exactly. For what? No, Cass. I wanted to enjoy it, and I have. I never expected it or asked for it, I've had a wonderful time, and now it's gone. I'd probably have wasted it anyway.' She grinned. 'You know I've never been any good with money.'

'I don't know what Lucas will say.'

'Then we shan't tell him.' Mum knocked back her ouzo. Obviously she'd been practising. Personally, I thought it was revolting.

'At least you're back in time for the baby.'

'Oh yes. Gracie's baby. How is she?'

'The same.'

'Iss fat,' said Greta helpfully.

'Is she still making a fuss?' Gracie had been making very heavy weather of what had been on the whole a pretty uneventful pregnancy, and Mum had little sympathy with her.

'Oh yes. You'd think that no one had ever had a baby before.'

'Poor Lucas.' Mum grimaced. 'And you, Cass. How've you been?'

'I've bought this gorgeous studio! You've got to come and see it.'

The next day, Mum visited my little attic.

'A garret. A real garret. Oh, Cass! How romantic!'

'Yes. Isn't it?'

'You're not leaving home, are you?' Mum said, eyeing the bed.

'Not exactly. But I can sleep here if I need to; if I want to work late. It'll be a bolt-hole if I need one.'

'That's all right, then.' Mum looked relieved. 'I'd hate you to leave home, Cass.'

'I know you would. But Mum, I'll have to go one day. I can't live at home forever.'

'Why not?'

'Because – because people just don't. I shall be twenty-nine next year. *Twenty-nine*. It's time I was a bit more independent.'

'I don't see why.'

'Mum, I'm an adult, with my own friends, my own career. With my pay from the gallery and the sales of my paintings, I may not be rich but I make enough money to live on my own. I don't know anyone else of my age who lives with their mother.'

'Are you ashamed of me? Is that it?'

'Don't be ridiculous, Mum. It's got nothing to do with being ashamed. It's to do with – with how I feel about myself.'

'And about me?'

'Well, yes. Perhaps. I think you and I maybe depend on each other more than we ought to. I love you, Mum. You know I do. You're my best friend. But we need to – separate a bit.'

'We separated when you were nursing. You were miles away then.'

'Yes. But I did keep coming home, didn't I?'

'To sort me out.' Mum's voice was bleak.

'Well, yes. Sometimes. But also to sort myself out.'

'So what are you going to do?' Mum asked, after a pause.

'Nothing at the moment. I've got my studio, and that's a start. And I'll just see what happens.'

But of course nothing would happen unless I made it happen, and I could see myself living at home forever unless I took some kind of initiative. Although life on the whole was good, I was feeling increasingly trapped by my situation. On the one hand, there was Mum, who undoubtedly did need me. Even if she felt free to take off to Greece for a couple of months, she did so in the knowledge that I would still be there when she got back, to support her as I had always done. But there was also that other problem; the problem I had carried with me all my adult life and which I felt powerless to address.

Given my circumstances, I suppose it was inevitable that when a man finally did make an appearance, he was to be much older than I was.

And, perhaps also inevitably, married.

Thirty-nine

I have often wondered about that phenomenon by which two people can know each other for some time, and then, quite suddenly, be struck by the same powerful spark of mutual attraction. But so it was with Edward and me.

My art classes had ceased a while ago, but we still saw each other from time to time when he came into the gallery with his paintings. We always passed the time of day, and he was generous with his encouragement when it came to my own work, but it certainly couldn't be said that we knew each other well; we were acquaintances rather than friends.

He was a softly spoken, gentle man, attractive rather than good-looking, with the stooping demeanour so often adopted by the very tall. Later on, I found it hard to imagine that I had failed to notice anything special about him, although I'd certainly admired and even envied his ability. He favoured oils rather than watercolours, and his stormy skies and blazing sunsets always reminded me of the seascapes of Turner. While my own style was very different, I would have given a great deal to be able to produce paintings as good as Edward's.

It was Humphrey who observed what was happening almost before I was aware of it myself.

'I think Edward is becoming rather attached to you,' he remarked, assembling matches and tobacco and beginning the complicated ritual of the pipe-smoker.

'And I like him.' We were having a leisurely cup of coffee in the course of an unusually quiet morning.

Humphrey eyed me thoughtfully.

'You know what I mean.'

I lowered my eyes, blushing.

'I thought so.' Humphrey took a puff of his pipe, and leant back in his chair. 'Be careful, Cass. That's all. Just be careful.'

'What do you mean?'

'I think you know what I mean.'

'Do I?'

'Yes, Cass. You do.' He looked at me over his half glasses. 'I'm very fond of you. I always have been. And I worry about you.'

'There's nothing to worry about. I'm fine.' My voice sounded bright and brittle, and even as I spoke, I knew it would take a lot more than I could manage to pull the wool over Humphrey's eyes.

'If you say so. But you're a vulnerable young woman, and Edward's – well, let's just say that there are complications in his life. He's also a lot older than you. I don't want you to do something you'll regret. Either of you.'

'I haven't done anything.'

'Yet.'

'I – we – haven't done anything,' I repeated. 'And there's no reason why we should.'

'If you say so.'

'I do say so.'

'That's all right, then.'

'Yes.'

'But you can always talk to me, you know.'

'Yes. I do know. Thank you.'

Afterwards, I thought about what Humphrey had said, and wondered exactly what it was that he had observed. Edward and I had spoken to each other no more than usual, and had spent no time at all on our own together. And if I had recently become acutely aware of his physical presence, of his smile and the tone of his voice when he spoke to me, then I found it hard to believe that anyone else could have noticed. Whatever it was that had developed between us was certainly there, but up until now it was as though it had been lying in wait, unacknowledged, biding its time until one of us should take notice and do something about it.

It wasn't until a week later that Edward asked me out.

'Would you care to come for a cup of tea and a bun before you go home? There's – a picture I'd like to discuss with you.'

'Yes. Thank you. I'd love to.'

It had been as simple as that. And while I knew that this had nothing to do with a picture and everything to do with Edward and me, it seemed the most natural thing in the world that we should get together like this.

'Thank you for coming,' Edward said, over tea and iced buns in the tea shop next door. 'I thought you might say no.'

'Why would I say no?'

'Because – because there's an attraction between us, and I thought you might think it unwise, I suppose.'

'There's nothing unwise about tea and buns,' I said, licking icing sugar off my fingers.

'You know what I mean, Cass.'

'Yes. I suppose I do.' After all, why else would we have chosen a corner table when the best tables – the ones in the window – were free?

'You probably don't know, but I'm married,' Edward said, after a long pause.

'I thought you might be, but I wasn't sure.'

'So I shouldn't be doing this at all.'

'Probably not. But then I suppose neither should I.'

'Things are – complicated.' Edward broke his bun into tiny pieces, and arranged them neatly round the edge of his plate. 'I do care very much for my wife.'

'Yes.'

'And I will never tell you she doesn't understand me.'

'Good.' I had never accepted that so many wives didn't understand their husbands. It had always seemed to me more likely that they understood them only too well.

'In fact, I shan't talk about her at all. Except to say that, in a way, we are already separated.'

'In a way?'

'I can't talk about it at the moment. Not yet. But can you just accept that anything – anything we do, you and I, can't hurt her. That I would never do anything which could cause her pain.'

'But surely—'

'Trust me on this, Cass. Please.' He picked up a fragment of his bun and placed it carefully in the middle of his plate. 'My wife is – unwell, and in a way, she still needs me. I will always be there for her. She hasn't anyone else. We have no children.' He looked up at me, and there was a deep sadness in his face. 'But we still need to be – discreet, you and I. There are people – family, friends – who might talk. Who might be upset.' He pushed his plate away. 'I don't want this to be spoiled by other people's gossip. You deserve better than that. I think even I deserve better than that.'

Looking back, it seems extraordinary that Edward and I could have been so frank and taken so much for granted at this early stage in our relationship. But that was one of the things I liked about him. There was no game-playing, no subterfuge, no pretending things were other than they were. He was very fond of me, he wanted a relationship, but he was married; and despite his mention of some kind of separation between him and his wife, the implication was that he and I could probably never be together. He had laid his cards on the table, and it was up to me to decide what I should do about it.

And yet in a way there was no decision to make. It was as though a path had been mapped out for us, and we were compelled to follow it. Right from the beginning, we both accepted it almost without question, together with the complications and problems that it might entail. There was no rosy mist obscuring the future; no feeling of live now, pay later; none of the blind, careless passion which I had been led to expect if ever I were to find love. I believe that we both knew that our relationship would not come without a cost, and that right from the start, we were prepared to pay it.

But of course, although it may not have felt like it at the time, I did have a choice, and I have often wondered how my life would have turned out if I had chosen a different course. Would I have met someone else? Would I ever have found the happiness and fulfilment that was to come? And perhaps above all, was I justified in committing an offence against a woman I had never met and who had certainly done me no harm, even if that woman were to be unaffected by it, as Edward had implied? I shall never know. We make decisions, and we live with the consequences. All I know is that I have never had any regrets.

On our second meeting, Edward drove me out into the country in his battered Morris Minor. It was a beautiful summer's evening, and we walked along the river bank and stopped at a pub for a drink. Edward didn't take my hand, and the only contact we had was when I nearly slipped in some mud, and he placed a hand on my arm to steady me.

We sat outside with our drinks, watching the ducks and swans drifting by among the reeds, and the reflections of the pale green boughs of willow arching into the water. I stole glances at Edward's big capable hands cradling his beer glass, his profile turned towards the river, the crinkle of tanned skin around his blue eyes, the slightly too long hair lapping his collar.

'We know very little about each other, Cass.' He turned and smiled at me, and for a moment it was as though that smile held everything I'd ever wanted.

I smiled back at him.

'What do you want to know?'

'Anything. Everything.' He laughed. 'Where do we start?'

'I don't know. I've never – done it like this before.'

'Neither have I.' He took a draught of his beer and wiped his mouth on his handkerchief. 'Maybe we'll just have to make up the rules as we go along.'

'So long as that's all we make up,' I said.

'So long as that's all we make up,' he agreed, and at last he reached for my hand. 'You have beautiful hands,' he said, turning mine over in his and examining the palm, then replacing it gently on the table in front of me like some small, precious object. 'Artist's hands.'

'And nurse's hands.' My skin still tingled where his hand had touched mine, and I was almost afraid to move my hand, as though I might break the spell created by that first moment of physical contact.

'Really? You're a nurse as well?'

So I told him all about my failed academic career, my years as a nurse and my subsequent breakdown. I told him about Mum and Lucas, about our eccentric domestic set-up and about the life and death of Octavia. I talked until the sun began to set behind the hills and the midges hovered in clouds over the water, and the tiny forms of bats streaked to and fro across the darkening skyline. And all the time, Edward listened. It was years since anyone had really listened to me like that, and it was almost like a drug. Only with difficulty did I finally manage to stop.

'Goodness. I don't usually talk like that,' I said. 'I'm sorry.'

'Don't be. I'm interested.' Edward smiled. 'Poor Cass. You haven't had it easy, have you?'

'Haven't I?' I'd never thought of my life as so very different from other people's, and certainly no worse.

'Well, you seem to have been through the mill. One way and another.'

'Maybe.' I fingered the stem of my glass. 'But I've been lucky, too. I have a wonderful family and some good friends, and I enjoy my job. Many people would envy me.' I drank the last of my wine. 'But what about you? Tell me about you.'

'Me.' Edward paused, gazing into his empty glass as though he might find in it the answer to my question. 'It should be easy, shouldn't it, but I've always felt happier listening than talking, especially when it comes to talking about myself.' He pushed the glass away and put his elbows on the table, resting his chin in his hands. 'I guess I'm a pretty ordinary sort of bloke; a middle-of-the-road artist, although I love what I do; not particularly well off, but then I've never minded much about money; with a banger of a car, a dilapidated cottage and a cat. No kids, though. I would have liked children.' He seemed about to say something else, then hesitated.

'Go on,' I said.

'And – and too old for someone as young as you.'

'Can I ask—?'

'Forty-five. Well, forty-five next week. And you are, what, twenty-five?'

'Twenty-eight.'

'That's still pretty young.'

'Not too young, though.'

'Don't you think so?'

'No. It's such a cliché, but really age isn't that important.'

300

Edward gazed out once more towards the river.

'You know, I can't believe this is happening. I've never done anything like this before. I never expected it, and I certainly wasn't looking for it.'

'No.'

'But you. It's different for you. You must have been looking for – hoping for someone to come into your life, Cass.'

'Not really.'

'Why ever not? You're young and beautiful. You must have had lots of boyfriends in the past. You must sometimes think about marriage and children. Don't all girls?'

'Perhaps,' I admitted. 'But then you see, my life's a bit – well, complicated, too.'

'Do you want to tell me about it?'

'Not now. Not tonight. It's – well, it's too soon.'

Edward nodded.

'There are no-go areas in my life, as you know, and you're entitled to yours. Never think you have to tell me everything, Cass. Just so long as we're honest with each other. I think that's all that matters.'

But of course I knew that if we were to have a relationship – an affair, even (how I hate that word, along with all its sordid connotations) – sooner or later Edward would have to know the secret which had darkened my life for so long, and I had no idea how I was going to go about telling him.

But just for the moment, just for the duration of that magic summer evening, with the last of the daylight staining the sky crimson and Edward once again reaching across the table for my hand, I would allow myself to be happy.

Forty

Our courtship – if an adulterous affair can be said to have such a thing – was slow and measured and tender. We behaved as though we had all the time in the world, pacing ourselves, basking in our developing love, and for the time being, asking little more than simply to be in each other's company.

Of course affairs, by their very nature, have their problems, the greatest of these being when and where to meet. I have never found subterfuge easy, and have always thought of myself as being a pretty straightforward and honest person, so it was hard having to take unnecessary bus rides so that Edward could pick me up in the next village, or smuggle him up to my studio when no one else was around (I had talkative neighbours).

And then there was Mum.

'What are you up to these days, Cass?' she asked me, after our third meeting. 'There's something you're not telling me.'

I hesitated. I had never lied to Mum, and yet I didn't want to tell anyone about Edward. Not yet, anyway. It was too soon, and I was still finding my way and getting used to the idea of him myself. Having to cope with Mum getting used to him as well was more than I could deal with, especially as she was bound to want to know every detail of our relationship. I would tell her one day, I decided, but not yet.

'I'm not up to anything,' I told her, 'or at least, nothing you need to know about at the moment.'

'Ah!' Mum's tone was triumphant, her radar as accurate as ever. 'A man! I knew it. How exciting! Tell me all about him. Where did you meet him? What does he—'

'Mum, please. Just don't ask. Not yet. I need – time. If you let the subject drop, I promise I'll tell you everything when I'm ready. If there's anything to tell,' I added, remembering that even the best affairs tend to have a sell-by date.

'If you insist.' Mum looked disappointed. Her own love life had recently run into problems (in the form of an avenging ex-wife), Greta was away, and Lucas and Gracie were preoccupied with their new baby daughter (Mum's take on grandmotherhood was ambivalent). She had evidently been hoping for a diversion in the form of my new romance, and now this was not to be. 'It's so boring of you, Cass,' she sighed. 'It's ages since you had a man, and now you won't even tell me who he is.'

'No, I won't. But I shan't tell anyone else, either' – Mum could be jealous where my confidences were concerned – 'and if anything exciting happens, you'll be the first to know.'

And she had to be content with that.

Only two things clouded my happiness. The first, obviously, was the fact that Edward was married. I had never considered myself to be the kind of person to have an affair with someone else's husband, and while Edward had made it clear that our relationship wouldn't interfere with his marriage, I still felt uncomfortable with the idea that somewhere out there was a woman whose happiness or stability might be compromised for the sake of my own.

And then there was the knowledge that sooner or later Edward was going to want more than just holding hands or a hug, and I had no idea how I was going to deal with this eventuality. I was twenty-eight years old, and had never even been kissed properly; how would he react when he found out? And what was I going to do? I gave much thought to the idea of sex with Edward, and a part of me longed for that closeness, that intimacy, that oneness which I had yet to experience with another human being. I found him physically very attractive; his smile and the touch of his hand had an effect I'd never experienced before; but my over-riding fear was greater than my desire, and the second he showed signs of taking things any further, something within me seemed to freeze.

For a while, Edward showed no sign that he was aware of any problem, and we had been seeing each other for some weeks when he finally brought the subject up.

'I think it's time we talked about this – this difficulty of yours, Cass.' We were lying companionably on the bed in my studio, sharing a bottle of wine.

'Yes.'

I could have asked what he meant; I could have prevaricated; there were lots of things I could have done to give myself more time. But Edward had been patient, and I owed him some kind of explanation.

'You know what I'm talking about, don't you?' He stroked my hair off my face and smiled down at me.

'Yes. Yes, I do.'

'But it's hard to talk about?'

'Very hard.' I brushed away a tear. 'I – I don't know where to start. And it's all so silly. You'll think me such a fool.'

'I won't. If something has caused you this much distress, how can you imagine I would ever think you a fool?'

'I know, I know. I'm not being fair.' I put down my glass and sat up on the bed, drawing my knees up to my chin, gazing out of the window at a sky stippled with tiny clouds. 'I suppose just finding the words is difficult. I've never told anyone before. Mum knows about it, but we don't talk about it any more. I suppose she feels guilty, and in any case, there's nothing she can do.'

'Perhaps there's something I can do.'

I laughed. 'That's the problem.'

'I thought it might be.' Edward sat up and pulled me to him. 'Try me, Cass. Just try me. What have you got to lose?'

'You,' I whispered into his chest.

'I don't think you'll lose me, however hard you try.'

'OK. I'll tell you. But do you mind if I don't look at you while I'm doing so? I think I'd find it easier.'

'You do what's best for you.'

I climbed off the bed and curled up in a small armchair facing the window, with my back to Edward. I fixed my gaze on the clouds, the blue of the sky, the vapour trail of a distant aircraft, and I began to speak.

'I was fourteen,' I said, and paused. I had never had to

put my experience into words before, and even finding those words was difficult.

'Go on,' Edward said. 'Just tell it as it happened. Try to forget I'm here.'

'We had this – cousin of Mum's living with us.' I swallowed. A chattering flock of starlings flew past the window and somewhere a door slammed. I heard the faint sound of Edward shifting his position behind me, and the louder sound of my own heart thumping in my chest. 'We called him Uncle Rupert. I never liked him very much.'

As I talked, the words seemed to flow more freely, as though they were gradually becoming disentangled from that part of my brain where they had been stored for all those years, and I found myself reliving the events of that dreadful afternoon. I did what Edward had suggested and imagined I was on my own, telling my story as though I were telling it to myself, omitting nothing, wondering at how every detail was still imprinted on my mind. Smells and sights and sounds which had remained hidden for years emerged as though I had experienced them only yesterday, and when I finally finished my story, I found that I was sobbing.

For a moment, time seemed to stand still, and I wondered what Edward was thinking. Would he think I was making a fuss about nothing? Or worse, would he think I was exaggerating or even inventing my story as some kind of excuse? I dared not turn round and look at him for fear of what I might read in his expression.

Then I heard the bed creak as Edward stood up and I felt the wool of his sweater against my cheek as he folded me into his arms.

'Oh, Cass.' His voice was muffled by my hair. 'You poor darling.' He fished a handkerchief out of his pocket and wiped my streaming eyes. 'I'm so so sorry. I don't know what to say.'

I shook my head, taking the handkerchief from him and blowing my nose.

'You don't have to say anything. What's there to say? It happened, it was a long time ago, and I should have got over it. In fact, until he died, I thought I had.' I looked round my bright little room; at the books and pictures, the easel set up in the corner, the simple furniture. 'He – he gave me all this. I should be grateful. But something stops me. Something was left behind, and I can't get rid of it. Something was – *spoiled*.'

'Cass, you do know I love you, don't you?' Edward said, after a moment.

'Yes. Yes, I do.' He'd never actually said it before, but I suppose I'd known from the beginning that he loved me.

'Well, in that case, you have to trust me. Somehow – *somehow* – we'll sort this thing out together.'

'Do you think we can?'

'Well, I don't know for sure. Of course I don't. But I do believe that if you love me half as much as I love you, we'll get through this somehow.'

'How?' I asked fearfully.

'We'll take things very very slowly,' Edward said, kissing the top of my head. 'And you must trust me.'

'I do. Of course I trust you.'

'That's a start.' He took my hand and helped me to my

feet. 'But let's leave it for now. I think you've had quite enough emotion for one day. Now, what did we do with that bottle of wine?'

Forty-one

Very gradually, with infinite patience and great tenderness, Edward began to lead me along the path to physical love. He refused to call it sex. Sex, he said, was for kids; kids who knew no better, who referred to 'having sex' as though they were having a cigarette or a drink and who looked upon it as just another form of recreation, like going out for a meal or to the cinema. Sex between loving adults was something quite different; something special. Edward had no time for the loveless couplings of the bike shed or the parked car, and while he admitted that he hadn't always been this idealistic – and confessed that few experiences were more disconcerting than waking up to find the wrong head on the pillow beside you – I gathered that for him such adventures had happened many years ago in his youth, and while not necessarily regretted, were certainly never to be repeated.

I thought of Mum, whose sexual activities, I knew for a fact, had taken place in all manner of venues, frequently with little or no love, and rarely with any regret. What would Edward have to say if he knew about her adventurous modus vivendi? And what would he think of her if they were ever to meet? In the end, I decided that it didn't much matter. What mattered was that Mum had found her way, and I was finding mine. I would never – could never – behave as Mum did, but neither could I judge her.

'Of course, in a way, our lovemaking has already started,' Edward told me some days later, as we walked hand-in-hand along our favourite river bank. 'It's about talking and listening as well as the physical part, and you're already so good at that, Cass. The rest will come naturally, I'm sure.' He turned to face me, taking both my hands in his. 'I will never do anything you don't want me to; anything to frighten or alarm you. All you have to do is trust me.'

A few days later, Edward kissed me. At first my body froze, and my ready response with it, but as he caressed my neck and shoulders and his lips gently traced my throat and cheek and forehead, I found myself relaxing in his arms. When the kiss finally came, I was more than ready for it, and I melted into it as though it was something I had been waiting for all my life.

'There. That wasn't so bad, was it?' he said.

I shook my head, too happy and relieved to say anything. Edward laughed at my expression.

'In that case, perhaps we ought to do it again.'

And this time I didn't hesitate.

After that first kiss, Edward encouraged me to lead while he followed, taking his cues from me, picking up on the small shy hints I gave as to what I wanted him to do. Sometimes, he almost seemed to be making me wait, as though he wanted to be absolutely sure that he had read my signals correctly, and when one hot night in August we finally did make love, I felt that if I had had to wait another second, I would have been unable to bear it.

'We did it! We did it!' I exulted, wrapping a sheet round my naked body and dancing round the room.

'Very romantic, I'm sure,' Edward remarked wryly, observing me from the bed.

'But can't you see what this means?' I sank down beside him. 'I'm OK. I'm normal. Everything's going to be all right.'

'I told you so.'

'Mr Smug!'

'Mr Smug seems to have made you pretty happy, and that can't be bad.'

'Oh, Edward! I still can't believe it. There's nothing – *nothing* – wrong with me. I'm a proper, whole woman.'

'I never doubted it for a minute.'

'Don't tease.' I lay back on the pillows. 'It's something people take for granted, isn't it? Like eating or breathing. I've looked at my body so many times and thought, if I can't use it – use it properly –give it to someone I love – then what's it all *for*?'

'Well, now you know.' Edward propped himself on his elbow and smiled down at me. 'And may I say, for a beginner, you were pretty amazing.'

'Do you think we ought to do it again? Just to make sure?'

'I think that's an excellent idea. We've got a lot of time to make up.'

I'd like to be able to say that from that moment I never looked back, and while in a way that's true, I still had disconcerting flashbacks and moments of something akin to panic. And I still couldn't look at Edward's body.

'I shouldn't worry too much about that,' he told me. 'It's not what it was.'

'Maybe not, but it's yours, and I ought to be able to accept it – all of it – because it's all of you.'

'Undress me, then.'

'*What?*'

'Undress me. Take my clothes off. You can do it in any order you like, stop if you want to, put things back on again if you want to. Imagine I'm a – doll.'

We were in my studio again, and Edward was sketching me. I was half-turned towards him, but couldn't see his expression.'

'Do you mean that?'

'Yes. Why not? I've undressed you often enough. I know the male body isn't as beautiful as the female. Well, not to me, anyway. And mine certainly isn't beautiful. But if it helps you to feel that you're in control, then maybe it won't be quite so alarming.'

'It's certainly an interesting idea.'

'You've moved your head!'

'Of course I've moved my head! It's not every day I get an offer like this.'

'Turn your face back a little to the left, chin down a bit – yes, that's fine.' Edward continued to draw, the strokes of his pencil making soft sweeping sounds across the paper. 'Well? What do you think?' he asked, after a few minutes had passed.

'It sounds a bit – artificial.'

'Can you think of anything better?'

'Not really.'

'Well, then.' He stood up to examine his drawing, then sat down and took up his pencil again.

'Won't you mind?'

'Mind? Why should I?'

'I don't know.' I shrugged. Maybe it was I who minded; my own reaction, rather than Edward's, that I feared.

So that evening, I undressed Edward, while he lay on the bed reading aloud from the instruction manual for my new steam iron.

'This is crazy,' I said, unbuttoning his shirt.

'"Ensure that the plug is correctly fitted." Carry on Cass.'

'But—'

'No buts. If I think about what you're doing, I cannot answer for the way my wicked body will react, and then the whole point of this operation will be wasted. This very boring leaflet is an excellent distraction. Now, where was I? Ah, yes. "Always use distilled water when filling your iron." Well, fancy that. "Turn iron to correct setting . . ."'

'I love your hairy chest.'

'Good. "Stand iron on its end when finished . . ."'

'I can't get your shoes off.'

'Try undoing them first. "Before seeking help, please consult the following checklist for problems. Is your iron switched on?" They must think people are frightfully stupid. "Check the fuse—"'

'Gosh. Purple socks! I never thought you were the kind of person to wear purple socks.'

'They were a present. Cass, will you please, please get a

move on. I can't manage to keep up my boredom levels if you don't. And will you please stop talking. How can I concentrate on this if you're prattling away all the time? "For address of your nearest stockist please phone . . ."'

It took a long time, but eventually I managed to remove all Edward's clothes. And of course, he was right. There was nothing to be afraid of. Edward's body, unlike Uncle Rupert's, was all of a piece; I hadn't been suddenly presented with one disembodied (and uninvited) part of it; he had already given me all of it, together with all of himself. His was the body of the man I loved, and yes, it was beautiful. How could I ever have thought it might be otherwise?

'I'd like to draw you,' I said, standing back and admiring him. 'If you just stay like that—'

'Don't you dare!' Edward leapt to his feet and pulled me back onto the bed. 'And now, if it's all right with you, I think I deserve some kind of reward.'

Forty-two

It's some hours now since my mother opened her eyes or gave any indication that she knows what's going on, and I'm reluctant to disturb her. The nurses have washed her and brushed her hair, but she looks desperately thin and frail, and has aged ten years in as many days. She would hate to know that she has been reduced to this dry fragile shell.

'Don't let just anyone see me when I'm dead,' she told me, only last week. 'I shan't be looking my best, when I'm dead. I don't mind you, Cass. And Lucas, if he wants. But not Greta. She'll only be too upset. And not Gracie. I don't want Gracie to see me. Being dead is – well, it's private, isn't it?'

I agreed that death was certainly private, and promised that all unwanted visitors would be kept away. She had seen Lucas's two daughters, who had visited her a few days ago, and had made it clear that she had said her goodbyes to them. And Mum has never seen eye to eye with Gracie. But there is still that one person; the person she so desperately wants to see. Every time someone opens the door, I hope it will be her, but despite several messages (missed trains, a lost mobile *phone), she still hasn't arrived. I know she will never forgive herself if she's too late, but the matter is out of my hands. All I can do is hope.*

Mum always minded about her appearance. She wasn't vain in the conventional sense, and spent little money on clothes or make-up, but she was proud of her luxuriant hair, her slender legs and enviable figure, and as she grew older, she mourned their inevitable deterioration.

'It's so unfair, being a woman,' she once said to me. 'It's as though nature is saying you don't need to look good any more, so everything starts to go downhill. It's different for men. Men seem to grow better-looking as they grow older.' She sighed. 'Of course, it's all about babies.'

'What on earth do you mean?' I asked her.

'Droopy boobs, saggy tum, grey hair, wrinkles. If you can't make babies, then you don't need to attract someone to make babies with any more, do you?'

'Oh, Mum, don't be ridiculous. You still look fabulous, you know you do. Besides, you don't want to make any more babies, do you?'

'No,' she admitted. 'But I'd still like to have the choice.'

Mum had looked on the menopause as an unwelcome intruder into her life, and she grieved for the passing of her fertility. It must have seemed especially poignant that it had come at a time when I was finally discovering myself as a sexually functioning woman, and while she rejoiced for me, it brought it home to her that she wasn't getting any younger. Of course, she still had relationships, and it appeared to me that she was as attractive to men as she ever was, but some of her gay confidence was lost, and recently there had been some interesting, not to say colourful, additions to the bottles and jars on her dressing-table.

I had told Mum just enough about Edward and our relationship to keep her happy, without disclosing those aspects I wanted to keep to myself. I have always been a private person, and while I didn't mind Mum telling me about her love life, I didn't always want to exchange her confidences for those of my own.

'When are we going to meet him?' was a question she asked increasingly often, and one which was becoming more and more difficult to deflect. The fact that he was married didn't work at all, since Mum had scant regard for marriage (although she had rarely had affairs with married men herself). I tried telling her that Edward felt awkward about his married state, but that didn't work either.

'What's to feel awkward about?' Mum asked. 'We're not here to judge him. Besides, didn't you say he was separated?'

I recalled Edward saying all those weeks ago that 'in a way' he and his wife were already separated, and while I had been reassured by his words, they inevitably raised more questions than they answered. But while I did ask him several times if he couldn't explain what he meant, he always refused.

'Don't you trust me?' I asked him once. 'Is that it?'

'Of course I trust you.'

'Then please tell me, Edward. Please. I feel as though I'm being – excluded from an important part of your life. I've told you all about me. Things I've never told anyone.'

'But this isn't just about me, is it? Someone else is

involved. You'll understand one day, Cass, I promise. I have – I have my reasons for keeping it to myself for the time being, but I will tell you.'

'Is she abroad? Is that it?'

'No. I only wish she was – could go abroad.'

'A long way away, then?' I persisted.

'No, not a long way away. Not a long way away at all.' He smiled, but his eyes were full of such enormous sadness that I couldn't bring myself to question him further. If Edward had promised me he would tell me what I wanted to know, then he would keep his promise. Meanwhile, I would just have to wait. As for Mum, she would have to wait, too. And while it would have been wonderful to celebrate our love publicly, to be seen out and about together without subterfuge and to be able to acknowledge openly our coupled state, secrecy seemed a small price to pay for my new-found happiness.

And so I remained in ignorance until the day when, quite by chance, I saw Edward's wife.

It was my half-day, and I had gone into town to do some shopping. I was waiting at the bus stop for my bus home when I saw coming towards me a wheelchair, pushed by a tall and very familiar figure. Edward was leaning down, speaking to the woman in the wheelchair, but even from a distance I could see she was only half aware that he was talking to her. It was like a flash photograph. In those few seconds, I took in Edward, the wheelchair, the woman huddled beneath a rug, with glazed unseeing eyes, the awkward angle of her head, the twisted hands. And then I turned and fled, before either of them should see me.

When I got back to my studio, I sat on the bed and wept. I wept for Edward and for the woman who was so cruelly crippled, but I also wept for myself. For if Edward really loved me, why hadn't he let me in on this part of his life? Why hadn't he trusted me to listen and to support him? That I had assisted in betraying a wife was bad enough. Doing it to someone ill, someone handicapped, someone at such a terrible disadvantage, seemed unforgivable.

When Edward came round that evening, I told him what I had seen.

'You could have told me. You *should* have told me. How could you have kept something this important – this *painful* – to yourself? What does that say about me? About our relationship?'

Edward shrugged helplessly.

'Please, Edward. Tell me all about her. You have to tell me now; now that I've seen her. I want to understand.'

'I don't know where to start.'

'Well, the beginning would be a good place.'

Edward sat down, gazing at the floor, his hands between his knees.

'We'd only been married five years,' he began.

'Go on.'

'We were going to a wedding. I was driving. There was – an accident.'

'And?' I prompted.

'She – Vanessa – was terribly injured. They didn't think she'd make it through the night, but she survived. Oh, Cass. It would have been so much better for her if she hadn't.' He took out a handkerchief and blew his nose. His head was bent and I couldn't see his face, but I believe that he was crying. 'She was so beautiful, Cass. Vibrant, happy, full of life. And now – well, you've seen her. Sometimes she recognizes me, but most of the time she's no idea who I am. I tried looking after her myself, but in the end I couldn't manage, so she lives in a home. They're very good to her, very kind, but there's not much anyone can do. I visit her once or twice a week; sometimes her family come and see her. Today was the first time I've taken her out in ages. I thought it might help, but I don't think she even realized she was outdoors.' He looked up at me and attempted a smile. 'So there it is. Now you know.'

'Oh, Edward. I'm so so sorry.' I knelt down by his chair and took his hand. 'But why didn't you tell me? Wouldn't it have helped, to tell me?'

'I didn't want you to feel sorry for me, I suppose. Or sorry for Vanessa. I didn't want you to be tied to me by pity, or because you felt you had to support me. And Vanessa . . . She has so little dignity left, and to be pitied by my lover – and you are bound to pity her, Cass; how could you not? – is so degrading, somehow.'

'The accident . . .' I hesitated. 'Was it – was it your fault?' Edward shook his head.

'A lorry came out of a side road and didn't see us. It hit the car on the passenger side.' He ran his hands through his hair. 'But I still feel responsible. I know there was nothing I could have done – goodness knows, I've replayed it over and over in my head – but there are all those "if onlys". If only I'd filled the car up the day before and we hadn't had to stop for petrol, if only we hadn't been running late, if only we hadn't been going to that wedding at all (we nearly didn't). If only.'

'How long ago did it happen?'

'Seven years.'

'How terrible. How absolutely terrible, for both of you.'

'Yes. Though I don't think Vanessa is aware of anything very much at all, which I suppose is a blessing. She likes her food, and seems to enjoy music. Sometimes I read to her, but I don't think she takes it in. It's such a waste, Cass. Such a tragic waste. I lost the woman I loved on the day of the accident. The Vanessa who's left is someone quite different. But I owe it to her to visit her, to make sure she's well looked after. To do the little I can.'

'And – her family?'

'Her parents are dead, but she has two sisters. I get on with them both, and they made it clear some time ago that if I – well, if I found someone else, they would understand, but they'd rather I kept it quiet. At the time, I never imagined that would happen, so I didn't give it much thought. But now there's you.' He sighed. 'I hate keeping it a secret – you and me – but I feel in a way it's the least I can do. To divorce Vanessa would seem unutterably cruel, when she's done nothing to deserve it.'

'But don't people round here know? They must have heard of the accident. News like that usually travels pretty fast.'

'We lived in Surrey at the time, but I couldn't bear to stay on in the house, so I moved up here where nobody knows us. I brought Vanessa with me and found her a place to live so I could still visit her.' He got up and walked over to the window. 'No one here knows about her, and it's best that way. I don't want sympathy for her or for me. You can have too much sympathy, you know, Cass. I think in a way I was trying to get away from that, too. I didn't want to be "poor Edward" any more. I just wanted to get on with my life.'

I think that at that moment I loved Edward more than I had ever loved him; for his caring, his loyalty and his integrity. And I ached for his loss and for the seven lonely, agonizing years which had followed.

'Humphrey told me that you – well, that you had problems,' I said now. 'How much does he know?'

'Humphrey knows everything. He's the only person I've told, and he's been such a good friend to me. He was probably trying to protect you, Cass; warn you off. He knows I can't offer you what you want.'

'How does he know what I want?'

'Well, I suppose it was an assumption. But he probably assumes you want marriage and children. Don't most women?'

'Not this one. Not necessarily.' I joined him by the window and took his hand. 'I've never been particularly interested in marriage. I suppose it's because I've never lived in a married household. Mum never wanted to get married, and she's managed all right. Of course, I'm not really like her. One relationship is enough for me. But marriage? To be honest, I've never really thought about it.'

'And now?'

'And now what?'

'What – what do you want to do? Now you know about Vanessa.'

I sighed.

'It's a difficult one. I hate to feel I'm taking advantage of her in some way. On the other hand, you say she can't really be hurt by anything we do.'

'I love you so much, Cass. I'm not sure I could cope without you now I've found you.' Once more, Edward's eyes filled with tears.

'Can I sleep on it?' I asked, after a moment.

He nodded. 'Of course. And I'll respect whatever you decide to do.'

But when it came to it, there wasn't really any decision to make. I think my mind was made up even before Edward left the room.

Forty-three

Living with a secret is never easy, but I probably coped better than many people because I've always been quite good with secrets. I had friends, but none of them particularly close, and except for Myra (who was very understanding and could be surprisingly discreet), I didn't tell any of them about Edward.

It was with some reservations that I finally told Mum about Edward's situation, having extracted from her a promise of absolute secrecy. Her reaction was typical.

'Oh, the poor man! How perfectly dreadful for him. I wonder if there's anything I can do to help. Perhaps I could go and visit his wife? Or even take New Dog to see her? They say people like that often respond to animals rather than humans. And New Dog is handicapped too, isn't he, so they've got something in common. I could go on the bus—'

'No, Mum. No!' Whatever Vanessa's state of mind, I was sure that there were few things she needed less than New Dog.

'Why ever not? Honestly, Cass. You're such a wet blanket sometimes.'

'Mum, I'm not telling you about this so that you can do something about it. I'm telling you because you're my mother and you wanted to know. There's nothing you can do for Vanessa. In fact it doesn't seem there's much anyone can do for her.'

'I could make her a cake. Most people like cake.'

'Mum, please. Just leave it, will you?'

For a moment, Mum looked crestfallen, then she brightened.

'But you can introduce me to Edward, can't you? There's nothing to stop you now. And after all, I do introduce you to my men-friends.'

This last was not strictly true, for while I had certainly met most if not all of Mum's lovers, it was as often as not when they were scantily clad en route for the bathroom, or in the kitchen waiting to be fed (usually by the long-suffering Greta). Mum rarely bothered with formal introductions.

'Well . . .' I hesitated. I had become accustomed to keeping my two lives separate, and wasn't sure how well they would mix. Edward was my refuge as well as my lover. Our life together was an oasis of peace in a generally troubled world. Would all that change if I were to bring him home?

'Oh, come on, Cass. I'll behave beautifully, I promise. I won't let you down.'

'It's not that. And I do want you to meet him, of course I do. But Mum, I don't want the others around. Not yet.'

'But Greta and Call Me Bill are family,' Mum protested. 'We don't have any secrets from them.'

'You may not have secrets from them, Mum, but I do. I'm

very fond of both of them, you know I am. But I don't want them knowing all about my personal life. I don't even want Lucas to know at the moment.'

'Oh, Lucas.' Mum sniffed. 'He's become so stuffy. I blame Gracie.'

It should be explained that Mum tended to blame Gracie for everything where Lucas was concerned, and this was not entirely fair on Gracie. For while she would never be the kind of daughter-in-law Mum would have liked (given her feelings about marriage, she would probably have preferred to have no daughter-in-law at all), Gracie was a perfectly nice girl; just a bit ordinary, and somewhat lacking in imagination. But she was a good wife and mother, and she seemed to suit Lucas, and that was really all that mattered.

I brought Edward home for tea and one of Mum's cakes, and they took to one another immediately. Edward thought Mum was 'so refreshing', and Mum considered Edward to be 'very charming, and so good-looking, Cass' (to my shame, I experienced a frisson of alarm, for Mum had been known to take up with younger men, and Edward was nearer Mum's age than mine). New Dog greeted him in a frenzy of leaping and licking, and true to her word, Mum appeared to have banished the rest of the household from the premises.

'Your mother is amazing,' Edward said to me on the way home. 'I've never met anyone quite like her.'

'I don't think there is anyone quite like her,' I said.

'And the way she talked about Vanessa. As though it was the most natural thing in the world for her daughter to have a married lover with a handicapped wife.'

'She wanted to go and see her.'

'Who? Vanessa?' Edward looked alarmed.

I laughed.

'Don't worry. I told her Vanessa was off limits. But Mum's like that. She looks for people to look after.'

'Does she look after you?' Edward asked.

'What a strange question.' I thought for a moment. 'No. Not really. She's best with sick people and animals, waifs and strays, that sort of thing. I don't think I count. When we were children, she tended to treat Lucas and me more as friends, except when we were ill. I think that's one of the reasons you make me so happy. I've never felt really looked after before.'

And it was true. If I thought about it, I don't think I had ever felt protected the way I did when I was with Edward. He was strong and sensible, calm in a crisis and good at making decisions. I could rely on him totally, and while I would happily have looked after him had the occasion demanded it, it was wonderful to have a relationship in which this was not a dominant factor. We never talked about it, but I'm sure we both recognized an element of father–daughter in our relationship, and I believe it was something we both needed. I had never had a father, and Edward was no longer able to look after Vanessa as he wanted to do. We had each found in the other something much more than simply a lover – although that was wonderful in itself – and I think we both helped one another to grow emotionally stronger.

My painting, too, improved greatly after I met Edward. Before, there had been a hesitancy, almost a shyness about my work. My paintings were nice enough, and people seemed to like them, but they had a self-effacing quality which reflected my own personality. Now, they became bolder, more assertive, and I was developing a real style of my own. I started experimenting in charcoal and pen and ink, and produced some pleasing sketches of Lucas's children (which I sold, since they were not to Gracie's taste). People began to commission drawings of their own children, and occasionally their pets, and I was happy to oblige. It made a pleasant change to be invited into people's homes to do my work, and I made several good friends in the process. I continued to work for Humphrey, who was beginning to talk of retirement and increasingly left the management of the gallery to me. For the first time in my life, I was fulfilled on all fronts, and happier than I had ever been.

And so the years passed. In time, I was able to buy my own small terraced house and convert the dining room into a studio, while Mum consoled herself for my absence by installing a new Lodger in my old bedroom. Edward and I spent as much time together as either of us needed (two artists living together doesn't always work), and an increasing amount of my work now involved commissioned drawings of babies and children.

It was almost my thirty-fourth birthday when Edward brought up the subject of children.

I was putting the finishing touches to a sketch of a sleeping baby. The child had adopted that position typical of babies, lying on its front with its knees drawn up. The soles of its feet peeped out from under a well-padded bottom, and one dimpled fist was visible beside the curve of a plump cheek.

I was pleased with the drawing and was leaning back to

admire it, when I became aware of Edward standing behind me.

'Cass,' he said, putting his hands on my shoulders. 'Would you like one of those?'

'One of what?' I reached for a pencil to sign my drawing.

'A baby of course. Cass, I think it's time you and I thought about having a baby.'

It may seem odd now, in an age when women clamour for the right to have babies with or without a partner, but Edward and I had never discussed the matter of children. Of course, I had thought about it from time to time; imagined what it would be like to have Edward's child; what it would be like to be a mother. But children had never featured very strongly in my plans and I had never been especially maternal. As a child, such dolls as I had were more likely to be used in games of cowboys and Indians, or subjected to bloodthirsty surgical procedures, than mothered in the conventional sense. And while I liked small children, I had never really considered having one of my own. So Edward's question took me by surprise.

'A baby? You and me?'

'Why not?' Edward sat down beside me.

'Do *you* want children?'

'Well, I certainly did, when Vanessa was – well, before the accident. Then I more or less said goodbye to the idea. But now – well, yes. I would like a child. Your – our child.'

'What's brought this on?'

'Anno Domini.' Edward laughed. 'Since I hit fifty, I realized that doors were beginning to close; doors that couldn't be reopened. There are so many things I'll never do now;

paint a masterpiece, climb Everest, learn to tap-dance . . . well, you know what I mean. But a baby – that's something I can do. Something we can do.' He spread his fingers. 'I haven't been able to do much for you, Cass. I haven't given you marriage or a home together, the usual things. But I can – could – give you a baby.'

'Goodness!' I was more taken aback than I would have imagined.

'I know. I think I'm even surprising myself. But just think about it. I know it's a big decision, especially for you. Between us, we can afford a baby, and I'll play my part. I'd be a good father.'

'I know you would. But it's not that easy, is it? I mean, what would people say?'

'You mean the unmarried thing?'

'No.' I laughed. 'With a mother like mine, the unmarried thing is hardly likely to be a problem, is it? No, I mean Vanessa, her family, people who don't know about us. Wouldn't I and my illegitimate offspring be a bit of an embarrassment?'

'I think we could get round it. After all, Vanessa's been ill for a long time, and I think her family have more or less guessed about you. They might even be pleased for me.'

'A baby. Our baby. It's certainly a thought. Can I think about it?'

Suddenly the streets were full of women with pushchairs, pregnant women, parents towing reluctant toddlers along busy pavements. No doubt they had always been there, but so far they hadn't been part of my agenda. Now, I found myself taking notice of them, surreptitiously peering into prams and even straying into shops selling baby clothes, where I would finger tiny dresses and sleep suits and try to imagine buying them for my own baby.

'What's that you've got?' Edward asked, when I was unpacking some shopping about a week after our baby conversation.

I held up a small fluffy blue rabbit.

'I couldn't resist it,' I told him.

'Is that – is that by any chance a present for Cass junior?'

'Or baby Edward. One or the other.'

'Oh, Cass! I'm so pleased!' He hugged me. 'I can't tell you how pleased.'

'Me too.' I put down the rabbit and returned his hug.

'When shall we start?'

'No time like the present. But not in front of the rabbit.' I replaced it carefully in its paper bag.

Forty-four

I hear footsteps flying along the corridor, coming towards us. I remember my nursing days, and the strict injunction never to run unless there was a fire or a dire emergency, but I know those footsteps, that breathless speed, even from behind a closed door. And when the door is flung open, I am not disappointed.

'Gran! Oh Gran!' Tavvy flings herself onto the bed, then turns to me. 'I'm not too late, am I? Dad met me and brought me straight here. Please tell me I'm not too late!'

'You will be, if you crush her. For goodness' sake be careful, Tavvy!' I stand up and pull her back off the bed, laughing in spite of myself, and then give her a huge hug. 'Oh, I'm so pleased to see you! You've no idea how pleased. She's been waiting for you for days. I didn't know how much longer she could hang on.'

'She looks so – so breakable. There's nothing of her.' The tears run down Tavvy's cheeks. 'Poor, poor little Gran. She doesn't deserve this.' She sits down by the bed and takes

Mum's hand in hers. 'Darling Gran. It's me. Tavvy. I'm here now.'

Mum's eyelids flutter, and there is the faintest ghost of a smile.

'I knew – knew – you'd – come.' Her voice is barely audible, and Tavvy leans down to catch her words.

'Of course I came. How could you think I wouldn't?' Tavvy strokes Mum's hand, then lifts it to hold it against her own cheek. 'I wouldn't let you do – do this without me, would I?'

Mum closes her eyes again, but the smile is still there, hovering, as though reluctant to leave her lips.

Tavvy weeps, noisily, helplessly, her mane of auburn hair – Mum's hair – falling forward over her face, her shoulders heaving with her sobs. Poor Tavvy. She and Mum have always been close, and I know she has had an appalling time trying to get here. I haven't seen her for nearly a year, and I scan her greedily, taking in the mass of freckles on her bare arms, her torn jeans and Save the Walrus (Walrus?) T-shirt, her sandalled (and far from clean) feet. She has lost weight, and I could swear she's grown a couple of inches. I hate to have had to interrupt her precious gap year, and yet I am so glad she is home and safe.

'Why didn't you call me before?' she asks now. 'You know I would have come.'

'I'd no idea it would be so quick. Besides, I wasn't to know you'd go off trekking into the jungle! Anyway, you're here now, and that's all that matters.'

*

It was my idea to name our daughter Octavia. Mum never actually suggested it, but I knew it was what she wanted, and it is after all a pretty name. She had tried to persuade Lucas to give it to one of his children, but he (or more likely, Gracie) was having none of it. And when the girls turned out to be as pleasantly ordinary as their mother, Mum felt vindicated.

'Anne and Sarah! I ask you! With names like that, what do you expect?'

However, I'm pretty sure that it wasn't so much the children themselves who bothered her as the fact that they had made her a grandmother, and that was something she told me she wasn't ready for yet.

'It sounds so *old*, Cass. Grey hair and lavender water and those enormous knickers with elastic.'

'And a shopping trolley,' I teased her.

'That too.'

'And flannel nighties.'

'Don't mock, Cass. It's not funny, growing old.'

But by the time Octavia came along, Mum had become used to her grandmotherly status, and was even heard to boast about it to disbelieving suitors ('No, really? You can't be! You look much too young!' was the response she expected and, as often as not, received). Nonetheless, I hoped that she would form a better relationship with my baby than she had with Lucas's, for while Lucas's children had a legion of grandparents, uncles, aunts and cousins courtesy of Gracie's family, Edward and I had few relatives.

But I needn't have worried, for Mum was besotted from the word go with the small bohemian who was our daughter. Refusing to wear the clothes other children wore, or play with the same toys, Tavvy went her own sweet way, and while she wasn't deliberately disobedient, nor even especially naughty, rules puzzled her. Whether she was talking to a stranger or picking flowers in someone else's garden, she quite simply didn't understand what she was doing wrong. 'But Mummy, I didn't *know*' was her oft-repeated refrain. The 'stranger' hadn't been strange at all; he was very nice. If she had a garden, she would be quite happy for someone to come and pick her flowers. What was the problem?

Beautiful, eccentric and imaginative, she spurned friends of her own age ('They just want to *play*, Mummy') but loved adult company and made a wonderful companion. She never needed to be entertained, and provided she had pencils and paper, was rarely bored. Her drawings from an early age were prodigious in quality as well as quantity, and if her school work was neglected in favour of her art, she came up with such plausible excuses that it was difficult to argue with her.

Edward adored her, and played a full part in her upbringing. We took it in turns to care for her, with help from Mum when the need arose, and she divided her time between our two homes. She never questioned this arrangement, seeming to enjoy the freedom and flexibility it engendered, together with her two bedrooms (not to mention the two cats – Tavvy loved cats). Whatever happened during the week, Edward and I always tried to spend the weekends together, and the three of us would have breakfast in bed on Sunday mornings; Edward and I with coffee and toast and the Sunday papers, and Tavvy in the middle with her boiled egg and soldiers.

It wasn't a conventional upbringing, but it worked, as I

tried to explain to Lucas on the one occasion when he took it upon himself to question our childcare arrangements.

'It's not normal, Cass. To live in two houses, the way you do, and push the child back and forth like a – like a tennis ball.'

'Tavvy's not pushed anywhere! She wouldn't put up with it, for a start.'

'And that's another thing. She's in very real danger of being spoiled,' Lucas said, as though being spoiled were on a par with being trapped in a burning building.

'Is that what Gracie thinks?' I asked mildly.

'Gracie did happen to mention that you might have problems later.'

'Well, do thank Gracie for me. I'm sure she'll be able to advise me if that ever happens.'

'There's no need to be sarcastic, Cass. We're only trying to help. After all, we have been at this game a lot longer than you.'

I thought of my two well-behaved nieces, who had probably never in their lives made a mud pie or climbed a tree (activities much favoured by Tavvy) and smiled. It was true that Sarah was beginning to show signs of rebellion, which Mum considered to be a promising start, but Anne appeared to be a lost cause. Gracie may not have been a particularly forceful character, but her genes more than made up for it.

'Of course you have, Lucas,' I said. 'I'll bear it in mind.'

Despite Lucas's warning, we had little trouble with Tavvy, and even her teens passed largely uneventfully. True, she could be wayward and moody, but no more than most teenagers, and as for the multiple piercings of her ears and the ring in her belly button, I thought they looked rather nice (the pierced eyebrow lasted only two days because Tavvy said it was too painful).

When Tavvy was sixteen, Vanessa died. Unsurprisingly, Edward was deeply saddened at the ending of a life which had been so cruelly cut off, and much angered by those who expected him to feel relief at what they imagined to be his long-awaited freedom. 'Now you and Cass can get married' was the often repeated refrain (our relationship had long ceased to be a secret), but we felt strangely reluctant to upset the status quo. We had lived separately for so long that the idea of such a major change was unsettling.

We asked Tavvy what she thought.

'Whatever do you want to get married for?' was her response.

'Isn't it what most people's parents do?' Edward asked.

'Most people!' scoffed Tavvy. 'No. We're all much better off as we are. Trust me. Besides, you two couldn't possibly live together. It wouldn't work.'

And I think she was probably right. We could manage the upkeep of our two modest homes, and we had our own routines and habits (not to mention the two by now ageing cats, who would no doubt fight). One day, maybe we would think again, but for the time being we were content. As for Tavvy, she flitted to and fro at will, as often as not staying with Mum. By now, Call Me Bill had died, and Greta was in poor health, so what with caring for her and seeing to sundry Lodgers, Mum had her hands full. Tavvy liked to go round 'to help', although I suspect that the two of them spent most of the time drinking tea and gossiping.

Humphrey was by now in his eighties, and had retired some years ago, but I stayed on as manager of the gallery. I continued to sell my paintings, but I had had to accept that I would never be good enough to make a living from my work, as Edward did.

But while Edward was undoubtedly good, Tavvy was better. Her paintings – wild, colourful and full of life, like Tavvy herself – delighted her teachers, and even before she left school several of them had sold. Many were exuberant abstracts in bright colours; bold swirls of paint interweaving or dancing across the canvas. Some were reminiscent of the French Impressionists (Tavvy particularly admired Gauguin), but there was a wildness and originality which were all her own. There was nothing shy about Tavvy's work; she had the courage I had lacked, and once she discovered oils, there was no stopping her.

'So you're going to be an artist, like your parents?' people would ask her, and Tavvy was always surprised.

'Just because I can paint doesn't mean that's what I'm going to do as a *job*,' she told me, exasperated at what she saw as a ridiculous assumption. 'No. I'm going to travel and have fun. Then I'll decide what I'm going to do.'

'Quite right,' said Mum, who had called in to see us. 'Aren't people silly?'

'Well, you've had to drop your other A levels, so your options are a bit restricted,' I suggested. 'Art seems the obvious direction, doesn't it? At least for the time being. You don't have to do it forever.'

My mother and Tavvy exchanged despairing glances.

'Dear old mum.' Tavvy patted my shoulder.

338

'She's just trying to be sensible,' my mother said, and they both rocked with laughter. They say the apple doesn't fall far from the tree; I think the apple that was my daughter had skipped a generation.

But even Mum had to agree that travel must be paid for, so when Tavvy got her one A level, she had to work to earn her gap year. Like Mum, she was not good at holding down a job, and managed to get through four within the first three months.

'People are so stupid,' she said, after three weeks as a chambermaid. 'Do they really think we don't find what they hide under their mattresses? I handed this customer his magazine, with a perfectly straight face, and said "I believe this is yours, sir", and he complained to the manager, and I was sacked.' She laughed, 'Oh, Mum. You should have seen it! All those naked bodies! And you've no idea what they were doing to each other. Men and women, two or three at a time, too. I wish I'd been able to keep it. Gran would have been fascinated!'

Eventually Tavvy found her niche, helping out at a day nursery, and while the manager frequently questioned some of the more unusual games she invented to entertain the children, her small charges and their parents thought the world of her.

After several months, Tavvy had saved up enough money for her expedition, and my house began to fill up with all the impedimenta of the backpacker. Wherever I went, I seemed to trip over camping equipment and hiking boots, insect repellent and mosquito nets. Typically, she had refused the services of gap year organizations or anyone else who might have been of assistance, preferring to plan her own itinerary. Her plans were typically vague, involving little more than, as she put it, 'taking off and seeing what happens', and were more than a little reminiscent of Mum's famous holiday.

'On your own?' I asked fearfully, when Tavvy told us of her intentions. 'Is it safe to go on your own?'

'Oh, Mum. Lots of people do it. I'll be fine.'

'I'd feel much happier if there was someone with you.'

'I did ask around, but no one wanted to come. Anyway, it'll be more fun on my own. I can do what I like.'

'Don't you always?' Edward asked mildly.

'Oh, Dad! Don't be so stuffy! In any case, isn't that what you love about me?'

'Surely you ought at least to have some sort of itinerary,' I said.

'Why? This will be much more exciting,' Tavvy said. 'I'll start with Peru, and see where that takes me. After all, if Peru was good enough for Paddington Bear, it's good enough for me.'

'Paddington Bear left Peru and came to England,' Edward pointed out. 'Perhaps he knew something you don't.'

'More fool he. Anyway, that's where I'm going. I've decided. And Gran thinks it's a great idea.'

'Gran would,' I replied, silently cursing my mother. For while she would no doubt be sleeping soundly in her bed while her granddaughter cavorted around the world, I was pretty sure I would lie awake worrying for weeks to come.

And so it was that one freezing November afternoon, Edward and I found ourselves waving our daughter off at Heathrow airport.

'She'll be all right,' Edward said, squeezing my hand, as we watched Tavvy making her way through into the departure lounge. 'She's nearly twenty, and she knows how to look after herself.'

'Yes,' I whispered, fighting back the tears, trying not to think of all the potential hazards lying in wait for the lone female traveller.

Tavvy looked back a last time; a slight figure weighed down by an enormous backpack and a cloud of bright hair under a battered straw hat. She grinned broadly and blew us a final kiss before disappearing from sight.

It seemed like the last curtain in the wonderful drama which had been Tavvy's childhood.

Forty-five

Another evening, another dusk, perhaps another night of waiting. Now, Tavvy and I sit on either side of Mum, holding her hands. There have been other visitors – Lucas, Greta, Edward with a flask of soup and some sandwiches – but Tavvy and I will stay here together until the end. It's what Mum would have wanted.

My mother sleeps. She hasn't stirred since Tavvy's arrival, but the faint smile still lingers on her face, and I believe she is at peace.

I tell Tavvy about her funeral plans.

'Black horses, Tavvy. Imagine! Where on earth are we going to find a black horse?'

'I know someone who's got a brown pony,' Tavvy says, after a moment. 'Would that do?'

'A brown pony . . . Oh, why not? I'm sure a brown pony will do nicely. Can it pull a cart?'

342

'I expect so,' says Tavvy, who knows nothing at all about horses. 'If not, we'll teach it.'

I think of all the things that will need to be done when Mum dies, and mentally add to the list teaching the brown pony to pull a cart.

'And flowers. She wants lots of flowers.'

'I should think so,' says Tavvy. 'A funeral wouldn't be a funeral without lots of flowers. Not wreaths, though. They're too – too—'

'Funereal?'

'That's probably it.' We both laugh.

'I'll miss her so much,' Tavvy says, after a moment, and begins to weep again. 'The world won't be the same without Gran.'

'I know.'

We sit on, chatting quietly, laughing, crying. Mum's breathing becomes increasingly shallow and erratic, and once again I find myself clinging tightly on to her hand, as though a part of me is still trying to hang on to her. When I look across the bed, I see that Tavvy is doing the same.

'We must let her go, Tavvy,' I say, reaching across to take Tavvy's hand in mine. 'We have to let her go.'

'Do you think she'll speak again?' Tavvy asks, through more tears.

I shake my head.

'There's no need. I think she's said all she wants to say. Now you're back, there's nothing to keep her.'

More time passes, a doctor looks in, a nurse asks if we're all right and brings us hot chocolate. Eventually, Tavvy and I both doze off, curled uncomfortably in our hospital chairs.

343

I must have fallen into a deeper sleep than I intended, for when I awake I am quite stiff and, for a brief moment, disorientated. But I know even before I open my eyes that Mum has gone. There is a stillness in the room; a silence which wasn't there before. The hand I hold in mine is still faintly warm, but my mother is no longer here. It's like coming into a room just after someone has left it: the embers are still glowing in the hearth; the seat of a chair still retains the warmth of the person who was occupying it; but there is no longer anyone there.

Tavvy wakes with a little cry.

'Oh, no!' She clutches at Mum's hand. 'She's gone! She didn't even say goodbye!'

'She did. When you arrived. That was her goodbye.'

Tavvy's head is bent and I know she's crying, but soundlessly this time. My own tears seem locked in my throat as though waiting for permission before they can be released. Somewhere, a church clock strikes, and an ambulance makes its noisy response to someone else's emergency; perhaps someone else's tragedy.

Eventually, Tavvy lets go of Mum's hand and stands up, gazing down at the small, still figure in the bed.

'So that's – it.' She sounds surprised.

'Yes. That's it.'

'So quiet for such a dramatic thing. The end of someone's life. You expect – oh, I don't know. A fanfare or something. Something more – important.'

'I know what you mean.'

'She didn't suffer, did she?'

'No. Not too much.'

'That's good. And you, Mum. You've lost your mother.'
She comes and puts her arms around me. 'Poor old mum.'

'I'll be all right.' I return her hug.

'You've still got me. And Dad.'

'Of course I have.'

Tavvy moves away, and stands silhouetted against the
light coming in from the corridor. Although she is so thin, her
stomach has a gentle and unmistakable curve, and she places
her hands over it protectively, as though challenging death to
seek out another victim. Catching my gaze, she gives a small
helpless shrug.

'I was going to tell you, Mum.' Her voice has the same
tone as it did when she was a little girl and was afraid I might
be cross with her. 'I did love him, you know. He said – he
said he'd stay with me. He promised to look after me.'

'But he didn't.'

'No. He didn't.'

The words hang between us, as though waiting for some
kind of resolution.

I take Tavvy in my arms again and hold her close.

'Poor Tavvy.'

'Oh, Mum. I've wanted you – needed you – so much.' She
sobs into my shoulder. 'I've been so stupid. How could I have
been so stupid?'

'It happens. These things happen. But we'll manage,' I
say, stroking her hair. 'It'll be all right.'

'Will it?' She lifts a tear-stained face to mine.

'Of course it will.'

'And – Dad?'

'You leave Dad to me.'

We stand there for a long time, holding each other, and I draw comfort from the warmth of my daughter's skin, her hair against my cheek, the small catch of her breath.

Outside the window, another dawn is lightening the sky; a new day is beginning; the last leaf detaches itself from a branch of the maple tree, and begins to spiral slowly towards the ground.